Also by Stuart McLean

STUART McLEAN

THE VINYL CAFE *Celebrates*

VIKING

VIKING

an imprint of Penguin Canada, a division of Penguin Random House Canada Limited

Canada • USA • UK • Ireland • Australia • New Zealand • India • South Africa • China

First published 2021

Some stories in this work were previously published in the following:
"The Waterslide" in *Extreme Vinyl Cafe*, "Birthday Present" and "Labour Pains"
in *Vinyl Cafe Diaries*, "Dave Cooks the Turkey" in *Home from the Vinyl Cafe*
and *Christmas at the Vinyl Cafe*, "The Laundry Chute," "Tree Planting," and "Opera"
in *Secrets from the Vinyl Cafe*, "Le Morte d'Arthur" in *Revenge of the Vinyl Cafe*,
"Odd Jobs" and "Love Never Ends" in *Vinyl Cafe Unplugged*.

www.penguinrandomhouse.ca

*Publisher's note: This book is a work of fiction. Names, characters, places and incidents
either are the product of the author's imagination or are used fictitiously, and any
resemblance to actual persons living or dead, events, or locales is entirely coincidental.*

Library and Archives Canada Cataloguing in Publication

Title: The Vinyl Cafe celebrates / Stuart McLean.
Other titles: Short stories. Selections
Names: McLean, Stuart, 1948-2017, author.
Description: Collection featuring ten never-before-published
stories and ten classic favourites.
Identifiers: Canadiana (print) 2021026411X | Canadiana (ebook) 20210264225 |
ISBN 9780735242647 (hardcover) | ISBN 9780735242654 (EPUB)
Classification: LCC PS8575.L448 A6 2021 | DDC C813/.54—dc23

Book design by Jennifer Griffiths
Cover images: (texture) © Katsumi Murouchi / Getty Images;
(dog and banner) © JenniferGriffiths

Printed in Canada

10 9 8 7 6 5 4 3 2 1

Penguin
Random House
VIKING CANADA

I bought a lamp at a craft show. It is a small table lamp, less than a foot high. It has an antique brass stand and a shade made of milky glass. It is too low to the ground, or, to be more precise, to the desk where I work, to shed any light and too reticent about the light-shedding business in any case—it tends to "glow" rather than illuminate, the light too soft to be of any help other than to the mood.

Yet in the mood-setting business, my little lamp is a prince among lamps. A day doesn't pass without it brightening my mood.

I turn it on every morning when I sit down to set about my work (which given the abundance of light in my office in the morning is akin to lighting a campfire on a summer afternoon). And maybe it's this essentially unessential quality, above its graceful milky-ness and its warm yellowness, that makes my little lamp so appealing.

As I sit at my desk, day in and day out, answering my phone, paying my bills, and scribbling away in between, I know that my lamp and I share this fundamental fact: neither of us is really necessary in this big wide world of light. But bidden, or unbidden, we are here nevertheless. Here by the grace of some big unknown thing. And while we are here, we will shine when we are called to, and do our best to shine as brightly as we can, shining away until the dark morning when someone will forget to turn us on.

February 6, 2003

STUART McLEAN,
"The Desk Lamp," from *The Vinyl Cafe Notebooks*

The Vinyl Cafe Celebrates

Kids, and Parents, and Grandparents

THE WATERSLIDE

I t was the dog days of summer and half the city was away. Even the mailman was on vacation. The neighbourhood was so quiet you could hear the spiders at work. There was absolutely *nothing* to do.

Murphy and Sam were lying on their backs, shoulder to shoulder, underneath Jim Scoffield's mulberry tree. There was an ant crawling across Sam's forehead. Both boys had their mouths stretched wide open.

Sam said, "This is crazy. It's been, like, an hour."

Murphy said, "It's been ten minutes. Do you give up?"

Sam said, "Do you?"

They had a bet. The first one to catch a mulberry in his mouth won.

A hot wind rustled the branches of the tree above them. The boys, sun dappled, watched the leaves turn from green to grey to green again. The clouds were doing summer things, but the berries weren't. Nothing was coming down.

It was the middle of the week in the middle of the summer. The neighbourhood had been reduced to sun, soft wind, and one lovelorn cicada vibrating at the top of the mulberry tree.

Murphy said, "It sounds like in *To Kill a Mockingbird*."

Sam said, "Once again I have no idea what you are talking about."

Murphy said, "The cicadas. Do you give up?"

Sam sat up abruptly. Sam said, "Okay. Whatever."

Murphy said, "I win."

SAM AND MURPHY were in the park. In the little kids' section. They were by the wading pool, draped listlessly over two of the swings. They were barely moving and all alone, except for a bored teenage girl who was pushing a toddler on the swing nearest the gate. The toddler, who was holding an orange Popsicle, was wearing diapers and nothing else.

A water truck swished down the street. They all looked up hopefully as it passed, as if it were going to stop and offer some relief from the heat. But it didn't even slow down. It was there and it was gone, and when it was gone the electric rattle of the neighbourhood cicadas was all that was left. You couldn't tell where they were. It sounded as if they were everywhere.

Sam said, "Cicadas, right?"

Murphy said, "Good. They live underground for seventeen years. Then, on the very same day, they all crawl out of the ground together, and climb to the top of the trees."

Sam said, "They live underground."

Murphy said, "Seventeen years."

Sam said, "What do they live on?"

Murphy said, "Root juice."

Sam said, "And then they all crawl out together. At the same time. After seventeen years."

Murphy said, "They only live for thirty days after that. They lay eggs, die, and it all starts again."

Sam said, "If I was a cicada, I'd stay underground."

Murphy said, "They eat them in China."

Sam said, "See."

Murphy said, "Stir-fry."

Sam said, "If we could get some, we could wok them up for my sister."

IT WAS LUNCH. They were eating at Sam's. Grilled cheese. Carrot sticks. Chocolate milk.

Morley was leaving for work, but she hadn't got out the door yet. She was standing in the middle of the kitchen with her hands on her hips. She was considering something.

"No," she said, "no videos. It's summer. It's a beautiful day. Play outside."

Sam said, "We're bored of outside."

Morley said, "That's funny. I thought you were bored of school. Adam Turlington is going to *summer* school. I bet summer school isn't boring."

ARTHUR, THE DOG, was lying in the cool dust under the back steps. Sam was holding a cup, dripping water on him through the slats.

Murphy said, "We should get the hose."

And that, more or less, is the moment it all began.

They called Peter Moore. They said, "Bring your bathing suit. And a sprinkler."

By the middle of the afternoon, there were five boys running around the backyard. Five boys and two sprinklers.

One sprinkler was attached to the garden tap and one was running out the back door, hooked up to the basement sink.

And the middle of the afternoon is when Rashida Chudary came by with little Fatima in tow. Rashida was on her way to the grocery store. She had stopped by with something for Morley. When no one answered the front door, she came around the back.

Fatima got sprayed. She squealed, but it was a squeal of delight. In fact, the tears only came when her mother said they had to go. One thing led to another, and Fatima ended up staying.

"We'll take care of Fatima," said Sam.

AND THEY DID—MAGNIFICENTLY. They unscrewed one of the sprinklers and replaced it with a nozzle. They set the nozzle to jet spray. They set Fatima on a chair on the back of the deck. They gave her the jet hose. Fatima blasted them with the hose as they ran around the yard.

Fatima stood on her chair, up on her toes, whirling the hose around with the intensity of one of those white-gloved traffic policemen, with their crisply ironed shirts and braids looping over their shoulders. Fatima was in a watery heaven.

It was, beyond a doubt, the most wonderful fun Fatima had had in her entire life—ever. Better than anything. Better than *Eid*.

When Rashida came to get her daughter after an hour, Fatima wouldn't leave.

Sam said, "She can stay. *We'll* bring her home."

When Sam and Murphy did bring Fatima home, Rashida gave them ten dollars.

"Sweet," said Murphy.

IT WAS MURPHY'S idea to pick Fatima up the next afternoon. But before Sam and Murphy headed off to her place, they spent the morning getting ready. They got Peter Moore to bring his wading pool over. They dragged Sam's old sandbox from a forgotten corner of the yard, and set it in the sun so the sand would dry out. They made lemonade.

Then the three of them walked over to the Chudarys' place and knocked on their door, standing on the stoop like three little Jehovah's Witnesses.

When Rashida answered, it was Murphy who did the talking.

"We were wondering," said Murphy, "if Fatima would like to come to our water park."

On the first day of their water park's operation, they got Fatima and Erik Schmidt's little brother Jürgen. They led Fatima and Jürgen through the sprinklers, let them spray the hoses, and watched them splash in the pool. After two hours, Peter walked the soggy and exhausted toddlers home.

Sam and Murphy stayed behind, putting everything back in place and mopping up the basement. They were almost finished when Peter marched into the backyard, with two ten-dollar bills. They had made twenty bucks.

MURPHY WENT TO his cottage over the weekend, which didn't really matter because it rained on Saturday. But they were back at it on Monday. Murphy, who had had two days to think about things, arrived with three white T-shirts and two days of pent-up plans.

They set up the backyard: the sandbox, the wading pool, and the sprinklers. Then Murphy produced the white T-shirts.

"We should look professional," said Murphy. They put on the white T-shirts and headed off. They were looking for customers.

That afternoon there were seven kids in the backyard. Four of them paying customers.

"Campers," said Murphy. "Not customers."

IT'S NOT CLEAR who thought up the waterslide. It *might* have been Fatima. Something about being the first kid there, the founding member of this club or camp or whatever this was—something, anyway, had given the normally shy four-year-old a massive injection of self-assurance. The highlight of each afternoon was the game they now called Jet Stream, the game in which Fatima stood on her chair, and whirled around and around with the hose, making them all run and squeal. Fatima, the smallest by a good half-foot, twisted and turned, running the backyard with the authority of a symphony conductor.

The waterslide could have been Fatima's idea. But no one remembers any more. And it doesn't really matter.

Old Eugene who lives next door was involved. It wouldn't have happened without Eugene. It wasn't his idea, of course, and no one ever tried to say it was. But he *was* involved. It wouldn't have happened without him.

Eugene had been watching since the water park first began. How could he not? Eugene, in his blue suit pants and his matching vest, the sleeves of his white dress shirt rolled to the elbows, had watched, sitting where he always sits on hot summer afternoons, on the old kitchen chair under his grape arbour. He was smoking one of his Italian cigars, nursing a tumbler of his homemade Chianti, tilting his chair dangerously backwards, his feet feathering the fence whenever he started to teeter.

The day the waterslide was born, Eugene, in the middle of his ninety-second summer, tilted dangerously back in his kitchen chair under the grape arbour, the fruit flies buzzing around him, and the children too. He had been wondering if he should open another bottle of the five-year-old Chianti, or try some of last year's batch, but then he had been taken over with the children and what they were trying to do. What in God's name were they trying to do? They had two slides they had removed from two playsets, and they were duct-taping them together. Or trying to. They seemed to be trying to make them into one long slide.

"Sam," called Eugene, in his throaty whisper, waving his spotted arm in the air. If it was a slide they needed, he had a better one. It was in his shed. He was pretty sure.

"Sam," he called again, coughing and spitting on the ground, gesturing at the shed at the bottom of his garden.

Eugene has one of just about everything down in the shed: gardening tools, household appliances, leftover construction supplies. And that doesn't even scratch the surface. There was also contraband, for instance: hidden bottles of eau-de-vie, secret cases of cigars.

He led the boys around his wife's flower bed, past his famous fig tree, under the grape arbour, between the rows of peppers and tomatoes, and into the earthy cool of the shaded shed.

When his watery eyes adjusted to the light, Eugene started Sam, Peter, and Murphy moving stuff around: an old refrigerator, a bureau, two hand-push lawn mowers. It was dirty work and they were getting hot and annoyed because they didn't understand what he was up to. Then they unearthed it. Eugene stepped back, and beamed, and the boys stood there in the sticky darkness without saying a word, struck dumb, staring into the back corner of Eugene's shed as if they had just uncovered the gold mask of Tutankhamen. It was the greatest treasure they could imagine—a long plastic tube. It was a portable industrial garbage chute, the kind you use when renovating houses to slide debris from the second floor to the yard. Eugene had packed the chute into the shed thinking someone might have a use for it some day. And now they did.

Sam and Murphy had been trying to build a waterslide that ran from the back deck down to the garden. A little slide. A modest drop. But by the time they had finished, by the time they had heaved Eugene's enormous plastic tube out of the shed, and dropped it over the fence, they had also heaved modesty out the window.

This was the waterslide to end *all* waterslides. This waterslide didn't start on the deck. This waterslide began at the second-floor bathroom window, traversed the family-room roof, looped around the clothesline pole, rolled over the picnic table, and ended in the back garden near the pear tree.

Fatima stood on the deck with her little arms folded over her chest as the boys worked, nodding occasionally, pointing at this and then at that, like the foreman at a construction site.

IT TOOK MOST of the afternoon to assemble it. The hardest part was connecting the slides from the playsets to Eugene's chute. They finally figured it out, and when they did, they all agreed it just might be the greatest waterslide built. *Ever.*

Any normal adult watching this unfold would have been seized by a spasm of anxiety and put a stop to it. But Eugene was the only adult watching. And at ninety-two, Eugene was a lot closer to boys, and the boyhood call to adventure, than he was to the anxiety levels of any normal adult.

What could possibly go wrong? After two wars and ninety-one and a half summers, the only thing Eugene worried about was his cellar of homemade wine, and the boys' slide wasn't going anywhere near that.

Fatima was the first one down. She bounced to her feet at the bottom like a trapeze artist. She confirmed it—it *was* the greatest waterslide ever built.

WORD SPREAD OVERNIGHT. No one actually *told* anyone. The news spread through the telepathy of childhood. By the next day, there wasn't a boy or a girl in the neighbourhood who didn't know about the waterslide in Dave and Morley's backyard. No *adults* knew about it. The boys disassembled it at the end of the afternoon. They spent the next morning putting it back together. They didn't believe they were doing anything wrong. They just had that intuitive understanding, shared by all children, that there are perfectly innocent things children do that adults are not equipped to handle.

No one was surprised then, the very next afternoon, when about twenty-five kids showed up. Or that everyone knew, without anyone saying anything, to wheel their bikes down the drive and lean them behind the house, so they didn't attract attention from the street.

What did surprise them, however, was the moment that second afternoon when Eugene, who had been watching the children quietly from his chair under the arbour for two days straight, stood up, went inside, and came out fifteen minutes later wearing nothing but a bathing cap and a knee-length blue bathing suit. He grinned, and waved at the kids, and then he propped his pruning ladder against the fence and climbed over, the veins on his knotty old legs throbbing with excitement.

It was Chris Turlington who started filming all this on his cellphone. It was his twin sister, Christina, who encouraged other kids to do the same, then edited the footage into a surprisingly slick video and posted it on YouTube.

Dave never would have seen it if he didn't work in a record store and his staff weren't attuned to this sort of stuff. A lot of people, apparently, are attuned. Tens of thousands, actually. *The Waterslide* became the most-watched video about an hour after it was posted. Everyone was talking about it. Though you understand when I say, everyone, I mean everyone of a certain age.

It was the Tuesday, I think. Although it could have been the Wednesday. It's hard to be certain about this. And it's not important. The days tend to blur together at the Vinyl Cafe, especially in the summer.

Anyway, it was the afternoon—that part is for sure. Dave was by the counter reading out loud from the back of a James Last album.

"Listen to this," he said to Brian, who has worked at the record store for years. "*This is a High Fidelity recording.*" Brian is Dave's oldest employee by far. Dave was reading this to Brian and to one of Brian's friends, who doesn't work at the store, but easily spends as much time there as Brian.

"*It is designed,*" Dave read, "*to play on the phonograph of your choice. If you are the owner of a new stereophonic system, this record will play on it. You can purchase this record with no fear of it becoming obsolete.*"

"What do you think?" said Dave. "Right or wrong?"

"Depends," said Brian.

"On what?" said Dave.

"On whether they're talking about the record as a concept or the concept of James Last."

"What ever happened to James Last?" said Dave.

"Exactly," said Brian.

Brian wandered behind the counter and dropped into the chair in front of the computer.

He typed *James Last* into Google. Fifteen minutes passed before Brian was heard from again.

"Oh, oh, oh," said Brian. "Have you seen this?"

Brian had given up on James Last and had flipped on YouTube.

"You have to see this," said Brian.

Dave wandered over and peered at the screen. Brian pressed play.

This is what Dave saw: a grainy and very shaky close-up of an impossibly old man struggling over a fence. Then there was a cut and a jerky shot of the back of a house. The camera pulled back, and Dave saw there were kids dancing on the back roof of this house. Then the shot zoomed in, and Dave saw something that looked like a bobsled run coming out the upstairs window.

There was something familiar about it all. "I think I have seen this before," said Dave. "This is like déjà vu."

Then the camera zoomed in on one of the kids dancing on the roof. The boy had one of those tiny Italian cigars in his mouth.

"I know this place," said Dave. "Is this a frat house? It looks like a frat house."

Dave leaned forward, squinting at the screen. The picture was so fuzzy it was hard to be sure. The camera zeroed in on the window. A small face and two hands appeared. Whoever it was, was holding a bottle in each hand and dumping the contents of the bottle down the slide.

"I think that's detergent," said Brian.

"Shampoo," said Brian's friend. "That's jojoba shampoo."

They all looked at him.

"I recognize the bottle," said Brian's friend.

"Ohmigod," said Dave.

"You ain't seen anything," said Brian. "It gets wicked better."

There was another edit and the camera focused on the old guy again. It was hard to make him out because the kids were gathered around him slapping him on the back. The old guy was doing something to his mouth.

"Ohmigod," said Dave again.

It was Eugene, of course, and Eugene was doing what he always does before he does anything that requires exertion. He was reaching into his mouth and removing his false teeth.

As Dave watched, the old man handed his teeth to a little girl who was standing on a chair holding a garden hose. The girl held the teeth high in the air. All the kids applauded. Now she was stuffing them into her pocket. She turned her hose onto the slide.

The camera left her to follow the old man inside the house. Up the stairs, into the bathroom.

Dave said, "Is this live?"

There was another edit. The old man was putting on a pair of nose plugs. There was a close-up of the shower. Two young boys were helping the toothless old man up onto the toilet and out the bathroom window. Then the point of view changed and the camera was outside again. It was on the ground, and there was the back of the house and then the camera zoomed in on the bathroom window. Everything was still for a few seconds, until—POW—the impossibly old man came flying out the window. He was sitting down and waving at the camera—until he hit the frothy spot where the boy had poured the jojoba shampoo. When he hit that spot, he flipped onto his back, gaining speed, his feet wiggling in the air. And that's when everything came into focus for poor Dave. The old man, it was, ohmigod, it looked exactly like Eugene from next door.

"I have to go," said Dave.

"It gets better," said Brian. "The whole point is the end. When he hits the garden fence."

But Dave was already out of the store.

SO DAVE MISSED the moment when Eugene flew out the bottom of the slide like he'd been shot out of a cannon. And he missed the part where Eugene smacked into the garden fence—the part where the old man struggled to his feet and stood there, toothless, covered with bubbles, his nose plug on, grinning madly, laughing, until he spotted his wife, Maria, on the other side of the fence. When he saw Maria glaring at him, his smile vanished, and his shoulders sagged.

"Busted," said Eugene, sadly, to the camera.

Dave, who was already through the front door, missed that part. He was gone like a shot, turning right, past Dorothy's bookstore, past Kenny Wong's café, thinking *Don't stop . . . there's no time to stop.* He had to get home, he had to . . . He got four blocks, four long blocks, but no more, before his poor pounding adrenaline-shot heart felt as if it were going to explode. He pulled up short, gasping for breath. This was ridiculous; he couldn't run all the way home. He needed to get a taxi. He got a taxi.

"Hurry," said Dave. "Hurry." Waving a twenty-dollar bill at the taxi driver.

IT WAS 4:30. The hottest part of the day was done. Sam and Murphy were on the back porch, sitting on the double hammock. Well, they were more slouched than sitting. Or sprawled. Inching back and forth, but barely. The perfect picture of summer indolence. As still as a hot wind on a summer lake.

Dave burst onto this scene like a dog with a fetched ball. Dave was all sweaty and panting and out of breath. Doglike Dave.

Murphy and Sam looked up at him from the hammock with sleepy boredom.

"Hey Dad," said Sam.

"Boys," said Dave.

"Hey," said Sam.

This was not what he had expected at all. This was the last thing he had expected.

He looked over the fence. Eugene was sitting where he always sat—under the grape arbour, tilting back on his kitchen chair, his arm in a sling.

Dave looked at Eugene and then at the boys. He walked over to the fence and nodded. Eugene nodded back and spat on the ground.

ONCE WHEN HE was a boy, Dave's parents gave him a dart set. He had begged them for the dart set. He couldn't remember why. But he wanted it, and they gave it to him for his birthday.

Now in those days, Dave's favourite show on television was *Circus Boy*, a show that chronicled the weekly adventures of a young boy called Corky, whose parents, the Flying Falcons, were killed in a high-wire accident. Corky was adopted by a clown named Joey and rode Bimbo the elephant in the show. He was played by, of all people, Micky Dolenz, later of Monkees fame. (Years later Dave and Dolenz and Mitch Ryder had a wolf of a night in London reminiscing about the TV show.)

The episode that had the biggest impact on Dave was about a knife-thrower and his wife. Dolenz didn't remember it. But Dave did. Dave remembered it vividly. The wife was tied to a board. The assistant put the blindfold on the knife-thrower and spun him in a circle. Dave remembered everything about the show—the way the blindfolded man threw the knives at his wife, the way the knives stuck in the board all around her.

Dave was maybe eight when that show was on the air. He took his little sister, Annie, into the basement, and he stood her against the basement wall, and he threw his new darts at her. The first one stuck in her knee. The second in her shoulder. After the second one, she said, "This is a stupid game," and ran upstairs.

Their mother fainted when she saw the darts sticking

out of her daughter. When Dave explained why he had done this thing with the darts, his father seemed to understand, though he did confiscate the dart set. Dave always thought well of his father that he didn't get mad. Or lecture him. It was an accident, and Dave wouldn't have done it again. His father knew that.

DAVE SMILED AT Eugene over the fence.

Dave said, "You okay?"

"Ahh," said Eugene, motioning toward the vegetable patch with his head. "Gardening accident."

Dave said, "Sorry to hear that."

Maria, who was sitting beside her husband, snorted.

Dave nodded and walked back to the boys in the hammock. "What have you boys been up to?"

"We watered the garden," said Sam.

"Front and back?" said Dave. He was looking around. The grass was wet; the bathroom window was closed. There were no children dancing on the roof.

"Just the back," said Sam.

"Looks like you did a good job," said Dave.

Except for a few telltale soap bubbles clinging to the pear tree, everything was in order.

Dave said, "You've probably done enough watering for the next little while."

"Yeah," said Sam. "Probably."

Dave looked at his son hard. Sam looked back, nodding his head.

Sam said, "We are pretty much through with the watering."

Okay, thought Dave, *my move*. He knew it. They knew it. The boys were getting up.

"We are going to the park," said Sam.

Line of least resistance, thought Dave. *Lead me on.*

"That's a good idea," said Dave. He dug into his pocket and pulled out a bill. "Why don't you stop by Lawlor's and get yourself an ice cream."

Sam glanced at Murphy.

Murphy patted his bulging pockets.

"That's okay," said Sam. "We've got money."

SCHOOL LUNCH

After supper, on the night before the first day of school, Morley sent Dave and the kids to Lawlor's Drugs to buy school supplies. Morley stayed home. She had already done clothes, shoes, medical forms, the dentist, and groceries.

Dave stopped at the magazines and said, "Choose what you need and I'll meet you at the cash."

Sam was first back. He dumped a handful of stuff on the counter and said, "There. Can I have gum too?"

He had chosen a Pink Pearl eraser, a package of five eraser tips that fit on the top of pencils, a bottle of Wite-Out, and a dispenser of Correcto-tape.

"What about something to put your mistakes into?" said Dave. "What about a binder? What about a pen?"

"Pencils," said Sam, "not pens."

He came back a few moments later with five pencils and a red three-ringed binder with Spiderman on the front.

"There," he said. "Can I have some gum?"

Stephanie chose an oversized nylon binder that zipped up, a package of six pastel-coloured Hilroy notebooks, a giant pack of loose-leaf, and a $49 fountain pen.

"No way," said Dave. "Put the pen back."

"Can I have gum?" she said.

The next time Stephanie floated up to the cash, she was holding five little cardboard boxes with cellophane windows.

"Labels," she said.

She had big white labels and small white labels and labels with fancy red borders and green-bordered labels, and a package of little red dots. There wasn't enough stuff in their house for all the labels she had.

"Please," she said. "I love peeling them off the paper. I love sticking them on things."

"Put the red dots back," said Dave. He had to draw a line somewhere. "And the fountain pen."

Dave bought himself a wooden ruler with a metal ink strip for old times' sake. A small blue notebook because the pages tore out so elegantly, and a pack of gum.

ON THEIR WAY home they stopped for ice cream. The world seemed perfect. The end of another summer, his children beside him with their new stuff, ready for the year ahead.

When they got home, Sam threw his bag on the couch.

"I got correction tape," he said. "You can cover anything."

"And an eraser," said Dave. "And pencils."

Morley was making tea. Stephanie spread her new notebooks out on the kitchen table.

"Should I use blue or green for history?" she said.

"What about the pink one?" said Morley. "I always used pink for history."

"That's ridiculous," said Stephanie. "Pink's for math."

Morley wasn't about to argue. It was the end of a long day. She had been grocery shopping before supper; she was tired. She had spent longer than usual in the supermarket, aimlessly gliding down the aisles looking for things she could put in her children's lunch bags. Something new, something surprising, something they would eat.

Just one day, she wanted one of them to come home and say, "Gee, lunch was good."

To hear that, just once, and you could die happy. Mostly what she heard was, "I hate vanilla pudding" or "Don't send those yogurts with the exploding aluminum lids."

Mostly what she got back was criticism and half-eaten lunches.

On the afternoon before the first day of school, the supermarket seemed to be full of parents like her, aisles of mothers and fathers trapped in the same vortex. Defeated parents with defeated eyes, staring into the middle distance in search of school lunch. Morley felt like she had tried everything in the store at one time or another. What kept her moving was the faint hope that there was a new idea on a shelf, somewhere.

She knew she was on a fool's mission. She knew even if she found something that they had never tried, she'd be crazy to buy it, her enthusiasm for unproved items tempered by the knowledge that anything the kids turned their noses up at would be *her* lunch until it was finished.

That's why she didn't buy in bulk any more. Because she had learned that when it came to school lunch, her children couldn't be trusted. Last year they said they liked mango juice. So she had bought flats of mango juice from one of those discount superstores. Carrying them from the car and stacking them in the basement. Enough mango juice to see them through Christmas. A pile of mango juice as high as her waist.

The first day she packed the first mango juice in their lunch, they both came home and denied ever liking it.

"Why did you give us that stuff?" said Sam.

Morley drank mango juice at lunch every day for two months straight. She used it to wash down the prune-apple cereal bars that no one else would eat. It was either that or throw the cereal bars out, and she was damned if she was going to do that. Even Arthur the dog would only eat them grudgingly, leaving little mounds of wet oats around the house. Which were not a pleasant thing to step in. Especially if you stepped in them unexpectedly in the night, in the dark. With bare feet.

This year for the first day's lunch, Morley bought kaiser rolls, and expensive salami, some crisp new apples, and chocolate milk. And not the little ones, the big ones—full pints. It was as tempting an array as she could think of—short of stuffing their lunch bags with licorice, something that she had considered doing. Two dollars' worth of licorice—each—and maybe a Coke, or a Red Bull. Nothing else.

"Gee, Mom, great lunch."

Short of stuffing their lunch bags with candy, the kaiser rolls and the expensive salami were the best that she could do.

The kids were in bed by ten. When she went into Sam's room to say good night, he was reading *Mad* magazine.

"Be careful," he said as she stepped over his clothes.

Sam had laid everything he was going to wear on the floor. The red T-shirt tucked into the jeans. His new sneakers sticking out from the bottom of the pant legs, like he could slide into them.

Morley knelt down in the darkness and pulled off a price tag that was still attached to the jeans.

Stephanie had all her notebooks stacked on her desk, all neatly labelled. She'd used the labels with the red borders for her name and put a large blank white one below it to fill in the name of the subject.

"It's like Christmas Eve," said Morley to Dave when she came downstairs. "It's like that perfect suspended moment on Christmas Eve when everyone's in bed and the presents are under the tree and the only thing left is potential. When everything has the possibility of perfection."

Before she went to bed, Morley looked in on both her children one more time. Sam was sound asleep on his back, his hands folded behind his head, a huge grin on his face. Stephanie still had her light on, reading.

"Lights off," said Morley.

And then she went back into Sam's room for a moment,

looking at him smiling in his sleep. Reaching out with her fingers and touching her son's grin.

And then she went to bed. And she lay in bed and thought about the year ahead. And she felt pleased. First day of school was like launching a new ship. The kids had been in dry dock all summer. Tomorrow it was time to push them out to sea again. Everything was shipshape. She had done everything she was supposed to do.

She began to run through the day in her mind. She got up and checked the alarm. It was set. Their clothes were ready, their books were ready. She'd bought a box of some awful cereal for breakfast, a cereal that would change the colour of the milk they poured on it to a bright pastel colour. A cereal with enough sugar in it to wake them up on the first early morning of the school year. And she imagined the perfect lunch that she'd prepare, the chocolate milk, the good salami, and she'd wrap the kaisers in Saran Wrap so they could see what she had made them.

She thought of these things and they made her smile. And then as she lay in her bed in the darkness Morley frowned: where were the lunch bags? Each child had a reusable nylon lunch bag with a Velcro fastener at the top. And the lunch bags hadn't crossed her consciousness all summer.

Morley frowned because she couldn't remember seeing them in the lunch-bag drawer where they were supposed to be. She rolled over so she was staring toward the bedroom door, toward the stairs, and she tried to remember if maybe she had washed the lunch bags. Maybe they were hanging in the basement. But she couldn't picture them there. In fact, she had no memory of them at all.

BECAUSE SHE WANTED the day to be perfect, Morley lay in bed and, in her imagination, she hunted through the kitchen. She did an inventory of the drawers and cupboards, but no matter where she looked, the bags were nowhere to be found. They weren't in the drawer where they belonged or the cupboard where she put things she wasn't using.

She lay there for maybe ten minutes thinking about the lunch bags before she was suddenly seized by a horrible notion. When the thought came, she sat up in bed abruptly. She knew exactly where the lunch bags were.

She'd passed them a hundred times since school was out. They were in the kids' backpacks, which were hanging downstairs by the back door, where the kids had left them in June. After the last day of school. Where they'd been all summer. Never unpacked—and festering.

Morley switched on the light beside her bed and crawled out from under the covers. She couldn't sleep without knowing the truth.

She retrieved Stephanie's backpack first, carrying it from the hook by the back door to the kitchen table. It must have weighed fifty pounds, crammed with every book Stephanie had used in grade eleven.

How could she have forgotten about this?

She pulled out the books one by one, and she made a pile on the kitchen table until she got to the very bottom of the backpack. And there at the bottom of the pack was a blue nylon lunch bag with a Velcro fastener, as flat as a pancake. Morley opened it slowly and peered inside.

Everything had fused together, the weight of the books squeezing the life out of the uneaten lunch so it had hardened into a leather-like strip.

Morley put the bag down and walked across the kitchen and got a pair of yellow rubber gloves from under the sink. She put them on and then she pulled at the leather thing in her daughter's lunch bag. It came out in one piece. It didn't resemble any kind of food Morley remembered having in her kitchen. In fact it didn't resemble food. It looked more like the pictures she had seen in *National Geographic* magazine of mummified bog people.

Sam's lunch bag was on the top of his backpack. Morley thought she remembered packing him a pear on the last day of school and a container of yogurt. One of the ones with the exploding aluminum covers. She pulled the lunch bag out of the backpack and opened it carefully. It was dark and damp in there, like a compost heap. And for a moment she thought of reaching in, and then she thought better of it.

Instead of reaching in, she closed the bag and put it back where she found it: at the top of Sam's backpack. And she hung the backpack up on one of the hooks by the back door. Then she picked up Stephanie's lunch bag, retrieved the piece of leather from the kitchen sink where she had tossed it, and placed it back in the nylon pouch. She dropped the lunch bag into the bottom of Stephanie's backpack and put the books on top. She hung it up by the back door too.

And then Morley went upstairs. She got into bed, but not before she had reset her alarm clock for fifteen minutes earlier.

She was giving herself and the kids a little extra time. So there would be time in the morning for the moment she now imagined as she lay under the covers—the moment when Sam and Stephanie were eating the sugary cereal, and she said, "Where are your lunch bags?" The moment when they shrugged sleepily, and she sent them to find the bags for themselves.

It was 1:30 in the morning. They'd be up in less than six hours. As she drifted to sleep, Morley thought of the bottle of Wite-Out on Sam's desk.

Morley had wanted so much to start her kids' school year off right. And oddly enough she was. On their very first morning, they were going to learn something. Something about taking care of your own stuff. Something about thinking ahead. Something about the shelf life of sandwiches and pears and yogurt. But Morley had learned something too. She might decide to go back to Lawlor's and get Stephanie that fountain pen. She might have to eat a week of salami sandwiches. She was prepared to do anything, anything, to make the year ahead a perfect year for her children. Anything but cleaning out those lunch bags.

FIREWORKS

They were bumping along the 104. Heading west, in Willy's one ton. Willy was behind the wheel. Dave was riding shotgun. Dave's son Sam was wedged in between them.

They crossed the Causeway in the late afternoon and were already past New Glasgow. Which meant they were making good time.

Willy said, "We could stop in Sackville. Take the kid to Mel's for dinner."

"Or to the Inn," Dave said. "We could take him to the Marshlands. Show him a little class." Dave winked at Sam.

Willy was wearing a black Def Leppard T-shirt and ripped jeans. Not exactly dressed for fine dining.

Willy said, "I'm in the mood for Mel's."

Sam said, "Is it *really* called . . . Sackville?"

THEY WERE SUPPOSED to fly home. Dave and Sam were. They had flown to Halifax, where Smith picked them up and drove them to Dave's mom's place in Cape Breton. Dave and Sam had come out to help Margaret and Smith with fall chores, putting the windows up and the garden frames away. They had return tickets home. But Dave ran into Willy in Kerrigan's, and Willy said, "I'm driving. If you want."

It was early autumn. The loamy smell of leaves in the chilly air.

"Leaving Tuesday," said Willy.

A Tuesday departure meant they could stay two days longer. It also meant Sam would miss a couple days of school.

"I'm okay with that," said Sam.

SO THERE THEY were. Sam in the middle, his eyes glued to the road, sliding into his father every time Willy took a corner too fast, which was most of the corners. The floor of the cab was already filling up with empty takeout cups, used paper napkins, spare change, and Willy's maps.

It was, in other words, perfect. Or as perfect as any twenty-two-hour road trip can be. It was working out just as Dave had hoped.

As they crossed the border from Nova Scotia into New Brunswick, Sam stared out the window at the flat land. There were huge towers rising up from the marsh like periscopes.

"Short-wave," said Willy. "They built it during the war."

As the spiderweb towers faded in the distance, Dave said, "We could go the long way you know, through Maine."

"Not crossing the border," said Willy.

"Might be fun," said Dave. "Stop and see Big Al in Bangor."

"Can't cross the border," said Willy, jerking his head toward the back of the truck. "Can't risk it."

In the old days, Willy used to haul cable for touring rock bands. But he wasn't a big man, and as the road cases got larger and heavier, and as he got older, the work got too hard. Don't get me wrong. Willy could still scramble up into the rafters of any arena like a monkey. The lifting and pulling just got too much. So instead, he learned the light board from Freaky Bottoms. He got into pyro a couple of years later.

"I have stuff back there," said Willy. Meaning in the back of the truck.

Dave glanced at his son. Sam was lost in a headphoned fog. Dave frowned at Willy.

Willy laughed. Shook his head. "Not that kind of stuff."

What Willy had back there were boxes of pyro left over from the tour he had just finished. Well, not exactly from the tour.

"It's complicated," said Willy.

The band Willy was working with had been up and down the eastern seaboard. The Carolinas, Virginia, Kentucky.

"We stopped in this little town," said Willy, "back in the hills. There was a hardware store. You wouldn't believe the place."

Willy described a screen door with a small bell, a wood stove with a little bucket for chew. The owner lived over the store. Just him and his dog. He showed Willy around. Willy loves that sort of thing.

"And there were boxes of stuff. Boxes of it. From the forties and fifties," said Willy.

"What kind of stuff?" said Dave.

"Pyro," said Willy. "Never seen anything like it. From a carnival or something. Big stuff. Show stuff."

The problem was it was sort of past its best-before date.

"But only by a decade or two," said Willy. "And I got it for a song."

Then he said, "I could lose my licence if I tried to cross back into the States with it."

Despite not wanting to risk the border, Willy, one hand resting on top of the steering wheel, the other riding the air currents out the window, didn't seem too worried about his cargo.

"The problem with the old stuff is the chemicals get unstable," Willy explained cheerfully. "Can't be trusted if it ain't stored right. Can be pretty, you know, *volatile*. Unexpected explosions. Things like that."

Dave twisted around and glanced at the back of the truck.

"Boom!" said Willy. And he laughed, deep and raspy, like a pirate.

WILLY PULLED INTO the gas station by the highway. He said, "I'm going to gas up before dinner."

After the stop for gas, they drove into town and ate at Mel's. Chicken sandwiches on sliced white. Real chicken. Real fries. Real shakes.

"This is good," said Sam.

As they walked back to the truck, Willy lit a cigarette. Dave made him walk down the street about a hundred yards away and smoke it there.

BACK ON THE highway, back on the road. Dave undid his sneakers and put his socked feet up on the dash.

He glanced at Sam. Sam was fiddling with the radio.

Sam said, "I'm trying to find some *good* music."

Dave looked over at Willy—who had been humming along to the radio. Willy shrugged and smiled.

Dave rested his head against the side window of the truck and gazed out into the dusk. He hadn't thought of firecrackers for years.

FIRECRACKERS WERE A huge deal in Big Narrows when Dave was young. Not the fancy ones. Not Roman candles and things like that. The little red ones. The ones that look like tiny sticks of dynamite. You light the fuse and they explode and *nothing else*—no stars, no sparkles. Just a flash and a good old utilitarian, boy-like bang.

You got them at MacDonnell's. MacDonnell's General Store. They came every autumn. Like apples. You dreamed of them all summer, and they arrived in the fall. So when the leaves began to turn, boys watched over MacDonnell's the same way they watched over the quarry pond for signs of ice.

"Are they here yet, Mr. MacDonnell?"

"When are they coming, Mr. MacDonnell?"

They came all the way from China. From the port city of Macau. And they came by boat, into New York City. Or so Mr. MacDonnell said.

"Slow boat from China, boys. We have to be patient."

No one, or no child anyway, ever suspected that Mr. MacDonnell might have stock left over from the previous season in his basement storeroom. Or would have understood, had they figured it out, what a favour he was doing them by making them wait. There can be abundance in scarcity, and the day the firecrackers finally appeared, there was an abundance of joy. The thought of it made Dave smile. The day they finally appeared was as good as Christmas morning.

Each package—they cost a nickel, or maybe a dime— was about the size of a deck of cards. And red inside and out. Each cracker was not only dynamite red itself; the package came wrapped in red *paper*. *Firecracker* paper. There was nothing like it anywhere—crispy, waxy—like tissue paper gone stale.

Anchor Brand, Alligator Brand, Black *Cat*, Black *Bat*, Black *Jack*, Black *Widow*.

The instructions, printed at the bottom of the label, in English, were identical on each pack.

Lay on ground, light fuse, and move away.

Yeah. Sure.

The little ones, Ladyfingers they called them, were maybe half an inch long, and boys like Johnny Flowers actually held them in their hands when they went off. Dave had seen this with his own eyes, but had never had the guts to try it himself.

Cherry bombs were the biggest, two inches long, two feet loud—guaranteed to blow the head off a Barbie doll if you taped enough of them to the doll's neck.

The best, like so much in life, were the ones in the middle. The one-inchers, the inch-and-a-halfs.

The firecrackers came in packs of twelve, or sometimes sixteen, and the wicks were made of strands of grey paper woven together so the firecrackers came in strings, designed for the Chinese practice of letting off the whole string at once—for a celebratory round of pop, pop, pop, pop, pop. . .

No kid in the Narrows would ever do that.

For children who counted their money by the penny, *that* would have been the most monstrous frivolity, a waste of explosive proportions.

And so October would come, and on the October day when the precious red packages finally appeared on the shelves, kids would flock to MacDonnell's in twos and in threes, and buy a pack, or if they could afford it, two. And then they would sit on a rock, somewhere out of sight, and carefully unravel the wicks, lighting the firecrackers one by one. If they had applied themselves as assiduously to their school work, the town might have boasted a Nobel Prize.

Mostly the firecrackers were set off at night. For what could be better, if you are between the ages of eight and sixteen—the prime firecracker demographic—than to be out after dark with a smouldering string and a pocket full of black powder.

Dave said, "What was the string called?"

Sam shifted and said, "What?"

Dave said, "I was just thinking. We used to use string to light firecrackers. I can't remember what we called it."

"I have no idea what you are talking about," said Sam.

Dave *did* remember that it had to be the right kind of string—soft cotton, hard to find in the Narrows in those days. But if it was the right kind, it would smoulder all night, just the sweetest of smells. When you wanted to light a firecracker, you held the smouldering string to the wick until it sputtered to life. The burning string meant you didn't have to find matches. Meant you could actually carry fire around.

"Punk," said Dave. "We called it punk. And I'm talking about firecrackers."

Firecrackers. They were like a storm in a tube—both thunder *and* lightning—and the kids lit them and threw them as if they were born for stormy nights.

The best place to set them off was the bridge.

You'd light the fuse and hang over the railing and hold on. One. Two. Three. Four. If you timed it exactly, it would explode right before it hit the water. Blow a hole in the river, the water rippling out for yards and yards.

The best place to set them off was the bridge. Or in the schoolyard. Or in the ball field.

Really it didn't matter. The best place was anywhere there were other kids. And in October there were always kids whirling around. Someone was always up to something.

Chan Gillespie once packed a chocolate-milk carton with baby powder and taped four cherry bombs to it. There were at least a dozen kids there to watch the night he set it off. When he did, the powder shot out of the bottom and the carton took off, like a fighter jet. It was awesome. The best theatre some of them would ever see. Ever.

Dave's friend Billy Mitchell had this idea you could take a bunch of packs, break the sticks open, collect the powder and pack it into a pipe, making a rocket that could launch a hamster into space. He had the hamster. And he built the capsule. He took his grandfather's old mailbox and covered it in tinfoil. They spent a weekend training the hamster. But Billy could never convince enough kids to pool enough powder to pack the six-inch copper pipe he had stolen from his father's woodshed. So that never went any further than talk.

As you might expect, firecrackers were dropped down chimneys by older boys. But mostly they were just lit and chucked in the air. Mostly it was just a Friday night in October, three boys in sneakers and windbreakers.

There were accidents of course.

One day Billy, Chan, and Dave were hanging out on the old railway tracks on the way to the church. Billy lit a one-incher, but it slipped out of his hand before he could toss it. The lit cracker fell into his boot. It didn't actually explode. But it didn't go out either. For a moment none of them moved. For a moment they just stood there, the three of them staring at each other in disbelief. Then they heard the firecracker flare with a whoosh, and it kept whooshing as Billy hopped around, screaming. Chan and Dave yelled, "Take your boot off, take it off," but they were backing away at the same time. Just in case. You never knew.

They had, after all, seen what could happen to a Barbie doll.

The firecracker didn't blow, but it did burn right through the side of Billy's boot, and burned Billy's ankle. Dave and Chan had to help him home. And that was it for firecrackers that year.

Kids were burned every year, but no one was burned seriously, not even Billy that day on the tracks. No one lost an eye, or any of those things you read about, and when October came, even eight-year-olds were allowed out at night, unsupervised, with a pack of matches, a piece of string, and their pockets full of mischief. That was the way it was back then. Everyone did it. And everyone knew what they were up to. How could they not? Nearly every night in October, the town was punctuated by the rat-ta-ta-tat of kids and their little explosives.

"DAD?"

Sam was poking Dave.

"Dad! Willy said, 'Do you want to stop?'"

"What?"

"Do you want to stop?"

Dave glanced at Sam. His son had given up on the radio. He was headphoned again and glowing.

Maybe the adults of his childhood had been a touch cavalier about safety, but Dave's generation had been overprotective. Sometimes he felt like his son was living a virtual boyhood.

It made Dave sad to think that Sam wouldn't have fire-cracker memories. The closest Sam had ever come to the explosives racket was the summer afternoon Dave had found him squatting on the sidewalk with a small hammer and a roll of caps—crouching there banging out little sparks. Someone had brought the caps from the States. Maybe even Willy.

"DAD?" SAID SAM again. "Do you want to stop?"

Dave looked over at Willy. Willy was grinning.

They were somewhere past Moncton. A ways still to Fredericton, on a stretch of highway where there is not a lot going on. They would soon be coming up to a little town with a service centre. And a little further on, a chip wagon, and a farm stand, and a motel and then about five minutes further, on the right-hand side if you're heading for Fredericton, there was an old quarry.

"Remember?" said Willy.

Willy had bought the explosives for no other reason than to watch them go off. He figured he'd find a place to light them when he got home. But this place was as good as any other. And now he had company.

When Dave spotted the quarry road he said: "There!"

And Willy pulled in.

"Careful," said Dave. The road was all gravel, and wash-boarded out.

So Willy slowed down. They drove to the end of the road and got out.

Sam said, "What's going on?"

Willy said, "It's showtime, son."

Sam helped Willy and his father unload the truck. Seven boxes in all, each one with a hand-painted label that looked like a circus poster. They humped them down to the bottom of the quarry.

When they were done, Dave put his hand on Sam's shoulder and pointed back up toward the truck. "You sit up there," he said.

Sam scrambled back up the slope and settled down on the lip of the quarry.

Willy was now on his knees, opening boxes and pulling things out. "This stuff is amazing. It's amazing."

Dave said, "Be careful."

Willy smiled his gap-toothed smile. "As always, bro."

And then he stood and called up to Sam, "You ready, son?"

Sam shrugged, and Willy bent over and lit the first one. For a moment there was nothing.

Dave said, "Nothing." And he took a step toward it.

Willy grabbed him by the shoulder and pulled him back.

Willy said, "Patience, brother. Patience."

Neither of them moved. Suddenly there was a whizz and a silver flare and then an explosion of indigo. And the entire sky, or all of the sky they could see from the quarry floor, was full of blue diamonds.

And Willy said, "Oh yeah."

And he lit another, and then another. The explosions shimmered off the quarry walls and flashed and flowered on the rocks, turning everything blue and red and yellow, but only for an instant.

"Beautiful," said Willy. "It's beautiful."

Blossoms and stars and diamonds. The sky telescoping in and out.

After twenty minutes or so, Dave noticed the flicker of headlights along the quarry lip. A car had pulled off the highway and was bouncing down the gravel road. Five minutes later he saw another and then another. Before long there were maybe fifteen or twenty lining the shoulder of the quarry. And Dave could make out the silhouettes of people standing there watching.

Willy said, "Golden Orbs of Pluto's Fire."

And golden orbs flew up into the night, and in the light of the orbs, Dave saw upturned faces and pointing fingers. A dad with a child hoisted on his shoulders. A young couple, their arms around each other, their heads together but tilted back. He saw them in the flash and then he didn't.

Willy said, "Waterfall of the Fire Cauldron."

Dave stopped watching the sky and began watching the people instead. Some sitting, some leaning on their cars. And then he said to Willy, "Your show," and climbed back up the hill. He found Sam and sat on the ground beside him.

"This is awesome," said Sam. "This is the best night of my life."

Dave put his arm around Sam's shoulders.

Willy called, "Golden Dragons Waken from Slumber."

There was another whoosh and a flare. Dave saw his son's face, this time in the golden glow, and he thought this is how he would like to remember him. When Sam grew up and left home and Dave wanted to remember him, he wanted to remember Sam just like this. Sitting there, on the edge of the quarry in the middle of the night, his head back, his eyes wide open, and a smile on his face. Surrounded by the deep inky sky—but also the whizz-bang joy of explosion and the smell of the smoke, the *oooo*s and the *ahhhhh*s and now, from the people all around, the applause.

Then he heard Willy's voice again. Willy was still down below, standing alone in the darkness.

"Red Stars and the Dance of Light."

Sam leaned into Dave, his small body heavy against Dave's chest.

"This is going to be a good one," he said.

THE MERMAID AND OTHER MYSTERIES

Sam is spending the weekend with his sister. They are sitting at the kitchen table in her second-floor apartment. They have just finished dinner. Pasta with a reddish sauce. Salad. And dessert.

They have been sitting there talking about their parents since they finished eating. About Dave and Morley. About their father's record store. About the theatre where their mother works. They have talked about Arthur, their old dog. Now they are talking about their grandfather. Dave's father, Charlie, from Cape Breton, who Sam never met.

"I remember his smell," says Stephanie. "He smelled like plaid."

Sam says, "That's not helpful."

"He used to play the ukulele," says Stephanie.

"When he drove his truck," says Sam. "I knew that."

"Steered with his knees," says Stephanie.

It is possible she never saw him playing the ukulele while he drove. It is possible that's only a story she heard, just the way Sam had.

"It's hard to tell the difference," says Stephanie. "But I think I can remember."

It would have been the sort of thing Charlie would do. Sing to his granddaughter as they drove down the hill to town. Turning toward her and throwing his head back. He knew the road by heart. She would have sat in the front. There would not have been a booster seat.

IT FELT LIKE it had happened. But it's hard for her to remember more. She was so young when he died. The memories she has are moments without context—like photographs in an album. There is one in the truck. There's another where she is sitting on his shoulders, ducking so she won't hit her head on a tree branch. But those could have easily been her father's shoulders she was sitting on. She thinks she remembers Charlie and a boat.

"A lobster boat, probably," she says.

"At least you met him," says Sam, reaching for another helping of dessert. "At least he knew you."

They don't do this often, these two. Reminisce. It's not that they are too young for it. Everyone likes to reminisce. Young and old. What is it to reminisce but to share stories that you star in.

Sam says, "Do you remember when I broke my arm?"

"That summer," says Stephanie.

That summer Dave and Morley left the two of them in Cape Breton with their grandmother. Stephanie was eleven.

Which means Sam was, what? Four. And Grandpa Charlie had, of course, already passed away.

Dave wanted to take Morley to some festival in New York State. So they all drove down to Big Narrows and stayed a few days together. And then Morley and Dave took off, leaving Sam and Steph with Margaret.

It was the first time their parents had left them. Dave and Morley thought it would be good for Margaret, and for them—quite frankly, *they* needed some time too.

"It was a bad break," says Sam. Meaning his arm.

And just like that, this little after-dinner communion—which has been rolling along so happily—is in danger of derailing.

The broken arm, which Sam has just remembered, comes, you see, with certain complications.

"You want some tea?" says Stephanie, getting up from the table and walking over to the stove.

She is playing for time. She is trying to decide if she is going to tell her brother the truth about the broken arm.

Stephanie has a history of this. Of truth telling.

Over the years, she has delivered numerous truths to her brother—many of which would have been better left withheld.

If she was here to defend herself, Stephanie would argue that she was only trying to be honest. Others might argue she was being a bit insensitive.

The spring he was only five, for instance, Sam believed with his heart and soul that the beans his mother had planted in the garden were going to grow into a giant beanstalk.

"Don't be silly," said Stephanie. This was after watching a week of Sam's careful watering.

"They are *wax* beans. They're the ones we have for dinner. The ones you *hate.*"

True? Certainly it was true. But another truth was that at twelve years old, ready to leave childhood behind, Stephanie was bored of her brother's cute credulity.

When Sam earnestly told her that their father could remove the tip of his thumb and then reattach it—"It is from a wound he had in the war"—Stephanie said, "Give your head a shake. To begin with he was never in a war."

Then she removed the tip of her own thumb.

"See," she said, wiggling her fingers in his face. "It's a trick."

There were others of course. Some of them of significance.

There is a difference between coming upon the truth of things in your own time, and having truth thrust upon you by others. And all this truthfulness, delivered with such moral certitude, meant Sam sometimes navigated the world with a certain tentativeness.

This reached its apotheosis the spring Sam was eight. A Friday night in June. Stephanie was babysitting. She invited some friends over. One of them brought a copy of *The Exorcist.* They encouraged Sam to watch it with them. When little Regan projectile-vomited onto the priest, Sam threw up too. If Sam hadn't been the kind of kid he was, a boy blessed with seemingly endless sup-plies of trust and hopefulness, his childhood might have ended right there.

Which brings us back to the broken arm.

There is Sam, sitting at his sister's kitchen table—reminiscing.

"I fell off the swing," he says.

And there is Stephanie, standing by her stove, mulling which way she should go with this.

Let me tell you the truth of it.

SAM DID FALL off the swing. And it was in Cape Breton, at their grandma's house, the summer their parents left them. That much is true.

Stephanie was pushing Sam. And, okay, in the passive-aggressive way of older siblings, she was pushing too hard. So when he fell, the trajectory of the swing launched him surprisingly far—his little arms and legs windmilling as he sailed over the yard.

When he landed, he landed on his funny bone. The elec-tric jolt that ran down his arm stunned him. He lay in the dirt for a second as the swing spun silently above him.

He didn't dare move. Because even though he was only four, he knew what had happened. He had broken his arm.

He lay there soundlessly, stock-still, and then he began to scream. A bit of showboating perhaps. Stephanie would certainly have said that.

Their grandmother ran out of the kitchen, wiping her hands on her apron.

"Sam," she said. "Sweetheart. Whatever is the matter?"

"My arm is broken," said Sam. "I broke my arm."

Standing there by her stove in her apartment all these years later, Stephanie can remember that moment perfectly. Her grandmother bending over and scooping up her brother. And she can remember following them inside the house, morosely.

Now, it was quickly apparent that telling Sam he was going to be all right was only making matters worse. He was dangerously close to falling into outright hysteria when Margaret changed tack. She picked up his arm, wiggled it a bit, and said, "Oh my goodness. No wonder you are crying. Your arm *is* broken."

Sam stopped crying on the spot.

Stephanie recalled that moment as if it were yesterday. Her brother turning to her across their grandmother's kitchen.

"See!"

Then looking back at Margaret, he said, "Do I need a cast?"

Without a second's pause, Margaret said, "Oh yes."

And that's when Stephanie started to cry because, well, because she had just broken her brother's arm, hadn't she? And they were going to have to go to the hospital, and the truth would inevitably come out, about her pushing too hard, and she would be sent to reform school.

"Do we have to take him to the hospital?" she said.

Margaret, who was operating at a highly evolved level of child care, turned and winked at her granddaughter and said, "I think we can handle this ourselves."

It was all very confusing.

Stephanie sat there watching as Margaret got an old, half-empty bag of plaster from the shed. And she watched her wrap Sam's arm in gauze, and then set the gauze with the plaster.

"I broke my arm," said Sam to his sister. "The bone snapped."

"Right through," said Margaret, who had begun to clean up.

She fashioned a sling out of a pillowcase.

"How long will I need the cast?" said Sam.

"Oh, it is a very bad break," said Margaret. "That cast is going to have to stay on overnight."

Then she made popcorn. And they sat by the stove, and they ate popcorn.

"WE WENT TO the hospital to get the cast," says Sam, interrupting Stephanie's reverie.

No, Stephanie is thinking, as she stands by her own stove, all these years later. *We didn't go to the hospital.*

She picks up her kettle and moves it to the stove top.

NOW YOU MIGHT wonder what harm there could be with her saying something right now. Sam, after all, clearly didn't break his arm. They cut the cast off the next morning. The whole exercise was rather sweet.

But the tapestry of our lives is made up of little bits of faded cloth—each worn piece stitched to another on the frame of memory. Is it so horrible that Sam believes he fell off the swing and broke his arm and they put on a cast and it healed overnight? One day the contradictions of that might occur to him. But for now, he soared through the air in an awful acrobatic falling, and when he landed, he snapped his arm, and he had a cast like so many of his friends.

It may be a curation of memory, but it was, after all, a magical two weeks—living there with their grandmother in that rambling old house, without their parents, for the first time in their lives. It was a time that *should* be mythologized.

It is no coincidence that this was the one and the same summer that Stephanie had her own encounter with myth. For that was the summer, the summer Morley and Dave left them with Margaret, the summer that Sam broke his arm, that Stephanie saw the mermaid.

LET ME TELL you about it.

Margaret's friend Mildred used to watch Sam in the afternoons, when he napped. While Mildred babysat Sam, Margaret would take Stephanie off on her own. To town—to the post office, to Kerrigan's for groceries, or to the Maple Leaf Restaurant for ice cream. Margaret was still driving Charlie's truck that summer. And sometimes, on the way home from town, they would park at Rock Beach, the way Charlie used to. Margaret would sit on the big flat rock at the back of the cove where Charlie liked to sit. Stephanie would sit beside her. And they would stare out at the lonely grey ocean.

One afternoon Margaret started to cry as she sat there. When Stephanie asked her why, instead of answering Margaret said, "Did your father ever tell you that if you shed seven tears into the ocean, a fairy will come out of the water?"

Stephanie had never seen a grown-up cry before. She had been staring at her grandmother with concern. The tears were virtually *running* down her grandmother's cheeks. She finally summoned the courage to speak.

"Can we try?" she said. "To get a fairy?"

Margaret shrugged. "No harm in that," she said.

They took off their shoes and set them on the rock. They picked their way over the stones to the edge of the water.

Stephanie walked right in. But Margaret knew how cold the water was. Margaret stopped at the edge.

Stephanie tugged on her arm.

"Come on," said Stephanie, trying to be as encouraging as possible. "You cry. And I'll count."

The moment Margaret put her feet in the salty cold ocean she stopped crying. It was just too cold to cry. Instead, she started to laugh at the foolishness of it—standing in the ocean trying to summon fairies.

"Grandma," said Stephanie, "why aren't you crying? Is something wrong?"

THAT WAS THE day Margaret began telling Stephanie the old stories.

They would sit in the kitchen in the evening when Sam had been put to bed. The kettle would be hissing on the stove; Margaret's knitting would be in her lap. And she told the stories that her mother had told her when she was a girl. Stories about all the sea spirits.

The little blue men who lived in the shallows looking for boats to sink.

The selkies, who looked like seals when you saw them in the dark, rolling sea but who could come onto the beach, shed their skin, and take human form.

"If you ever marry a selkie," said Margaret one night, with great seriousness, "you have to burn the skin."

"Why, Grandma?"

"Because if all you do is hide the skin, the selkie will find it. And when they find their skin, they will leave you and return to the ocean and never come back."

"I would never marry a selkie," said Stephanie.

Margaret shrugged.

"Anyway," said Stephanie, "how would I know?"

"A woman always knows," said Margaret.

"Probably by the smell," said Stephanie. "Probably they smell like seaweed."

Margaret told her about leprechauns.

"A leprechaun," said Margaret, leaning forward with great seriousness, "is not a little person the way they say in the books. A leprechaun appears to us in the form of an old man."

She said it twice.

"Just like an old man," she said.

Then she said, "If you ever catch a leprechaun, he has to grant you three wishes. And once he has done that, you have to let him go."

Stephanie said, "Was Grandpa a leprechaun?"

"God spare me," said Margaret. "I never thought of that. But it's well possible."

Stephanie said, "Did you ever ask him for three wishes?"

"I never had to," said Margaret. "He was always granting my wishes *before* I could ask."

"Maybe that is why he died," said Stephanie. "Maybe he ran out of wishes."

Margaret said, "Maybe he did."

ONE AFTERNOON MARGARET took Stephanie to Ellen Burnett's house so Ellen could read her cup.

Ellen used an old brown teapot her mother favoured, with no strainer in the spout, so you were sure to get plenty of leaves. And real porcelain teacups, from England. Old ones, with a good diameter at the bottom—not too narrow but not too wide either.

Ellen knew just how a girl Stephanie's age would like her tea.

"Lots of milk and three sugars," she said, not asking.

Margaret nodded.

Stephanie drank her sweet, milky tea until there was only a little left in the bottom of the cup. Then Ellen told her to hold the cup in her left hand and turn it three times to the right.

Stephanie, who had no idea what was going on, nodded earnestly.

Right before she began, Ellen Burnett put her hand on Stephanie's head and said, "As you do it, I want you to think of the future. I want you to think of what is going to happen to you."

Stephanie said, "But I don't *know* what is going to happen to me. I'm only eleven."

Ellen said, "Hush now. You do as I say and *I* will tell you what is going to happen."

Stephanie turned the cup carefully, one, two, three times. She did it again, the other way, then flipped the cup upside down into the saucer.

It was only after she turned it upside down that Stephanie realized she had been concentrating so hard on turning it the right way that she had forgotten to think of the future.

She was about to admit that, but Ellen Burnett said, "Perfect." And she decided not to say anything. Why mess with perfection?

Ellen picked up Stephanie's teacup and the three of them leaned forward and peered inside.

Stephanie has no memory of what Ellen then told her.

ON THE WAY back from Ellen's, Margaret and Stephanie went for a walk on Logan's Beach. They took their shoes off and left them by the wooden sidewalk where the sea grass ends and the sand begins. The tide was out, and the beach was wide and flat, and the fog was rolling in. It wasn't an afternoon for a walk, but they walked all the way to where the sand ends at the rock point.

It was just after they started back that Steph looked over her shoulder and saw the girl on the rocks at the point's end. As soon as she noticed her, the girl slid into the water—her hair, a flash of green, and in Stephanie's mind's eye, below her waist, a flippered tail.

"Grandma," she said, tugging on Margaret's hand.

It was foggy. It was hard to see the point from where they had stopped. Probably it was a seal. Possibly it was someone swimming. A girl from town, maybe. Maybe a girl from town who had told a boy to meet her on the beach and he didn't come. Maybe the boy had recently moved to town and the girl wanted him to be her boyfriend and she was heartbroken. Aren't mermaids heartbroken?

"Grandma," said Stephanie, "did you see it?"

But Margaret shook her head.

That night as they were going to bed, Stephanie said, "Grandma, do you believe all those stories you told me?"

Margaret leaned down and squeezed Stephanie's hand. She said, "Don't you?"

AND THESE ARE the moments Stephanie is remembering as she stands by the stove in her kitchen waiting for the water to boil.

Her little brother, still sitting at her table, is lost in his own dreams of that long-ago summer.

"We went to the hospital to get the cast," he says suddenly. "I don't really remember that part too well."

She makes up her mind. She turns and she says, "No, Sam. We didn't go to the hospital."

The kettle begins to whistle, and she turns off the stove and carries it to the table. She pours the boiling water into the teapot, the steam rising in her kitchen for a moment like Cape Breton fog.

"We didn't go to the hospital," she says. "The doctor came to the house. He put the cast on right in the kitchen."

"I was so young," says Sam. "It's hazy. I think I remember we made popcorn."

"I remember that," says Stephanie.

She sits down and smiles at her younger brother.

"Sometimes," says Sam, "when we are young, we read things, or see movies, or people tell us stories, and they get jumbled. And we think we saw them. We think we are remembering but what we are remembering is something we have heard. Murphy told me that. We see things that we have never really seen."

And that is true. Sometimes we imagine things.

And sometimes, if we are lucky, we walk along a beach holding our grandmother's hand, and the fog rolls in. And we glance back over our shoulder into the fog and glimpse things that no one else sees.

Stephanie is remembering the rotten smell of seaweed, the raucous call of the sea birds, the grey roiling sea that rolls on and on. The little blue men who wait in the shallows to make mischief with boats, the seals that can shed their skin and turn into people, and how fairies come out of the water if you shed seven tears. And she is remembering, too, the way the waves run up at your feet and suck the sand away so you feel as if you are sinking. And the way tea leaves lie in the bottom of teacups.

She fills her brother's mug and she smiles.

"Here's to Grandma," she says.

Birthdays
and Holidays

BIRTHDAY PRESENT

The day Morley turned forty—a Tuesday afternoon that seems long ago and far away now—her friend and neighbour Mary Turlington came over after lunch with a little box wrapped in gold foil. It was just a token. The sort of trinket women give to each other to mark special moments. It was a ceramic creamer in the shape of a cat—the creamer's handle fashioned from the cat's tail, the cream designed to purr out of the cat's mouth. It was the sort of thing you would pass with a smile and a shake of your head at a garage sale. But, if you happened to get one from your best friend on your fortieth birthday, it would be the sort of thing you might grow fond of, the way you grow fond of certain Christmas decorations.

Women understand these things. In fact, only women possess the grace to pull something like this off. A man is not likely to drop in on a friend, unannounced, on his friend's birthday, and give him a ceramic creamer in the shape of a cat. Not in a thousand years. And if he did—if, say, Bert Turlington were seized by some inexplicable spasm and bought Dave a ceramic creamer for his birthday, wrapped it, and took it to his house after dinner—no matter how cool it was (because a cat creamer could possess a certain retro coolness), the transaction would leave a trail of awkwardness and confusion that could hover between Bert and Dave for . . . well, quite possibly for the rest of their lives. For months they would avoid each other, in case the subject of the creamer arose.

But Mary isn't Bert, and Morley isn't Dave, so on Morley's fortieth birthday, Mary Turlington knocked on Morley's front door after lunch, holding her purse in one hand and the wrapped creamer in the other.

When Morley opened the door her eyes were watery and red. She was holding a wad of Kleenex. She looked as if she had been weeping. She had, in fact, been weeping on and off all morning.

"Morley," said Mary right away, "what's the matter?"

Now that's another thing a man wouldn't do. If Bert knocked on Dave's door to give him a ceramic creamer in the shape of a cat (of course it wouldn't be in the shape of a cat, it would be in the shape of a dog) and Dave answered the door with tears in his eyes, Bert would not ask what was wrong. Not if he was thinking clearly. If he was thinking clearly, Bert would do one of two things. He would remember something he needed to check at home: "I'll be back in a minute," he might say. Or, if he wasn't overwhelmed with the need to escape, if he wanted to stick around, Bert still would not risk an emotional encounter. He would help by handing his friend a plausible excuse. He wouldn't ask,

"What's the matter?" He would say, "You cutting onions?"

But because she is a woman, and therefore possessed of an emotional fearlessness, Mary looked at Morley's red and watery eyes and she drove right to the heart of the matter. Mary said, "Morley, what is the matter?"

Morley's shoulders began to shudder. She opened her mouth, but no words came out. She shook her head, turned, and walked into the kitchen.

Mary followed her.

They sat at the kitchen table.

Finally Morley said, "How could he live with me so long and not know I would hate it?"

"You mean tonight?" said Mary.

"I don't want a birthday party," said Morley. "I hate birthday parties."

Morley had, in fact, hated birthday parties since she was a little girl, hated them ever since she could remember.

She hated birthdays so much she had burst into tears at her own fifth birthday party the moment everyone began to sing "Happy Birthday."

Morley didn't like being the centre of attention.

And she hated everything else about birthday parties. She hated greeting people at the door. She hated games like Pin the Tail on the Donkey. She hated bursting balloons. She even hated presents. When she attended her friends' birthday parties, Morley would watch them unwrap their presents with her heart pounding, her anxiety rapidly escalating. She would grow frantic because she wanted the birthday girl to like her present the best.

The year she turned seven, Morley sat in front of her pile of wrapped presents and started to weep. "I don't want to open them," she said to her mother between sobs. She was certain there would be a present she wouldn't like. And she was sure everyone would know. She was afraid she would hurt someone's feelings, afraid she wouldn't be a good enough actor.

And now, thirty-three years later, Morley felt much the same about the neighbourhood party Dave had planned for her fortieth birthday. She didn't want to be the centre of attention on her fortieth birthday. She was afraid she wouldn't be a good enough actor.

She had hoped the day would just slip by.

Dave had known that she would *say* that she didn't need a party. So he hadn't told her about it until two days beforehand.

She begged him to call it off.

"But I've already invited everyone," he said.

Morley didn't want the entire neighbourhood knowing she was forty. "You announced it?" she said.

"Not exactly announced," said Dave. "I asked people to come. To a party."

"You announced it to the neighbourhood," said Morley.

"Just people we know," said Dave.

"You told them I was forty?"

"Well, *turning* forty," said Dave. "Not actually. Forty. Not yet. Technically."

This was information that Morley had not planned on releasing. She didn't want children on the block running around chanting, "Lordy, Lordy, your mom's forty!" It was a fact she had thought they could keep within the privacy of their own home.

"It is just so insensitive," said Morley to Mary Turlington. She was fiddling with the little cat creamer as she talked.

"What do you guys normally do?" asked Mary. "What do you do on his birthday?"

"I never throw a party," said Morley defensively. "Never. Ever.

"Last year," said Morley, "I gave him ballet tickets."

"Oh," said Mary, nodding.

"The year before," said Morley, shutting her eyes, "I gave him a Shaker blanket box."

"And the year before that?" asked Mary.

"Cooking class," said Morley.

"Cooking class," said Mary.

"I enrolled him in a vegetarian Indian cooking class," said Morley.

"He must have liked that," said Mary.

"Actually," said Morley, "I'm not sure."

IF TRUTH BE told, it wasn't just the notion of being the centre of attention that was upsetting Morley. Honestly, a part of her was charmed that her husband had planned to make a fuss over her fortieth birthday. But she was anxious about the *kind* of fuss her husband might organize.

As Morley understood it, Dave's notion of a party involved a keg of beer, a few bags of chips, and a crowd of people drinking the beer on empty stomachs.

"I hired caterers," said Dave.

"You what?" said Morley.

"I have hired caterers," said Dave. "You don't have to do a thing. The caterers will come in the afternoon and bring the food and set everything up. They'll clean up before they start, and they'll clean up when they're finished."

What could she say? He wasn't begging her, but almost.

So the party was on. And that's why Mary found Morley crying on the day she turned forty.

THE CATERERS WERE supposed to arrive at three.

Morley had agreed to go out for the afternoon. She would get her hair done. She would have a facial. She would go shopping. They would leave a key under the mat. The caterers would let themselves in and get ready.

"No cleaning, no cooking, no nothing," Dave had said. "You go out. You come home. Everything will be ready."

"I have to get ready to go," said Morley to Mary Turlington. She stood up and began to clear off the table.

"Let the caterers do that," said Mary.

Morley looked around her kitchen. There was a laundry basket on the counter. There were dirty breakfast dishes in the sink. There were footprints on the floor.

"I was going to wash the floor," said Morley.

"No cleaning," said Mary.

"I can't leave the house like this," said Morley.

"Yes, you can," said Mary. "That's the deal. Right?"

So off she went.

AND AT TEN past five, there she was, walking up the street toward her house. Except she wasn't walking up the street—she was swinging.

Forty years old and Morley had just had her first facial. Her first manicure. She felt elegant. She felt sophisticated. Her hair was light and bouncy. It felt as if it was swaying back and forth like TV commercial hair. She glanced down at her hands. Her nails were sparkling. Her face was glowing. She was moving with grace. She sensed that her posture had improved. She was standing tall. She was utterly . . . presentable.

She held her nails up to her face, and she looked around the street and she thought, *Please, Lord, let this be the moment I run into someone I haven't seen for years.*

And then she was thinking about what was waiting for her. She was thinking that, in a moment, she would walk into her house, and there would be a caterer to greet her. She thought how good it was to be rich. *My servant is waiting,* she thought, *my servant who has been with me all these years. I should give him the weekend off.* And that made her smile, and she thought, *How would I cope without him? I don't even know where he keeps the coffee.* She laughed out loud and thought how wonderful it was to be so calm and elegant. How wonderful it was to have a faithful servant laying out plates of hot food on your dining room table while you sashayed along the street looking so good that birds were falling out of the very trees you were walking under.

Morley could hardly wait to get home. She would breeze into the kitchen, check one of the dishes casually, as if this were something she was used to doing. And then she would go upstairs and stand in front of the mirror and check herself. She would look so good.

It was five-twenty when she walked in the side door.

She expected to be wrapped in the steamy aroma of a kitchen going full blast. She expected her dining table to be groaning with hot plates and platters. She expected hors d'oeuvres and entrees, salads and desserts. She expected an abundance—no, she expected an overabundance, she expected excess.

She walked in the side door and up into the kitchen and stopped dead in her tracks.

She looked around in disbelief.

There was a laundry basket on the counter. There were dirty breakfast dishes in the sink. There were footprints on the kitchen floor. Not only was there no food, there was no sign of a caterer anywhere. There was a deficit of caterers.

She phoned Dave at work.

Dave wasn't at work.

"He left an hour ago," said Brian, who comes in part-time. "He said to tell you he went to get a keg of beer."

"A keg of beer?" choked Morley.

"And chips," said Brian.

Morley's mouth fell open.

She hung up.

"That was a joke," said Brian. But she didn't hear him.

Brian phoned back.

"That was a joke," he said. "Dave went to buy flowers. Is everything okay?"

"The caterer isn't here," said Morley.

"Don't worry," said Brian. "He'll show up."

"But people will be here in less than an hour."

"Those guys work fast," said Brian. "Don't worry."

Okay, thought Morley.

She went upstairs and stood in front of her full-length bedroom mirror. Her elegance had evaporated. She looked distressingly familiar. Her hair, which had been so flouncy on the street, had flounced into a tangled mess.

She looked at the clock radio. Five-thirty.

The invitation had said six.

She went downstairs to the kitchen. The laundry basket was still on the counter, the dishes still in the sink, the footprints still on the floor.

The telephone rang. She looked at it with apprehension.

"Hello?" she said.

It was a man. An unfamiliar voice.

"Is that you, Mrs. Dave?"

"Yes," said Morley. "Who is this?"

"I am Frank. Your server," said the voice on the phone.

"Frank," said Morley. "Where are you?"

The voice said, "I am right here. Where are you?"

Morley said, "I'm in the kitchen."

There was an uncomfortable pause.

The voice on the phone said, "I don't see you."

Morley said, "Well, where are you?"

The voice on the phone, Frank, said, "I am in the kitchen too."

There was another pause. A longer pause.

Then Frank said, "I don't think you are in the kitchen. When are you coming home?"

Morley said, "Frank. Where are you exactly?"

Frank said, "By the stove."

Morley couldn't help herself. She glanced across her kitchen towards the stove. She almost said, "No, you're not." But she suppressed the impulse and said, instead, "Frank, what house are you at?"

"I am at your house," said Frank. "Fifteen Chestnut."

"Frank," said Morley, "we don't live at Fifteen Chestnut."

Morley could hear the gears grinding in Frank's brain.

"But," said Frank triumphantly, "if you do not live here, why am I all set up for your party at Fifteen Chestnut?"

"Frank," said Morley, "we live at Fifty Chestnut."

There was another pause. Longer still.

"Frank," said Morley, "why did the people at Fifteen Chestnut let you in to set up for a party they're not having?"

"You are not home yet," said Frank.

"Frank," said Morley, "how did you get in?"

"There were men working on the deck," said Frank. "*They* let me in."

"Frank," said Morley, "I don't want to upset you . . . but I think you're in the wrong house."

Morley had the portable phone in the crook of her shoulder. She had already picked the laundry basket off the kitchen counter. She was running upstairs. She stopped on the landing.

"Frank," she said. "Don't cry."

"I just lit the Sterno," he said. "All the food is in the warming dishes." Frank's voice had risen an octave. He said, "The house wasn't ready for a party. It took me an hour to tidy everything."

Then he said, "What happens if you come home?"

"Frank," said Morley. "Frank, stay calm. I have a plan."

"This is not a good situation," said Frank. "I have no training for this."

"Frank," said Morley. "Listen to me. I want you to turn the warming plates off. I want you to walk up the street. No, Frank, listen to me. I want you to run up the street. I want you to run up the street to my house. I want you to run to Fifty Chestnut Street. There is a station wagon in the driveway. I am going to put the key in the ignition. Bring everything down here."

There was a sob on the other end of the line. Frank said, "What about the Millers, Mrs. Dave?"

"Who are the Millers, Frank?" said Morley.

"There is an envelope here on the counter by the fridge. It is addressed to Mr. Don Miller. If you don't live here, is it possible that Mr. Don Miller does?"

Morley took a deep breath. She said, "The Millers aren't expecting you, Frank. I am."

She felt as if she were in the thick of a hostage taking. She felt as if she were trying to talk a hostage taker out of his hideout.

"Mrs. Dave," said Frank, "what happens if the Millers come home and find their house tidy and clean and smelling of chicken pot pie and vegetable cannelloni?"

"Frank," said Morley, watching herself in the mirror, "that is a risk we are going to have to take."

IT TOOK FRANK five minutes to get down the street. When he knocked on the front door his face was white.

"Frank," said Morley, "the key is in the car."

"Mrs. Dave," said Frank. He was wringing his hands. "You don't understand. You don't understand how much I cleaned up there. The house . . . it doesn't look like the same house any more."

"Just go, Frank," said Morley. "We won't say anything to anyone. Just go and get the food."

Frank was nodding his head. But he was staring into the middle distance and he wasn't moving.

"Frank!" shouted Morley.

The tires squealed as he backed onto the street.

Halfway up the block he honked his horn, jammed on his brakes, and swerved around a man on a bicycle.

It was Dave.

DAVE WATCHED IN disbelief as his car screeched to a halt. He watched as a man he had never seen before, a man in black pants and a white shirt, leapt out of his car and ran into Dr. Caudwell's old house.

Dr. Caudwell had sold his house just before Christmas.

Before Dave could work out what to do, the man ran out of Dr. Caudwell's old house carrying a large chafing dish. He threw it in the back of Dave's station wagon. And then he ran back into the house again.

Dave couldn't believe his eyes.

He was witnessing a robbery.

As he watched, the man came out carrying another piece of silver.

Without stopping to think, Dave dropped his bike and began to lumber along the street. He launched himself across the sidewalk at Frank, feeling like Sergeant Preston of the Yukon—about to get his man—but looking, sadly, more like the last kid chosen on the schoolyard football team. Frank looked up at the last moment and stopped dead in his tracks, watched Dave fly by him like an off-target human cannonball. Dave hit the car instead of Frank and slid to the ground. Frank stared in amazement as Dave struggled to his feet. Frank couldn't believe his eyes when this strange, deranged man shook himself off and came at him again. This time they went down in a tangled heap.

Frank had been carrying a dish of tomato bisque. When the steaming soup hit Dave's chest, he looked down and saw what he determined was his own blood and gore streaming down his flannel shirt.

"I have been stabbed," Dave screamed. "Help me!"

And that's when the second car pulled into the driveway.

And Don Miller stepped out.

He surveyed the scene and pulled out his cellphone and called the police.

It took a while for everyone to calm down.

For Dave to understand he hadn't halted a crime in progress.

For Frank to stop fretting about Dave's chest wound.

When they did straighten things out and they all went inside, Don Miller couldn't believe what Frank had done to his house. The house had been full of contractors when Don had last seen it. Frank had rolled up the painters' drop cloths and swept up the sawdust and lugged a table up from the basement.

They were standing in the empty living room.

"It looks incredible," said Don Miller.

"I know," said Frank.

And that is when Don Miller said, "My wife and kids come in tonight. But we're staying in a hotel until Monday, when the movers come. Why don't you leave everything here? Why don't you have your party here?"

And that's when Dave said, "Only if you bring your family."

THERE IS SOMETHING liberating about a house without furniture. There is something musical about voices when they bounce off empty walls. There is something about the way bare wood floors invite people to move—to slip, to slide, to become dancers.

Dave loaded up a box of his favourite party albums— *Let It Bleed* by the Rolling Stones, *OK Computer* by Radiohead, *Hip Hug-Her* by Booker T. and the M.G.'s, *Aretha's Greatest Hits.*

By the time Don Miller arrived with his wife and two kids, the music in the living room was cranked. People were dancing.

It was a grand party.

Frank recovered his equilibrium and glided around the house with his bow tie askew and his sleeves rolled up. People perched on countertops with plates in their laps. People sat all the way up the stairs sipping wine from glasses and beer out of the bottle. Someone ordered pizza for the kids.

At eleven-thirty, while they were dancing in the living room with their shoes off, Morley leaned against Dave and said, "I feel like a teenager."

Which is exactly what Sam, eleven years old, said not five minutes later to Molly Miller, age twelve, as he smoked his first cigarette with her in the Millers' garage.

THE MILLERS COME from Indian Bluff, Saskatchewan, a town of two thousand people, where Don taught high school and Susan worked in the bank.

"This is great," said Don Miller to Dave as they leaned against the kitchen counter just before midnight. "We were scared of coming. I don't mean tonight. Not to this. To the city. Susan was offered an opportunity and we had to try it. But we were scared we wouldn't meet anyone. We were scared Molly would meet the wrong kind of kids."

By the time they brought out the cake, Morley had forgotten it was her birthday. Mary Turlington had got at the icing anyway and it now read *Happy Birthday Morley* across the top and *Welcome Home Millers* on the bottom.

Don Miller gave a speech, and he was funny and everyone applauded and no one even noticed Morley when she sat down quietly in a corner and opened her presents.

It was a perfect night. A night of spilled drinks and laughter and general youthfulness. A perfect night to turn forty.

Sometime after midnight Sam came to Morley and said he didn't feel good.

"I think I'll go home," he said.

"Too many Cokes," said Morley.

"I smoked," said Sam.

"Oh," said Morley. "That always makes me feel sick."

"Me too," said Sam. "Do you think I'll get cancer?"

"Probably not," said Morley. "Do you think you can quit?"

"I think so," said Sam. "I'm going to quit tomorrow."

IT WAS WELL past midnight when Dave and Morley slipped quietly in the back door of their house. Dave poured himself a glass of water and leaned against the kitchen counter.

"Was that okay?" he asked.

Morley walked across the kitchen and put her arms around Dave's neck. She leaned into him and whispered in his ear.

"One more dance," she said. "One more dance."

And they danced slowly around the kitchen. Dancing to the sounds of night cars and crickets.

There was a laundry basket on the counter. There were dirty breakfast dishes in the sink. There were footprints on the floor.

It was perfect.

DAVE COOKS THE TURKEY

When Carl Lowbeer bought his wife, Gerta, *The Complete Christmas Planner*, he did not understand what he was doing. If Carl had known how much Gerta was going to enjoy the book, he would not have given it to her. He bought it on the afternoon of December 23rd. A glorious day. Carl left work at lunch and spent the afternoon drifting around downtown—window shopping, and listening to carollers, and falling into conversations with complete strangers. When he stopped for coffee he was shocked to see it was 5:30. Shocked because the only things he had bought were a book by Len Deighton and some shaving cream in a tube—both things he planned to wrap and give himself. That's when the Joy of Christmas, who had sat down with him and bought him a double chocolate croissant, said, *I think I'll stay here and have another coffee while you finish your shopping.* The next thing Carl knew, he was ripping through the mall like a prison escapee.

On Christmas Eve, Carl found himself staring at a bag full of stuff he couldn't remember buying. He wondered if he might have picked up someone else's bag by mistake, but then he found a receipt with his signature on it. Why would he have paid twenty-three dollars for a slab of metal to defrost meat when they already owned a microwave oven that would do it in half the time? Who could he possibly have been thinking of when he bought the ThighMaster?

Carl did remember buying *The Complete Christmas Planner*. It was the picture on the cover that drew him to the book—a picture of a woman striding across a snow-covered lawn with a wreath of chili peppers tucked under her arm. The woman looked as if she was in a hurry, and that made Carl think of Gerta, so he bought the book, never imagining that it was something that his wife had been waiting for all her life. Carl was as surprised as anyone last May when Gerta began the neighbourhood Christmas group. Although not, perhaps, as surprised as Dave was when his wife, Morley, joined it.

"It's not about Christmas, Dave," said Morley. "It's about getting together."

The members of Gerta's group, all women, met every second Tuesday night, at a different house each time.

They drank tea, or beer, and the host baked something, and they worked on stuff. Usually until about eleven.

"But that's not the point," said Morley. "The *point* is getting together. It's about neighbourhood—not about what we are actually doing."

But there was no denying that they were doing stuff. Christmas stuff.

"It's wrapping paper," said Morley.

"You are *making* paper?" said Dave.

"*Decorating* paper," said Morley. "This is hand-printed paper. Do you know how much this would cost?"

That was in July.

In August they dipped oak leaves in gold paint and hung them in bunches from their kitchen ceilings to dry.

Then there was the stencilling weekend. The weekend Dave thought if he didn't keep moving, Morley would stencil him.

In September Dave couldn't find an eraser anywhere in the house, and Morley said, "That's because I took them all with me. We're making rubber stamps."

"You are *making* rubber stamps?" said Dave.

"Out of erasers," said Morley.

"People don't even *buy* rubber stamps any more," said Dave.

"This one is going to be an angel," said Morley, reaching into her bag. "I need a metallic-ink stamp pad. Do you think you could buy me a metallic-ink stamp pad and some more gold paint? And we need some of those snap things that go into Christmas crackers."

"The what things?" said Dave.

"The exploding things you pull," said Morley. "We are going to make Christmas crackers. Where do you think we could get the exploding things?"

There were oranges drying in the basement on the clothes rack and blocks of wax for candles stacked on the ping-pong table.

One day in October Morley said, "Do you know there are only sixty-seven shopping days until Christmas?"

Dave did not know this. In fact he had not completely unpacked from their summer vacation. Without thinking he said, "What are you talking about?"

And Morley said, "If we wanted to get all our shopping done by the week before Christmas we only have"—she shut her eyes—"sixty-two days left."

Dave and Morley usually *start* their shopping the week before Christmas.

And there they were, with only sixty-seven shopping days left, standing in their bedroom staring at each other, incomprehension hanging between them.

It hung there for a good ten seconds.

Then Dave said something he had been careful not to say for weeks. He said, "I thought this thing wasn't about Christmas."

He immediately regretted his words as Morley left the room. And then came back. Like a locomotive.

She said, "Don't make fun of me, Dave."

"Uh-oh," thought Dave.

"What?" said Morley.

"I didn't say that," said Dave.

"You said 'uh-oh,'" said Morley.

"I thought 'uh-oh,'" said Dave. "I didn't *say* 'uh-oh.' Thinking 'uh-oh' isn't like saying 'uh-oh.' They don't send you to jail for *thinking* you want to strangle someone."

"What?" said Morley.

Morley slept downstairs that night. She didn't say a word when Dave came down and tried to talk her out of it. Didn't say a word the next morning until Sam and Stephanie had left for school. Then she said, "Do you know what my life is like, Dave?"

Dave suspected—correctly—she wasn't looking for an answer.

"My life is a train," she said. "I am a train. Dragging everyone from one place to another. To school and to dance class and to now-it's-time-to-get-up and now-it's-time-to-go-to-bed. I'm a train full of people who complain when you try to get them into a bed and fight when you try to get them out of one. That's my job. And I'm not only the train, I'm the porter and the conductor and the cook and the engineer and the maintenance man. And I print the tickets and stack the luggage and clean the dishes. And if they still had cabooses, I'd be in the caboose."

Dave didn't want to ask where the train was heading. He had the sinking feeling that somewhere up ahead someone had pulled up a section of the track.

"And you know where the train is going, Dave?" said Morley.

Yup, he thought. *Off the tracks. Any moment now.*

"What?" said Morley.

"No," said Dave. "I don't know where the train's going."

Morley leaned over the table.

"The train chugs through the year, Dave. Through Valentine's Day and Easter and then summer holidays.

Through a town called First Day of School and past the village of Halloween and the township of Class Project, and down the spur line called Your Sister Is Visiting. And you know what's at the end of the track? You know where my train is heading?"

Dave looked around nervously. He didn't want to get this wrong. He would have been happy to say where the train was going if he knew he could get it right. Was his wife going to leave him? Maybe the train was going to *D-I-V-O-R-C-E*.

"Not at Christmas," he mumbled.

"Exactly," said Morley. "To the last stop on the line— Christmas dinner. And this is supposed to be something I look forward to, Dave. Christmas is supposed to be a heartwarming family occasion."

"Christmas dinner," said Dave tentatively. It seemed a reasonably safe thing to say.

Morley nodded.

Feeling encouraged Dave added, "With a turkey and stuffing and everything."

But Morley wasn't listening.

"And when we finally get through that week between Christmas and New Year's, you know what they do with the train?"

Dave shook his head.

"They back it up during the night when I am asleep so they can run it through all the stations again."

Dave nodded earnestly.

"And you know who you are, Dave?"

Dave shook his head again. No. No, he didn't know who he was. He was hoping maybe he was the engineer. Maybe he was up in the locomotive. Busy with men's work.

Morley squinted at her husband.

"You are the guy in the bar car, Dave, pushing the button to ask for another drink."

By the way Morley said that, Dave could tell that she still loved him. She could have told him, for instance, that he had to get out of the bar car. Or, for that matter, off the train. She hadn't. Dave realized it had been close, and if he was going to stay aboard, he was going to have to join the crew.

The next weekend he said, "Why don't I do some of the Christmas shopping? Why don't you give me a list, and I will get things for everyone in Cape Breton?"

Dave had never gone Christmas shopping in October. He was unloading bags onto the kitchen table when he said, "That wasn't so bad."

Morley walked across the kitchen and picked up a book that had fallen on the floor. "I'm sorry," she said. "It's just that I like Christmas so much. I *used* to like Christmas so much. I was thinking that if I got everything done early maybe I could enjoy it again. I'm trying to get control of it, Dave. I'm trying to make it fun again. That's what this is all about."

Dave said, "What else can I do?"

Morley reached out and touched his elbow and said, "On Christmas Day, after we have opened the presents, I want to take the kids to work at the food bank. I want you to look after the turkey."

"I can do that," said Dave.

DAVE DIDN'T UNDERSTAND the full meaning of what he had agreed to do until Christmas Eve, when the presents were finally wrapped and under the tree and he was snuggled, warm and safe, in bed. It was one of his favourite moments of the year. He nudged his wife's feet. She gasped.

"Did you take the turkey out of the freezer?" she said.

"Yes, of course," said Dave.

Of course he hadn't. But he wasn't about to admit that. He wasn't about to tell Morley he couldn't hold up his end of a bargain. So Dave lay in bed, his eyes closed, his body rigid, the minutes of the night dragging by as he monitored his wife's breathing.

Forty minutes went by before he dared open an eye. "Morley?" he said softly.

There was no answer.

Dave gingerly lifted her hand off his shoulder and when she didn't stir, rolled himself off the bed in slow motion, dropping like a shifty cartoon character onto the carpet beside Arthur the dog. A moment later he periscoped up to check if Morley was still sleeping and saw her hand patting the bed, searching for him. He picked it up, looked around desperately, and then shoved the confused dog onto the forbidden bed. He placed Morley's hand on Arthur's head, holding his breath as they both settled. Then he crawled out of the bedroom.

There was no turkey in the basement freezer. Dave peered into it in confusion. He lifted an open package of hot dogs. Then he dove his upper body into the chest freezer, his feet lifting off the ground as he rattled around inside, emerging a moment later empty-handed and panicked. He ran upstairs and jerked open the freezer in the fridge. Bags of frozen vegetables tumbled out as he searched it frantically.

There was no turkey in the upstairs freezer either. Dave stood in front of the fridge as if he had been struck by a mallet—so stunned that he was able to watch but not react to the can of frozen orange-juice concentrate as it slowly rolled out of the open freezer and began a slow-motion free fall toward his foot. He watched it with the dispassionate curiosity of a scientist.

The metal edge of the orange-juice container landed on his big toe. Before he felt the pain shoot up his leg and settle exquisitely between his eyes, there was a moment of no pain, a moment when he was able to formulate a thought. The thought was, *This is going to hurt.* Then he was stuffing his fist into his mouth to stop himself from crying out.

That was the moment, the moment when he was hopping around the kitchen chewing on his fist, that Dave realized that looking after the turkey, something he had promised to do, meant *buying* it as well as putting it in the oven.

Dave unloaded both freezers to be sure. Then he paced around the kitchen trying to decide what to do. When he finally went upstairs, Morley was still asleep. He considered waking her. Instead, he lay down and imagined, in painful detail, the chronology of the Christmas Day waiting for him. Imagined everything from the first squeal of morning to that moment when his family came home from the food bank expecting a turkey dinner. He could see the dark look that would cloud his wife's face when he carried a bowl of pasta across the kitchen and placed it on the table she would have set with the homemade crackers and the gilded oak leaves.

He was still awake at 2 A.M., but at least he had a plan. He would wait until they left for the food bank. Then he would take off to some deserted Newfoundland outport and live under an assumed name. At Sam's graduation one of his friends would ask, "Why isn't your father here?" and Sam would explain that "one Christmas he forgot to buy the turkey and he had to leave."

At 3 A.M., after rolling around for an hour, Dave got out of bed, dressed, and slipped quietly out the back door. He was looking for a twenty-four-hour grocery store. It was either that or wait for the food bank to open, and though he couldn't think of anyone in the city more in need of a turkey, the idea that his family might spot him in line made the food bank unthinkable.

At 4 A.M., with the help of a taxi driver, Dave found an open store. There was one turkey left: twelve pounds, frozen tight, Grade B—whatever that meant. It looked like a flesh-coloured bowling ball. When he took it to the counter, the clerk stared at it in confusion.

"What is that?" said the clerk suspiciously.

"It's a turkey," said Dave.

The clerk shook his head. "Whatever you say, buddy."

As Dave left the store, the clerk called after him, "You aren't going to eat that, are you?"

HE WAS HOME by 4:30 and by 6:30 he had the turkey more or less thawed. He used an electric blanket and a hair dryer on the turkey, and a bottle of Scotch on himself.

As the turkey defrosted, it became clear what Grade B meant. The skin on its right drumstick was ripped. Dave's turkey looked as if it had made a break from the slaughter-house and dragged itself a block or two before it was captured and beaten to death. Dave poured another Scotch and began to refer to his bird as Butch. He turned Butch over and found another slash in the carcass. *Perhaps*, he thought, *Butch died in a knife fight.*

As sunrise hit Dave through the kitchen window, he ran his hand over his stubble. He squinted in the morning light, his eyes dark and puffy. He would have been happy if disfiguration was the worst thing about his turkey. Would have considered himself blessed. Would have been able to look back on this Christmas with equanimity. Might eventually have been able to laugh about it. The worst thing came later. After lunch. After Morley and the kids left for the food bank.

Before they left, Morley dropped pine oil on some of the living-room lamps.

"When the bulbs heat the oil up," she said, "the house will smell like a forest." Then she said, "Mother's coming. I'm trusting you with this. You have to have the turkey in the oven—"

Dave finished her sentence for her. "By 1:30," he said. "Don't worry. I know what I'm doing."

The worst thing began when Dave tried to turn on the oven. Morley had never had cause to explain the automatic timer to him, and Dave had never had cause to ask about it. The oven had been set the day before to go on at 5:30 P.M. Morley had been baking a squash casserole for Christmas dinner—she always did the vegetables the day before—and now, until the oven timer was unset, nothing anybody did was going to turn it on.

At 2 P.M. Dave retrieved the bottle of Scotch from the basement and poured himself a drink. His hands had begun to shake. There was a ringing in his ears. He knew he was in trouble.

He had to find an oven that could cook the bird quickly. But every oven he could think of already had a turkey in it. For ten years Dave had been technical director of some of the craziest acts on the rock-and-roll circuit. He wasn't going to fall to pieces over a raw turkey.

Inventors are often unable to explain where their best ideas come from. Dave is not sure where he got his. Maybe he had spent too many years in too many hotel rooms. At 2:30 P.M. he topped up his Scotch and phoned the Plaza Hotel. He was given the front desk.

"Do you cook . . . special menus for people with special dietary needs?" he asked.

"We're a first-class hotel in a world-class city, sir. We can look after any dietary needs."

"If someone brings their own food—because of a special diet—would you cook it for them?"

"Of course, sir."

Dave looked at the turkey. It was propped on a kitchen chair like a naked baby. "Come on, Butch," he said, stuffing it into a plastic bag. "We're going out."

Morley had the car. Dave called a taxi. "The Plaza," he said. "It's an emergency."

He took a slug from the bottle in the back of the cab. When Dave arrived in the hotel lobby, the man at the front desk asked if he needed help with his suitcases.

"No suitcases," said Dave, patting the turkey, which he had dropped on the counter and which was now dripping juice onto the hotel floor. Dave turned woozily to the man behind him in line and, slurring slightly, said, "Just checking in for the afternoon with my chick."

The clerk winced. Dave wobbled. He spun around and grinned at the clerk and then around again and squinted at the man in line behind him. He was looking for approval. He found, instead, his neighbour Jim Scoffield. Jim was standing beside an elderly woman whom Dave assumed must be Jim's visiting mother.

Jim didn't say anything, tried in fact to look away. But he was too late. Their eyes had met.

Dave straightened and said, "Turkey and the kids are at the food bank. I brought Morley here so they could cook her for me."

"Oh," said Jim.

"I mean the turkey," said Dave.

"Uh-huh," said Jim.

"I bring it here *every* year. I'm alone."

Dave held his arms out as if he were inviting Jim to frisk him.

The man at the desk said, "Excuse me, sir," and handed Dave his key. Dave smiled. At the man behind the counter. At Jim. At Jim's mom. He walked toward the elevators one careful foot in front of the other.

When he got to the polished brass elevator doors, he heard Jim calling him.

"You forgot your . . . chick," said Jim, pointing to the turkey Dave had left behind on the counter.

THE MAN ON the phone from room service said, "We have turkey on the *menu*, sir."

Dave said, "This is . . . uh . . . a *special* turkey. I was hoping you could cook *my* turkey."

The man from room service told Dave the manager would call. Dave looked at his watch.

When the phone rang, Dave knew this was his last chance. His only chance. The manager would either agree to cook the turkey or he might as well book the ticket to Newfoundland.

"Excuse me, sir?" said the manager.

"I said I need to eat this *particular* turkey," said Dave.

"That *particular* turkey, sir." The manager was non-committal.

"Do you know," said Dave, "what they feed turkeys today?"

"No, sir?" said the manager. He said it like a question.

"They feed them. . ."

Dave wasn't at all sure himself. Wasn't so sure where he was going with this. He just knew that he had to keep talking.

"They feed them chemicals," he said, "and antibiotics and steroids and . . . lard to make them juicier . . . and starch to make them crispy. I'm allergic to . . . steroids. If I eat that stuff I'll have a heart attack or at least a seizure. In the lobby of your hotel. Do you want that to happen?"

The man on the phone didn't say anything. Dave kept going.

"I have my own turkey here. I raised this turkey myself. I butchered it myself. This morning. The only thing it has eaten is. . ." Dave looked frantically around the room. What did he feed the turkey?

"Tofu," he said triumphantly.

"Tofu, sir?" said the manager.

"And yogurt," said Dave.

It was all or nothing.

The bellboy took the turkey, and the twenty-dollar bill Dave handed him, without blinking an eye.

Dave said, "You have those big convection ovens. I have to have it back before 5:30 P.M."

"You must be very hungry, sir" was all he said.

Dave collapsed onto the bed. He didn't move until the phone rang half an hour later. It was the hotel manager.

He said the turkey was in the oven. Then he said, "You raised the bird yourself?" It was a question.

Dave said, "Yes."

There was a pause. The manager said, "The chef says the turkey looks like it was abused."

Dave said, "Ask the chef if he has ever killed a turkey. Tell him the bird was a fighter. Tell him to stitch it up."

THE BELLBOY WHEELED the turkey into Dave's room at quarter to six. They had it on a room service trolley covered with a silver dome. Dave removed the dome and gasped.

It didn't look like any bird he could have cooked. There were frilly paper armbands on both drumsticks, a glazed partridge made of red peppers on the breast, and a small silver gravy boat with steam wafting from it.

Dave looked at his watch and ripped the paper armbands off and scooped the red pepper partridge into his mouth.

He realized the bellboy was watching him and then saw the security guard standing in the corridor. The security guard was holding a carving knife. They obviously weren't about to trust Dave with a weapon.

"Would you like us to carve it, sir?"

"Just get me a taxi," said Dave.

"What?" said the guard.

"I can't eat this here," said Dave. "I have to eat it. . ." Dave couldn't imagine where he had to eat it. "Outside," he said. "I have to eat it outside."

He gave the bellboy another twenty-dollar bill and said, "I am going downstairs to check out. Bring the bird and call me a taxi." He walked by the security guard without looking at him.

"Careful with that knife," he said.

DAVE GOT HOME at six. He put Butch on the table. The family was due back any minute. He poured himself a drink and sat down in the living room. The house looked beautiful—smelled beautiful—like a pine forest.

"My forest," said Dave. Then he said, "Uh-oh," and jumped up. He got a ladle of the turkey gravy, and he ran around the house smearing it on light bulbs. *There*, he thought. He went outside and stood on the stoop and counted to twenty-five. Then he went back in and breathed deeply. The house smelled like . . . like Christmas.

He looked out the window. Morley was coming up the walk . . . with Jim Scoffield and his mother.

"We met them outside. I invited them in for a drink."

"Oh. Great," said Dave. "I'll get the drinks."

Dave went to the kitchen then came back to see Jim sitting on the couch under the tall swinging lamp, a drop of gravy glistening on his balding forehead. Dave watched another drop fall. Saw the puzzled look cross Jim's face as he reached up, wiped his forehead, and brought his fingers to his nose. Morley and Jim's mother had not noticed anything yet. Dave saw another drop about to fall. Thought, *Any moment now the Humane Society is going to knock on the door. Sent by the hotel.*

He took a long swig of his drink and placed his glass by Morley's hand-painted paper napkins.

"Morley, could you come here?" he said softly.

"There's something I have to tell you."

MARY TURLINGTON AND POLLY ANDERSON'S CHRISTMAS COLLISION

As everyone knows, Polly and Ted Anderson host their annual Christmas party, their "At Home," on the second Saturday of every December. It is a tradition. It started as a small gathering—just a few couples over for drinks before dinner—but it has become the neighbourhood event of the year. Everyone marks the Anderson Christmas party in their calendar months in advance. Everyone keeps the second Saturday in December free.

Even Mary Turlington. Especially Mary. Mary adores Polly's party. The fancy hors d'oeuvres, the exotic drinks, and that magical moment at the end of the night, when Ted lights the candles on the branches of the Andersons' tree and everyone gathers in the living room to sing carols, the happy crowd spilling out into the hall.

Now, of course, Mary wishes that it was *her* husband, Bert, and not Polly's husband, Ted, lighting those candles. Mary wishes *she* was the one who hosted the grand neighbourhood soiree.

If you want to throw a gold-medal party, it is hard to top Christmas.

As far as Mary is concerned, no other holiday offers the grandeur of it: the thematic possibilities for decorations and music, costumes and food, presents and children. Christmas is kind of it.

Except for maybe a surprise party. Mary has always wanted a surprise party. But you can't throw a surprise party for yourself. Although she has considered it.

Believe me, Mary has considered *all* the options.

The year her son Adam turned twelve, for instance, Mary said to Bert, "Thirteen, next year."

And Bert said, "Before you know it, we'll have a teenager."

Mary said, "I have been wondering about his bar mitzvah."

Bert said, "We're Presbyterian."

If truth be told, when Christmas comes, with its message of goodwill and fellowship, and its story of peace and love, instead of embracing the attendant feelings of generosity and good spirits, Mary sometimes slips on the heavy cloak of envy.

She can't help herself. At Christmas, she is Robin to Polly's Batman, Marlowe to Polly's Shakespeare, McCartney to Polly's Lennon.

And then one day this fall, word got out that Polly *wasn't* going to throw her famous party this year.

It was Gerta Lowbeer who told Mary. It was an off-the-cuff remark. But the kind of off-the-cuff remark that has been known to start revolutions.

Like most incendiary claims, it had a passing familiarity with the truth. Polly had wondered aloud if people were tiring of her party. "The Terriers didn't come last year," she said. "Or the Schellenbergers."

Like most perfectionists, Polly was suffering a crisis of confidence. All she needed was some reassurance. And she got that in droves. But not before Mary had heard the coaxing call of Polly's abdication.

And when a dancer hears music, she will always find a floor to dance on—especially if it is a tune she has been waiting to hear. When Mary learned Polly was vacillating, Mary jumped.

With the best of intentions, mind you. It wouldn't be Christmas without a neighbourhood party. And who better to step into the breach than her?

And so it was, late in November, that everyone in the neighbourhood received two invitations. One from the Turlingtons, and one from the Andersons. Or, more to the point, one from Mary and one from Polly. Both for the second Saturday in December.

WHEN THEY REALIZED what had happened, neither woman stood down. As far as Polly was concerned, standing down was out of the question. It was her neighbourhood obligation. Her responsibility. People counted on her.

And Mary? Well, Mary was far too wound up to consider it. She was not only going to hold a party, she was going to out-Polly Polly. Not out of spite, you understand. Out of enthusiasm. Like I said, think Lennon and McCartney.

No one knew what to do. Everyone was talking about it.

"We've always gone to Polly's," said Carl Lowbeer.

"We opened Mary's invitation first," said Gerta.

The gracious thing, of course, would have been for *Mary* to cancel. To phone everyone and explain her mistake. Reel in her invitations. Maybe replace them with a New Year's levee, or an Easter brunch, or . . . a bar mitzvah.

But if the voice of graciousness whispered, Mary didn't hear it. In Mary's mind everyone was coming to *her* party. And that was the end of that. Mary had moved on. She had already chosen her signature colour.

"It is so obvious," she said to Bert after weeks of fussing. "I can't believe it took me so long. The best colour is no colour at all."

"Obviously," said Bert. Who didn't have a clue what she was talking about.

"White!" said Mary. "A *white* Christmas."

She would transform their house into a palace of white.

"The painters are coming tomorrow," she said to Bert. "They are going to do the walls and the floors."

"Excellent," said Bert, thinking, this wasn't excellent at all.

MARY STARTED WORKING on the wreath the following weekend. For the front door.

"It will be the first thing people see," she said. "Like a billboard on the edge of town."

She set herself up in the basement. She started with pine boughs—spray-painting them white.

"What an improvement!" she said, stepping back to admire her handiwork.

She laboured on the wreath for three days. When she was finished, she called Bert and Adam to give her a hand. "I need help," she said.

The three of them struggled up the stairs as if they were carrying a sofa.

"It's a little bigger than your average wreath," said Bert, sweat pouring from his forehead.

It was so oversized they couldn't fasten it to the front door. They used pulleys and chains to suspend it from the lintel over the door.

"That *should* hold," said the consulting engineer.

The wreath was perfect if all you were going to do was look at it from the sidewalk. But if you wanted to *use* the door, you had to crawl through the hole in the middle of it.

"No problem," said Mary, hoisting herself through, demonstrating. "It's fine."

The problem was Mary couldn't leave well enough alone.

"What it needs is complexity," she said.

"What?" said Bert, trying to be helpful.

Mary added a sprig of holly, which she had, of course, painted white. And she kept adding things. Christmas balls. And walnuts. Chestnuts. And oranges. Something new every day. Everything coated in a light inking of white or silver.

As the days passed, Mary's wreath looked more like a ghostly cornucopia than a Christmas ornament. And every morning she would dab it with peanut butter and bacon fat to attract birds.

"Real birds," she said.

A pigeon began to roost in the wreath. The mailman refused to come near the door any more. Mary put a plastic container in the driveway and told the mailman to leave the mail in the bin.

"Coward," she muttered, slipping through the wreath, swatting at a squirrel as she went.

AS MARY HOMED in on the party weekend with the intensity of a guided missile, the rest of the neighbourhood watched its approach with growing anxiety.

Lunchtime. The back booth of Kenny Wong's café. Carl Lowbeer, Bernie Schellenberger, Jim Scoffield—and Dave, who had summoned them together. The neighbourhood was heading for a collision and someone had to do something.

So the four of them ate lunch, and talked about what that something might be. What could or couldn't, should or shouldn't be done, and when they were finished, of all the hare-brained schemes they considered and might have settled on, of all things, they settled on Dave's.

THEY SET UP in the room over his store. They taped a large map of the neighbourhood onto the ping-pong table. By early December there were enough coloured pins sticking in the map and lists stuck to the walls that the room looked like a military headquarters.

"We have the neighbourhood divided into squads," said Dave. "Each squad has a captain. Each captain has a schedule."

It was the first captains' meeting. Dave, and Dorothy, and Carl, and . . . well, there were at least twelve of them around the table.

The plan was simple. Both Mary and Polly would be told the other party had been cancelled. But in fact, everyone in the neighbourhood would attend both parties simultaneously.

"How are we doing that?" said Carl. Captain of Squad One.

"You each have four families," said Dave. "In a minute Jim is going to hand out your maps and schedules."

At their assigned times, each captain was to slip their four families out the back door of whichever party they were at and rendezvous with the designated teenage drivers, who would be standing by.

"The drivers," said Dave, "will ferry you back and forth."

If everything went as planned, the squads would hop back and forth from one party to the other. And neither Mary nor Polly would be the wiser.

WITH A WEEK to go, it seemed as if they were going to pull it off.

"Everyone has RSVPed. Everyone is coming," said Mary to Bert.

But as any general will tell you, the thing about battle plans is battles *never* go as planned. Especially when they are lubricated with frosty glasses of candy-cane cocktails and white liquor icicles.

But I'm getting ahead of myself.

Before you knew it, it was the second Saturday in December. Six P.M. Look. There are Bert and Mary standing at their front door. In front of Mary's White Wonderland. The walls and floors inside the house are painted palace-white. The sofa and chairs, the end tables and dining-room buffet are draped in white linen. There are platters of white canapés and pitchers of frosty beverages everywhere.

Look at Bert, perspiring slightly, in his white suit, white leather shoes, white top hat and gloves. And Mary, in her set of white-feathered angel wings. The two of them look as if they have been plucked off the top of a wedding cake.

And there, a few blocks over and across the park, on the other side of the neighbourhood, are Polly and Ted, standing under a candy-cane arch at their front door. Polly is handing each guest a festive cocktail as they arrive.

And look! There is Dave. Standing in the room over his record store. He is staring at the map on the ping-pong table. There is a black walkie-talkie dangling from his wrist. He is bringing the radio up to his mouth now.

"Squad One!" he says. "This is Big Turkey! GO!"

Carl and his squad of families—twelve people in all—are the lead-off group. They go in Polly's front door, throw back their cocktails, and once the second group arrives, Carl and his squad slip out the back. They run down the alley like a pack of prison escapees, heads ducked below the level of the back fence so they can't be seen.

They are heading for the red garage at the end of the lane where the drivers are waiting to speed them the seven blocks over to Mary's.

A mere fifteen minutes after they went in Polly's front door, Mary is greeting them at her front door with one of *her* festive white wine spritzers.

Carl peers at his drink, shrugs, and throws it back. Before you know it, Dave is on the radio telling him it is time to head back again.

"Whoa," says Carl, as he staggers out the back door.

"Hang in there," says Dave. "You're doing great."

AS PEOPLE ARRIVED at each house, both Mary's and Polly's living rooms filled up. Perhaps neither house was as full as Polly's usual crowd, but flying about, handing around hors d'oeuvres and drinks, all Polly or Mary really registered were the new faces and the lively atmosphere.

So good that people are really mingling this year, thought Polly as Ruth Kelman hurried past her to the other end of the room.

So the first few transfers went off without a hitch. It was a little later that the hitch began uncoupling.

OUT IN THE front yard, Bert was staring at Mary's wreath. It was so full of "complexity" people could hardly get through it.

"I'm going to move it," said Bert. "I'll put it back up in the morning."

It took four of them to carry it: Bert got Adam and the twins to help him. When they tilted it on its side to get it through the back gate, five-year-old Dierdre Lewellen tumbled out into the snow.

"It's about time!" said Dierdre with her hands on her hips. "I have been stuck in there for over an hour."

Carl Lowbeer and his squad were peering out from behind the garage. They had been heading to the back door when Carl caught a glimpse of a white pine cone edging around the corner of the house. He called his group to a halt and watched, dismayed, as Bert and *his* team leaned the wreath against the back door.

When Bert and the others went back to the front of the house, Carl tiptoed up to evaluate things. He stood on the wreath and leaned over to knock tentatively on a kitchen window. No one came. He knocked again and saw Mary rush into the kitchen with an empty platter. He dove for the shadows of the garage before she saw him.

His group were way too tipsy to navigate the wreath. So Carl pried open a basement window and began funnelling them through one by one. By the time everyone was inside, it was time to head back to the Andersons again.

"Not until we warm up," said Carl, clutching a mug of White Russian eggnog. His second.

"Second?" said Dave over the walkie-talkie.

"Third?" said Carl. "I may have losh count."

The truth is that everyone may have lost count.

Of course, each time a group moved from one house to the other, glasses of cheer were thrust into their hands. Everyone was getting . . . what do I say? . . . exuberantly cheery. And a cheeky streak of independence had begun to appear.

As Carl and his group tumbled out the basement window, Gunner Olsen staggered in the front door, scooped a plate of white asparagus from the dining-room buffet, and pranced out again.

"What are you doing?" said Mary, as he danced by her.

"No worries," said Gunner. "I'll be back."

One boisterous squad declined their drive and set off cross-country. When last seen they were carrying a pitcher of Mary's white wine spritzers and a plate of white chocolate rum balls. *They* hadn't been heard of since.

Down in Mary's basement, an abandoned walkie-talkie crackled to life. "Big Turkey to Squad Four. Over."

Jim came on the radio instead. Jim said, "We've lost Squad Four, Big Turkey. Squad Three set off to find them."

Things were breaking down.

Dave, who was making one last effort to coordinate everyone from the room over his record store, gazed at the map on the ping-pong table. He brought the radio up to his mouth and pushed the red transmit button.

"Squad Three," said Dave. "Squad Three. This is Big Turkey. Over."

No one was answering any more. The party had gone rogue.

Faced with the growing difficulties of getting in and out of Mary's, everyone had settled at Polly's. And they were refusing to move.

Except for Gunner, who had decided *his* contribution to the night was to get as many of Mary's snacks over to Polly's as possible.

MARY STOOD BY the sink, mopping her brow. She couldn't figure it out. She had been tearing between the kitchen and the dining room all night. Each time she placed a fresh plate of appetizers on the buffet, there was an empty plate to take away.

She was certain she had prepared an excessive amount of food. Yet even though there seemed to be fewer and fewer guests, she was running out. Something was going on.

She opened the freezer. She pulled out the last plate of rum balls. She had been hoping to save them for Christmas Day. As she set them on the counter, she thought she saw someone duck behind the garage. It had been happening all night.

And it was at that moment, a floor below her, that Rick Moore sat up, burped, and looked blearily around. Rick was the leader of the missing Squad Four. He had come through the basement window an hour ago and promptly fallen asleep on one of the rec-room couches.

But now he was awake, peering around; and as far as he could see, the house seemed to be leaning precariously to the left. Whose house it was exactly he couldn't recall. But he knew the important thing was for him to get out before it collapsed.

Upstairs, Mary was arranging the rum balls on her last silver tray. She picked up the platter, moved it to one hand, smoothed her white skirt with the other, and then burst into the living room with a flourish. The living room was completely empty.

Except for Rick, who had stumbled upstairs behind her. He blinked at her, dimly remembered his mission, grabbed her arm, and said with a slur, "Come on. We gotta get to the other place."

As he hustled the bewildered Mary out the front door he pointed at the rum balls and said, "Good. Bring the snacks and save Gunner a trip."

Rick got Mary around to the backyard and into the last of the shuttle cars that was waiting at the end of the alley. Five minutes later they were standing in front of the Andersons' house.

Mary couldn't believe it when Rick shoved her through the door. Everyone was there.

Finally she understood what was going on. She felt a surge of affection. After all these years. Bert had organized her a surprise party!

Mary stood by the door staring at everyone, and waiting for them to yell "Surprise!" But instead, the room fell deathly silent.

Mary began noticing things. In slow motion. A plate of her white cheddar toast points on the coffee table. Rashida Chudary grinning awkwardly with one of Mary's white snowflake shortbreads balanced on the edge of a teacup saucer. Dave standing next to the fireplace, a goofy line of her White Russian eggnog above his upper lip.

In the silence, she saw Gerta Lowbeer bend over and pick up a bowl of her white pepper macadamia nuts. Gerta was holding them out to her.

Mary took one reflexively. And that's when Polly flew out of the kitchen and the entire room swivelled as one, like they were watching a tennis match. The door flew open, Polly sailed in, everyone turned, looked doubly horrified, and then as one they turned back to Mary.

It was Polly who broke the silence.

"Oh good," she said, when she saw Mary. Polly was the only one in the room who had no idea that something was amiss. "I was wondering when you would get here. Did you get something to eat? There are the most extraordinary treats. Gunner really outdid himself this year."

And that is when Polly noticed that the room was strangely quiet. And she looked around, befuddled.

But only for the briefest moment.

Because in that briefest of moments, a thousand expressions crossed Mary's face. Her shoulders tightened and then relaxed, which made it look as if her angel wings had begun to flap. And then she smiled, and she said, "Thank you, Polly. You know I wouldn't miss one of your parties."

Of course she should have said that weeks ago. She should have said that when she realized she had been misinformed and Polly was still having her party. She should have stepped aside graciously.

She was, as they say, a little late coming to the party. But they also say, better late than never.

The room slowly filled with chatter again, and as it did, Mary whispered something in Dave's ear and Dave slipped out the door, heading back to her house to collect Bert, Adam, the twins, and the snacks that Gunner had missed.

IT WAS MAYBE an hour, maybe two, before *Polly* finally put it all together. Everyone else was still around and about, still chatting away. But the night was clearly winding down. Polly had begun tidying up. And Mary was helping her, carrying what was left of the white asparagus and the shortbread cookies into the kitchen. Polly had just picked up a plate of whitefish pâté when she realized Mary was in a white dress and snowflake pantyhose. That's when the penny dropped.

Polly had considered doing a white theme herself. And having considered it, she had no trouble recognizing it.

They were alone in the kitchen now. The two of them. Polly had just put a platter high on a shelf over the fridge when she turned and looked at Mary and said, "Next year," and this was the closest they would ever come to actually talking about *this* year.

"Next year," she said. "Let's do the party together. Your food. My house."

It was a small act of grace. Of generosity. But it came from Polly's heart.

Mary was about to say something, but before she could, Ted appeared through the swinging door and said, "It's time to light the tree. Where are the matches?"

Polly pointed at a drawer in the kitchen and said, "You always take so long to get them going. Where's Bert? Get Bert to help you."

As Ted went looking for Bert, Polly put her arm around Mary's waist and steered her through the door. When the carolling began, the two of them were standing together beside the tree.

The night traditionally ends with that boisterous old carol "We Wish You a Merry Christmas." When they got to it, Polly leaned close to Mary and whispered:

"I love this one."

Soon the entire room was dancing that dangerous line between singing and outright shouting.

Oh, bring us some figgy pudding
Oh, bring us some figgy pudding
Oh, bring us some figgy pudding
And a cup of good cheer

THE CHRISTMAS SEASON is many things to many people. To some it is the story of the birth of Jesus—the story of peace, and love.

To others it is a time of goodwill and fellowship, a time to gather together, with family and friends, in schools and in homes, in churches and in theatres.

Some just like the decorations and the lights and the warmth they give; finding light at the darkest time of the year.

Others just like the music.

Even the little ones were singing along now. Stomping their feet and waving their hands in the air.

And Mary and Polly too, singing along at the top of their lungs, the night's escapades completely forgotten. The two of them doing what women are so good at doing—moving on. Living with a little victory, and a little defeat. And if ever there need be proof of miracles, surely this would suffice.

"Here we go," said Polly, resting her hand on Mary's shoulder. "Everyone now!"

We won't go until we get some
We won't go until we get some
We won't go until we get some
So bring it right here

THE VINYL CAFE CELEBRATES

Beginnings

THE WORLD'S SMALLEST RECORD STORE

The first time the kid stole a record Dave missed the whole thing. In his defence, he was distracted. There was this other guy hanging around the store at the time. Full of questions. About suppliers and vintage records, the turntable by the easy chair. This. That. Everything.

Meanwhile, the kid was doing *his* thing in the blues section, although it has never actually been called the blues section in Dave's store. Back when Dave had names for each section in his store, he had a sign hanging over the blues records that read, SHE NEVER LOVED YOU ANYWAY. The sign was still there in the days I'm talking about.

Anyway, the kid had his back to the counter. He was wearing tight jeans and a bulky army surplus coat. The coat was the tipoff. And Dave completely missed it.

"Haven't seen *these* for years," said the guy with all the questions. He was pointing at the goldfish bowl of plastic centres for 45 rpm records.

"Where do you get them anyway?"

Now, normally, that's the kind of question Dave would enjoy.

"Actually," he would say, "I got them from Sarnia." And then he would tell the whole sorry story, about how the company that made them went out of business, and how he had bought a wooden crate, the size of a casket, full of the things.

It's how he spends the better part of *most* days. Talking about things like plastic record centres with his regular customers. But this guy *wasn't* a regular customer. And besides, there was something about him that was annoying.

It was around then that the kid left the store. He nodded at Dave as he slouched past the counter. Dave nodded back, absentmindedly. It was only hours later, long after the kid was gone, and the annoying guy had left, that the penny dropped.

Dave was tallying up the day's receipts when he stopped and stared across the store. That kid. The kid in the army coat. The kid had been stealing records. The way he walked by the counter. He might as well have been waving the record over his head. It had happened right under Dave's nose.

It was Mr. Question Guy's fault. Mr. Question Guy had distracted him.

THEFT HAS NEVER been a *big* problem in Dave's little store. And it certainly wasn't back then. The chains lose four, maybe five, percent to what they coyly call "shrinkage."

Dave loses hardly anything. His store after all *is* pretty small. Right from the beginning, he proudly claimed it to be the world's *smallest* record store.

Anyway, he was, and still is, usually there behind the counter. Who is going to shoplift when the owner is staring at you?

Sheesh. He couldn't believe he had missed the kid. He glanced at the clock. He was running late.

Now, Dave is many good things: a thoughtful friend, an easygoing neighbour, a loyal husband, and a loving father. One thing he's not, however, is graceful.

He lives with grace, but he doesn't *move* with grace. He is not what anyone would call an elegant or stylish man.

Except for this moment. This moment when he closes his store. He has done it so many times he can do it with the easy unselfconsciousness of a dancer. For two or three minutes at the end of every day, and almost always when he is alone, Dave is Fred Astaire.

He slips the scroll from the cash register into his pocket. He reaches out and lifts the arm off the turntable. He leans over and flicks off the lamp. He slides the money out of the cash register and into the night-deposit bag.

This day's take was $127.84 in cash, $35 in IOUs, and $8 in Canadian Tire money, which Dave has accepted at par from the day he opened.

If it wasn't for the kid, not a bad day.

He left the cash drawer open; then his arm floated out and hit the light switch.

All that was left was a few fluid steps out the door and the swift twirl of the lock—and Dave would leave the stage for another day.

HE WASN'T SURPRISED when the kid showed up a week later. Dave spotted him the minute he walked through the front door. If he had wanted to shut him down he could have. He didn't, however, want to shut him down. He wanted to figure him out.

There was something about the kid that fascinated Dave. He was an awkward-looking boy. Maybe sixteen. All arms and legs. He was flipping through the records filed under *D*.

Okay, was he a dork or a dude? The thought made Dave smile.

And it was that thought that made Dave decide what he was going to do next. He wasn't going to stop the kid. He was going to play "What If?" instead.

What if . . . What if, what?

Okay. If the kid took the new Dylan, Dave would let him go. If he took Duran Duran, he would nail him. Dylan or Duran Duran? Dude or dork?

Dave walked to the front of the store. He stood on a chair and fiddled with the speakers by the front door. He was giving the kid a chance to make his move.

When he came back to the counter, the kid had moved to the back of the store. This was a little like chess. *My move,* thought Dave. Dave went over to the *D*s. The Dylan was gone. The kid had won fair and square.

He would have to get him next time. Which happened to be that weekend.

The kid walked in on Saturday evening, just before closing. As soon as he saw him, Dave thought, *Okay, enough is enough. This has got to stop.*

He waited until they were alone. And when they were, Dave walked over to him and put his arm on the kid's shoulder.

"Hey," said Dave. Friendly enough.

The kid stiffened and turned around. Dave was smiling. He had his hand out, ready to shake hands.

And, *oh yeah*. The kid had a record squished under his armpit. No doubt about that.

Dave's hand was still extended.

"My name's Dave," he said. "I've seen you around a couple of times."

The kid took Dave's hand awkwardly. What else could he do? Dave shook it—energetically. The kid gasped. Dave was shaking the record loose.

The kid leaned against the bin of records.

Nice move, thought Dave.

"My name is Nick," said the kid.

The kid looked terrified. He was squirming up and down against the crate like an elephant scratching on a tree. He was trying to shift everything back into place.

Dave couldn't help himself. He liked the kid. He decided to give him one last chance.

Dave said, "Do you like Dylan, Nick?"

The kid nodded. But he seemed apprehensive. As if he knew something bad was coming his way.

Dave smiled. Dave said, "What about Duran Duran?"

Dave was playing "What If?" again.

The kid said, "Duran Duran? I hate Duran Duran."

Dave said, "Good answer."

Then, without thinking about what he was doing, on an impulse he never understood but grew to be proud of because it worked out so well, Dave offered the kid a job.

"A job?" said the kid. He looked even more scared.

"Yeah," said Dave. "I need some help. After school. You look like an honest guy."

Things were definitely not going the way the kid had expected them to go.

The kid said, "Working. Like what?"

"Helping out," said Dave. "Stocking, cleaning. Looking out for shoplifters. That kind of thing."

The kid swallowed. The kid said, "I don't think so."

"Good," said Dave, without missing a beat. "Why don't you start tomorrow? Minimum wage. Except for tomorrow of course. You've already been paid for your first four hours."

Dave clapped him on the shoulder and gave him a last friendly shake. The album the kid had pressed against his body fell to the ground.

Dave pretended not to see it.

"See you tomorrow," he said. And he turned and walked back to the cash.

The kid picked up the record and put it back in the crate where he got it.

On the way past the counter he stopped and said, "My name isn't Nick. My name is Scott."

Dave said, "I'm still Dave. See you tomorrow."

AND SO WENT the days at Dave's little record store. This was, as I have said, a number of years ago. When his daughter Stephanie was still young. Scott, no surprise, fit right in. He was, it turned out, a Bob Dylan scholar. He had a collection of over twenty-five Dylan albums, none of them commercially released.

He mastered Ringo, the game of flipping record centres across the store at a moving turntable. They used a home-made catapult assembled from a mousetrap. In his third week, he scored the first-ever "Brian Epstein" by landing a centre directly on the spindle. A feat that Dave had decided was impossible. To celebrate, Dave closed the store and they all went out for lunch, including the store's only other employee in those years, Brian, who invented the game. Dave had called him in specifically for the celebratory meal and paid him for the afternoon.

Things were good. Everyone got a small raise at Christmas.

So when the lawyer's letter arrived, it came, as they say, like a bolt out of the blue.

A cease-and-desist letter, from a guy who owned a place called the Vinyl Cafetorium. A store that was, according to this letter, legally the world's smallest record store. The store owner had, according to the letter, trademarked that phrase.

The letter informed Dave that he had to remove any and all signs that mentioned the size of his store, or a complaint would be filed in the provincial court seeking an injunction to stop him from exploiting the phrase.

"What?" said Kenny Wong, when Dave burst into his café waving the letter.

"That's what it says," said Dave.

"Take down the signs?" said Kenny.

"Or," read Dave, "they will seek compensation for damages both actual and statutory. Whatever that means."

"That," said Kenny, "means war."

THEY WENT TO check out the Vinyl Cafetorium that night. In Kenny's 1984 Lada. Dave was riding shotgun. Scott was in the back seat. It was almost ten. They figured the shop would be long closed. It was supposed to be a drive-by, a reconnaissance.

The store was lit up like a riverboat.

THE WORLD'S SMALLEST RECORD STORE. OPEN 'TIL MIDNIGHT said the marquee over the front door. On the door itself was a smaller sign: WE MAY NOT BE BIG, BUT WE'RE SMALL.

The same motto Dave had scrawled on the back of an envelope on one of the very first days his shop was open.

He had it pinned on the bulletin board by the cash. It's there still.

"But his store is huge," said Dave.

"It's not *huge*," said Kenny.

"It's way bigger than my place," said Dave.

"Well, how hard is that?" said Kenny.

"It's like one of those British pubs," said Dave.

"The fake ones," said Kenny.

"They're trying way too hard," said Dave.

The walls were exposed brick. There were posters on the pillars.

"The place is cool," said Scott. "The posters aren't all messed up like yours."

"That's because mine are real," said Dave.

Dave lifted a pair of binoculars to his eyes. He could make out a vintage pop cooler by the front door. It had COCA-COLA emblazoned across the front of it. Along the side of the room was a long counter, with an espresso maker sitting prominently in the middle of it. This was years ago, before you saw espresso machines everywhere. Way before Kenny got his. Behind the espresso machine, there was a guy in a white apron who looked strangely familiar.

"I know that guy," said Dave. "He used to come into the store and ask questions. It's that Mr. Question Guy. I can't believe it. That guy was spying on me."

That's when Ted Anderson walked out of the shop, carrying a large plastic bag.

"That's Ted Anderson!" said Dave.

Ted Anderson is a neighbour and one of Dave's regulars.

"Quisling," muttered Dave, reaching for his door handle.

He was about to jump out of the car. Kenny reached over and put his hand across Dave's chest. Kenny said, "Let's go."

Scott said, "Before we go, can I get an espresso?"

DAVE COULDN'T BELIEVE it. Back in the early eighties, when everyone else had been talking about expansion and growth, Dave had happily stayed small. He had resisted the urge to update, and renovate, and redecorate. He had *intentionally* set his bar low. Really low. And now someone was telling him he wasn't even big enough to be small.

He met Bert Turlington the next evening in the park. Bert is a criminal lawyer. They often walk around the park at night.

When he finished filling Bert in, Dave said, "Can we fight it?"

Bert said, "It's not what I do. But I know a guy. One of the best. He'll help you. But I have to tell you two things."

They were standing by a tree while Arthur poked around.

"The first thing is, he's very expensive. Conservatively, it could cost you about the price of a new car. A nice one."

Dave said, "What's the second thing?"

Bert said, "If the guy really has a trademark, you aren't going to win."

Dave said, "We won't win."

Bert said, "But you should do it anyway."

Dave said, "On principle."

Bert said, "Principle schminciple."

Dave said, "Then why?"

Bert said, "My friend needs the work."

A FEW DAYS later, Mr. Question Guy walked into the store. Right out of the blue. As bold as can be.

He walked in with the confidence of a prairie evangelist, and before Dave could do or say anything, he set a briefcase on the counter and said, "I thought we could settle this like gentlemen."

Then he pulled a binder out of his briefcase and said, "It's all in here."

And it was. The entire concept: design, marketing, strategy, product lines. The Vinyl Cafetorium. WE MAY NOT BE BIG, BUT WE'RE SMALL.

"Now listen," said the man. Dave still didn't know his name. "Listen," said the man, "here are your options. You can close down or you can keep going. But if you keep going, you are going to eventually close down because you can't compete against us. The smart decision would be to buy a franchise. Get in on the ground floor."

Dave said, "You are offering me a franchise?"

The man beamed. "That's exactly what I'm doing."

The man said, "The initial investment—"

Dave said, "Wait now. You're telling me I can make an investment in the . . . the Cafetorium? Just to keep my place?"

"Oh no," said the man. "You can't keep your place. We have final approval of locations. And we would never approve this location. I mean. You know." He waved his arm around Dave's store.

"We have our eyes on a lovely space in a little strip mall in the West End Industrial Park that I think would work out perfectly for you."

Dave suggested he leave.

"You should go," he said.

Or words to that effect.

DAVE WENT INTO the Cafetorium the next day. It was a Tuesday morning. The quietest morning of the week. He wasn't doing anything except fretting and he couldn't stand it any longer. He dropped the blind on the front door and reached under it and set the hands on the little raccoon to say he would be back in an hour. He went upstairs and poked around the storage room for a disguise.

He found the perfect thing. A suit, with a dress shirt and tie. It took him three tries to get the knot right. Even then, the skinny end stuck out by about three inches.

As he headed out, he grabbed his lunch. If anyone asked, he was going for lunch, that's what he was doing. He had no idea what he was going to do when he got to the Cafetorium. He didn't have a plan. He just *had* to see the place again. He was acting on impulse.

As he walked along, he was telling himself he wouldn't go in. He would simply walk by. Then his neighbour Mary Turlington breezed past him without a second look. He felt invisible.

When he got to the shop, Mr. Question Guy was nowhere to be seen. There was a young woman behind the counter. She had the store's sound system cranked loud. She was playing Duran Duran. Before Dave knew it, he was at the back of the store, furtively unwrapping his lunch. A sardine sandwich. When it was open he took a bite and slipped the rest of it onto a shelf above a heater.

He went back the next day. He couldn't stop himself. He had to see what had happened.

"There's an odd smell," he said to the woman.

"It's been here all day," she said. "It's driving me nuts."

He felt a pang of guilt. It wasn't her fault. He ordered a chocolate milk and gave her a generous tip. He headed to the back of the store to fetch the offensive sandwich. Halfway there he spotted the poster on a pillar.

DON'T BE FOOLED BY IMITATIONS, read the poster. THIS IS THE REAL DEAL. THE OFFICIAL WORLD'S SMALL-EST RECORD STORE.

Dave sighed. When he got to the back of the store, he muttered, "You think you're so small. I'll show you small." Instead of removing the sardine sandwich from the shelf, he placed the glass of milk beside it and left.

On Saturday he called the store from a pay phone. He used a fake name. He ordered a copy of *Trout Mask Replica* by Captain Beefheart. That would keep them busy. He had no intention of ever picking it up.

He had become Wile E. Coyote. Mr. Question Guy was the Road Runner. Pretty soon Dave had an Acme catalogue of plots rebounding inside his poor little head.

He'd pay an exterminator to park his van outside the store with a big sign in the window that read: EMERGENCY CALL.

He'd hire, what's his name, the guy with the ukulele, to stand outside and play the same song over and over. Maybe "Pop Goes the Weasel."

He spent half an hour flipping through the Yellow Pages under "Deliveries (manure, fresh)."

It's all he talked about.

IT WAS SCOTT who brought him to his senses one night.

It was a delicate moment. For a sixteen-year-old, Scott handled the moment with surprising sensitivity.

He put his hand on Dave's shoulder and said, "Have you noticed that you might have lost your mind?"

"He is stealing my ideas," said Dave, pushing Scott away. Standing up. Pacing. "He wants to steal my store," said Dave.

"Yup," said Scott.

"So what do you expect me to do?" said Dave.

"What would be best," said Scott, sixteen years old and not yet shaving, "is nothing."

"Nothing?" said Dave.

"Exactly," said Scott. "Nothing is exactly what you should do."

Then he said, "I went over there last week. I went through the whole place. And you know what? You're right. The coffee is terrible. And you know what else? He doesn't have *Blood on the Tracks*, or *Blonde on Blonde*. He doesn't even have *Highway 61 Revisited*. He'll be out of business in a year. All you have to do is wait him out. I know this guy stole your idea. But believe me, all you have to do is wait."

"You don't know what it feels like," said Dave.

"Maybe," said Scott. "But I know a little about theft. And I know robbing an idea is nothing compared to having one. The guy is nothing. *This* place is the real deal."

And that . . . was that.

A COUPLE OF months passed before Dave visited the Cafetorium again.

He almost didn't recognize the place. The sign was still up, but it had been shifted to the right. What *had* been the left side of the store was now an entirely new business— electronics. And the Vinyl Cafetorium, now half its original size, was little more than a coffee shop with a few racks of albums crammed against the wall across from the espresso machine.

Dave smiled. It might have been *small*, but it wasn't much of a record store. That's when he noticed the sign by the door. It said WORLD'S SMALLEST RECORD STORE . . .

WE MAY NOT BE BIG, BUT—and this is the part that delighted Dave. Someone had spray-painted over the words WE'RE SMALL. Now it said, WE SMELL.

Dave laughed out loud. Scott. For sure.

And Scott was right. It is easy to steal an idea. It's better to have one. And it's better still if you believe in the ideas you have.

As Dave headed home he was thinking about how much he was looking forward to going to work the next day.

It would be, he was sure, a quiet day. Not many customers. Just a few sales. Business, no doubt about it, would be slow. As usual, he would spend more time at the turntable than at the cash. And that wouldn't bother him one bit.

In fact, he couldn't think of anything in the world he would enjoy more.

OPERA

D ave's mother, Margaret, had a difficult summer. She couldn't get warm. Everyone kept complaining about the heat and Margaret thought, *Are they nuts? It's freezing here.* At the beginning of July her daughter, Annie, drove up from Halifax. Annie found Margaret in her garden, wearing a sweater and a toque. Annie was wearing shorts and a T-shirt.

Margaret stared at her daughter and said, "Aren't you cold?"

On Sunday, as Annie was getting ready to leave, Margaret said, matter-of-factly, "Will you come up for my birthday? It's going to be my last."

"It was eighty-two degrees when I left," said Annie to Dave on the phone. "She was wearing a scarf. And gloves."

Dave and Annie and their families all went for Margaret's birthday. Dave and Morley gave her a garden diary, bound in leather.

"You can use it every year, to keep track," said Dave, flipping through the diary for her. "There's a place for everything. When things come up. The first frost."

"Don't be silly," huffed Margaret. "Just how many years do you think I've got left?"

It was Annie who bought her mother the tickets to the opera—to the Lincoln Center in New York City, to a Saturday afternoon at the Met.

Margaret said, "I can't possibly go to New York."

"Why not?" said Annie.

"I have nothing to wear," said Margaret, buttoning the top of her cardigan.

WE STUMBLE ON the great loves of our lives in the oddest ways. Opera came to Margaret when she was a little girl. It arrived in the form of Doogie MacDougal—of the Ignish MacDougals, not the North Shore MacDougals.

Like his daddy, and his daddy before him, Doogie MacDougal was born and raised to the sea. He was a sailor four years on the *Margaree*, a rusty cargo ship that worked the eastern seaboard down to the Caribbean. Four years to sea, and he would have been gone forty more, except Doogie tore his shoulder to shreds in Boston unloading pallets of raw sugar. His arm twisted in a cargo net, yanking him fifteen feet in the air. He screamed like a seagull.

Doogie ended up in a New York hospital for a month and a half. A week before he was released, Angus MacDonnell showed up. He stood at the end of the bed, smoking, and said, "A man could get a job to the theatre if he wanted."

Doogie said, "I don't know squat about theatre."

Angus took a drag of his smoke and said, "Now tell me what's the difference between hauling ropes to change a scene and tying off a pallet. Rope's rope."

Doogie shrugged, and two months later he was drinking at McSorley's and working at the Met.

This was before unions. Before theatre schools. Half the backstage crew were crippled Bluenosers. Like Angus had said, rope's rope.

This was at the old Met, the one on Thirty-ninth and Broadway, before that building was torn down and the opera moved into the Lincoln Center. Back when Margaret was eleven years old. Back when Dr. Sandberg was the only person in Irish Bay who owned a radio. On Saturday afternoons, as many as fifty people would cram into his living room. Dr. Sandberg would turn his radio up and they would listen to their Doogie MacDougal at work. *Saturday Afternoon at the Met.* Milton Cross on the CBC.

That was in the early thirties, before the war.

Margaret, eleven years old, would go with her mother. They would dress up and sit on Dr. Sandberg's couch, leaning against each other, applauding with everyone else every time Milton Cross described a scene change. They could hear the audience in New York applauding too, and in her mind's eye Margaret could see Doogie MacDougal of Irish Bay, Cape Breton, standing on the stage of the Metropolitan Opera House in New York City, in front of the gold curtain, taking his bows. Doogie MacDougal gets caught up in rope and Margaret gets caught up in opera, and seventy-two years later there's probably no one in the country who has heard more of the Saturday afternoon broadcasts from the Met on the CBC than Margaret MacNeal from Irish Bay, Nova Scotia.

Sure enough, it was Doogie MacDougal who opened the door, but it wasn't Doogie who kept Margaret coming back. From the beginning she was swept away by the passion of the music. Opera is a world moved by storms and, living by the ocean, Margaret understood the eloquence of stormy weather. She was born into a world battered by elements beyond anyone's control. So she felt at home in this universe of villains and spurned lovers.

Opera was a world that made her feel worldly. By the time she was fourteen, Margaret had persuaded her father to buy a radio of their own, and every Saturday Margaret would sit in the parlour listening to her opera. You would think a parent could ask for nothing more, but Margaret's mother and father soon learned opera was leading their daughter astray.

The first time Margaret was moved to liquor, she was sixteen. Home alone, listening to *Tosca*, Margaret was overcome by the passions of Italy. The call of red wine stirred in her soul. There was no wine in the house, of course, or anywhere in town, except for the church. But that didn't stop Margaret. Margaret took one of her father's beers and mixed it with grape juice. She was passed out on the sofa when her parents came home. Sixteen and head over heels in love—drunk with love—all Margaret needed was a man.

As she got older, after she had found that man, she still pursued her first love. She listened every week, and she followed the lives of the stars—especially Maria Callas. Callas who lived on the edge. Callas who lived dangerously. Callas who left her husband for that rat Aristotle Onassis.

Margaret devoured all the gossip-page news about them. How Callas met Onassis at the film festival in Venice. How he came to London and threw a party for her at the Dorchester Hotel. How he decorated the room with thousands of roses and invited Churchill and Gary Cooper and Douglas Fairbanks Jr. Soon after the party, Callas sold her apartment in Milan and moved to Paris—moved so she could be on Onassis's route between London and Monte Carlo. It was pure love. And in the face of such love, Onassis dumped Callas for that Jackie Kennedy. Callas died of a broken heart. Her ashes were sprinkled over the Mediterranean where Onassis sailed his yacht.

Callas didn't just sing opera, she lived one. Margaret longed to live as recklessly as Callas. When Margaret met Charlie, she loved him to death, and she decided the most reckless thing she could do was marry him. After they were married, Margaret tried to love her Charlie as recklessly as she could.

Charlie loved music too. Margaret taught him about opera. He taught her to sing. They sang together driving the car, and they sang together doing the dishes. Margaret loved Charlie so much that even if Enrico Caruso had flown to Big Narrows and rented the Starlight Room at the

Breakwater Hotel, filled it with carnations and thrown a party for Margaret, inviting all the great Canadian personalities, like Stompin' Tom Connors and Foster Hewitt and Mister Dressup, Margaret wouldn't have given him an ear.

But now Charlie was gone, and Margaret felt just like Maria Callas—alone, a lonely old widow who couldn't get warm—except Margaret was living in a house in Big Narrows instead of an apartment in Paris.

ANNIE PHONED HER mother at the end of August and said, "I can't come to New York with you. The orchestra is going to Japan. They changed the dates."

Annie plays in Symphony Nova Scotia.

"Is there someone else you could ask?" asked Annie.

Margaret cast around town. Bernadette and Winnie both said they would be delighted to go to New York with Margaret. But they both said the same thing about the Met. "Do we have to go to the opera?" they asked.

Margaret phoned Annie in Halifax. "Couldn't the orchestra go to Japan another time?" she asked.

Annie said, "I'll get more tickets. We'll go to New York after Christmas."

Margaret said, "Christmas is a long time away. I don't know about after Christmas."

They both knew what she meant. She meant, I'll be dead after Christmas.

"Don't be silly," said Annie.

Margaret agreed to go in January. But she still had those birthday tickets sticking in the hall mirror, and they were making her crazy. Her kids were so wasteful. The way they used the telephone, calling all the time, as if long distance cost nothing. And now Annie was prepared to see these birthday tickets go unused. She couldn't let them go to waste. She phoned Gallagher's.

Arnie Gallagher is Big Narrows' one-man band. His store on Water Street serves the town as florist, funeral home, gift store, and travel agency.

"When's your flight?" asked Annie when she called a day later.

"Monday," said Margaret. Margaret omitted telling her daughter that she was going alone, omitted mentioning that flying had seemed like such an indulgence that she had bought a round-trip bus ticket. The Narrows to Sydney, Sydney to Halifax, Halifax to Montreal, Montreal to New York: thirty-eight hours straight.

It was while the bus was pulling out of Schenectady that Margaret began talking to Charlie. They had always planned to go to New York. It was going to be their big trip, their opera hajj . . . their pilgrimage. They were going to visit all the stations of the cross. Then Charlie died, and here she was, going alone.

For years Margaret had written down their plans in a pink Hilroy notebook. Unfortunately, all her plans were gleaned from *The New Yorker* magazine. For years Margaret had had the only subscription in Cape Breton. Unhappily, she cancelled it in fury in 1987, when William Shawn was forced to step down as editor. All her New York information was at best fifteen years out of date.

SHE ARRIVED AT the Port Authority bus terminal in New York City at seven-thirty in the morning. Margaret, who had barely closed her eyes for two nights, had finally fallen into a deep sleep not an hour before. When the driver shook her awake, she had no idea where she was. She humped her suitcase onto Forty-second Street in a daze. She was hungry and overwhelmingly tired. She stared at the river of yellow taxi cabs, at the early-morning crush of the city. Instead of the rush of excitement she had been expecting, Margaret felt fear. The buildings were so tall and packed together that she could barely see the sky. Suddenly New York didn't seem like such a good idea.

"Charlie?" she said, looking all around, her hand at her throat.

A man on Rollerblades was heading down the sidewalk, toward Margaret. He had spiked hair and tattoos, and pins everywhere. There were pins in his nose and in his ears and in his lips and through his cheek. This "pin man," who was—oh my God, he was wearing a skirt—this "pin man" cut by Margaret on his Rollerblades, and she felt the flap of his skirt on her legs. She thought to herself that no one had mentioned anything in *The New Yorker* about pin men in skirts who brushed by you on their Rollerblades when you were standing on the sidewalk minding your own business.

And they hadn't mentioned the noise either. She had never read about the honking horns. Margaret backed up and leaned against the bus terminal. She felt dizzy. The wall felt grimy. Dirty. For five minutes she leaned against it. Then a man carrying a black briefcase walked by her, stopped, turned, and handed her a dollar bill. She was too stunned to give it back. Her legs were shaking.

She went back into the bus station and sat on a bench. She and Charlie had planned to stay at the Algonquin Hotel. When she had phoned for a reservation, Margaret couldn't believe what they wanted for a room. She went to number two on their list: the Chelsea.

Somehow Margaret got herself going. Somehow she found the subway. It was terrifying. It reminded her of Margaret-Anne Madigan's vacuum cleaner—loud and dark and dirty. She got on the wrong train. It was heading north, which was not the way she should have been going, but she was too frightened to get off. Like the man in the song, she rode around and around for an hour and a half.

It was noon before she finally asked for help. She found herself standing on the corner of 125th and Adam Clayton Powell Jr. Boulevard, in the heart of Harlem, right across from the Apollo Theater, where Billie Holiday and Ella and Duke and Count Basie and Aretha Franklin had all performed.

Margaret felt utterly exhausted, utterly defeated, utterly depressed. She was utterly alone. Her feet throbbed. This wasn't the way she had imagined it at all. She must have been out of her mind to leave home. What had she been thinking?

She crossed the street and rubbed the lucky tree stump in front of the Apollo. She and Charlie were going to rub the stump together and make a wish.

"Wish you were here, Charlie," she said.

She dug out her guidebook. The Chelsea Hotel, where Mark Twain and Tennessee Williams had both stayed (and, as Dave liked to point out, where Sid Vicious had killed his girlfriend Nancy), was at the other end of town. Margaret couldn't stomach the idea of going back into the subway. She waved at a taxi cab.

She climbed into the back seat and squinted at the driver through the thick plastic security panel. He said something to her she didn't understand. Margaret realized he must have been asking her where she wanted to go.

"It's a long story," she began. "My husband died twelve years ago. . ."

She tried to explain about Charlie and the Algonquin. The driver kept interrupting. He wouldn't let her finish. All Margaret's fatigue and fear and disappointment merged into one big ball of frustration. She leaned right up to the thick plastic window separating them and yelled.

"The Chelsea Hotel, goddammit!"

The driver nodded and peeled off so abruptly that Margaret was slammed into the back of the seat.

"Oh my goodness, Charlie," she said, reaching for the door handle.

That was when she noticed that her driver, who was snaking in and out of the traffic as if he were running an obstacle course, looked nothing like the picture of the man on the taxi licence posted in the back with her. Margaret thought this man, who had clearly murdered the real driver, was taking her somewhere that wasn't the Chelsea Hotel, probably somewhere like a waterfront warehouse, where he would rifle her bag, take her things home to his mistress, and then dispose of her.

She would have jumped out of the cab, but he was driving too fast to get out. She reached into her purse and took out a knitting needle. She knocked on the glass. "Chelsea Hotel," she yelled again, waving the needle at him.

The driver looked horrified. His wife, who wanted him to work in the bakery business with her brother, kept telling him that he would get someone like this one day. "Why can't you stay home and work in Yonkers instead of driving weirdos and drug addicts all over the city?" she had said that very morning. He sped up. When he pulled up in front of the Chelsea, both he and Margaret jumped out of the cab and started to yell for help.

After things were cleared up, Margaret checked into the Chelsea in a haze, so exhausted she didn't notice anything about the historic hotel. She went to her room and fell asleep, waking up at suppertime sweaty and disoriented. For the second time that day, she had no clue where on earth she was.

The man at the front desk told her she should eat dinner at the Venus Coffee Shop around the corner on Eighth.

Margaret made her way unsteadily down the street. When she turned the corner and spotted the little café, she felt comfortable for the first time since she had left home. It had ten booths and twelve seats at the counter. It reminded her of the Maple Leaf Restaurant in Big Narrows. She ordered the roast turkey dinner with cranberry sauce and mashed potatoes. As she left, she nodded at the woman eating alone at the booth beside her. The woman, short-haired and rotund, was wearing a grey sweatshirt that said *World's Greatest Grandmother* on the front. She had ordered the turkey dinner too.

It was Wednesday night. According to her notebook, Margaret was supposed to go for a walk through Greenwich Village on Wednesday night. But Margaret didn't feel safe walking alone. Instead she sat in the small hotel lobby under a papier mâché sculpture of a fat lady on a swing and watched the people coming and going. Just as Margaret was about to go to bed, the lady from the coffee shop walked in the front door carrying a large purse and a handful of shopping bags. *She must be staying at the Chelsea too,* thought Margaret. Margaret watched her as she went by, wondering where *she* had been, all alone.

The next morning, the lady was sitting in the same booth at the Venus when Margaret arrived for breakfast. She had on a new sweatshirt. This one read *Ohio—So Much to Discover.* The woman had a map of the city spread out on her table. She was consulting a guidebook as she ate.

Margaret still had two days before the opera. She no longer knew how she was going to fill them. She wasn't tramping around this city alone, that was for sure. She wasn't getting on the subway again. Or in a taxi. The city was crazy. Maybe there was something on television she could watch.

On her way back to the hotel, Margaret walked by a woman on the corner selling something. The thin, olive-skinned woman looked about fifty. She was sitting on a milk crate with cartons stacked all around her. Margaret stopped to watch. The cartons were full of a strange oval fruit, the skins a soft blend of red and green and gold. The woman was holding a frighteningly huge knife. With a few deft strokes, she peeled the beautiful fruit, revealing its golden yellow flesh. Then she stuck it on a stick like a Popsicle and, right before Margaret's eyes, cut into the flesh five, ten times, twirling the fruit around and around on its stick. When she finished, it looked like a flower. For a moment Margaret forgot where she was. For a moment that became five minutes, and then ten, and then fifteen, Margaret stood on Eighth Avenue staring in awe at this fruit artist. She stood there until the woman made eye contact, smiled, and pointed at her fruit on a stick. Margaret had to have it, wanted more than anything in the world to walk down the street eating this beautiful juicy thing—whatever it was.

"Two dollars," said the woman.

"I'm from Canada," said Margaret.

"Mexico," said the woman, pointing at her chest.

Margaret wanted to ask what the fruit was, but she was too shy. She smiled at the woman and walked away feeling adventurous. When she bit into the fruit, juice ran down her chin. It was unlike anything Margaret had ever tried. It tasted not quite like a peach but almost. Firmer than a peach. Part peach, part grape, part tropical island. It was delicious. When she got to her hotel, she still had half her fruit left. She decided to walk around the block while she finished it.

"I can do that, Charlie," she said quietly.

When she came back to the fruit lady, she bought another.

"What is this?" she asked.

"Mango," said the lady.

Margaret walked around the block in New York City all by herself eating the second mango of her life.

"I love mangoes, Charlie," she said.

On her third pass, all smiles and juice stained, Margaret put out her hand to take another fruit that the woman was handing her. This time the fruit lady wouldn't let Margaret pay. Margaret was stuffed. She didn't want to refuse, but she didn't know what to do with it.

There was a man sitting on the sidewalk by the hotel, collecting spare change. On an impulse Margaret held the mango out to him.

"Would you like this?" asked Margaret. "I'm full."

"What is it?" asked the man.

"It's a mango," said Margaret.

"Thank you," said the man, reaching out to take it. "I've always wanted to try a mango."

So this is New York, thought Margaret as she walked away. She was vibrating.

She took a deep breath and walked right by her hotel. She crossed Seventh Avenue and then Sixth and then Fifth. She had no idea where she was going. She kept looking behind her, making sure the landscape hadn't changed, making sure the city wasn't rolling up behind her, making sure there was a way back. Then she stopped checking. There was too much to look at up ahead. She saw a lacy iron sculpture of a steam shovel in Madison Square Park that reminded her of the Seal Island Bridge over the Bras d'Or, just outside of Sydney.

She cried when she came upon the statue of Gandhi striding through his little flower garden in Union Square. The city that had seemed so grimy only hours before suddenly seemed to be welcoming her. The noise that had felt so overwhelming felt overwhelmingly full of life. The people seemed friendly, not frightening.

The next morning Margaret got up and bought a mango and headed off in a different direction. By opera morning she had been all over. The East Side. The West Side. All around the town. She was so jazzed by everything she had seen that she did something on Saturday morning that surprised even her.

She was waiting for the elevator to take her up to her room when the doors opened and the woman whom she had been seeing at the Venus Coffee Shop stepped off. Today her sweatshirt read *Akron: City of Invention*. They smiled at each other, and then the woman walked toward the front door. Margaret watched her go. And then, without thinking, Margaret called her.

"Excuse me," she said.

The woman turned, and in one of the greatest acts of courage of her life Margaret said, "Excuse me. I was wondering, I have two tickets for the opera this afternoon, and I was wondering if you would like to go with me. I'm sure you have other plans, and I know you may not like opera—no one seems to—it's just I hate to see the ticket go to waste, and my husband, Charlie, was supposed to come, but he died. I mean, it's twelve years ago now. I'm so sorry to bother you. I feel foolish."

"I was just going for lunch," said the woman.

"Of course," said Margaret, turning back to the elevator.

"That's okay," said the woman, turning to the front door, then suddenly turning back again.

"Wait," said the woman, recklessly, "I would love to go to the opera. But I don't have anything to wear."

"I am sure it wouldn't matter," said Margaret. "But we have to leave in an hour. My name is Margaret. I'm from Cape Breton."

"I'm Rose. I'm from Ohio," said the woman. "What about lunch?"

"We don't want to eat before the opera," said Margaret. "People who know about these things don't eat. If you eat you get sleepy. We'll have a snack during the intermission."

"Oh," said Rose, looking anxious.

"When we get there, we'll go to the maître d' at the Grand Tier Restaurant and order something for the intermission and it will be ready for us. That's what Andrew Porter of *The New Yorker* magazine used to do. Then afterwards, we'll go to the Algonquin for supper. The Algonquin is a famous hotel. That was the plan, anyway."

They took the number nine local train to the Sixty-sixth Street station. Even in the early afternoon, the Lincoln Center was magnificent—the fountain, the two huge Chagall paintings in the windows. It was so much grander than Margaret had imagined.

And when they got their seats, there was the great gold curtain, just like the one she had imagined Doogie MacDougal bowing in front of.

As they settled into their seats, Margaret turned to Rose and said, "I was just thinking about Leonard Warren."

In the spring of 1960, Leonard Warren, who was playing Don Carlo in Verdi's *La Forza del Destino*, finished singing an aria and was just about to launch into the rousing *cabaletta* that begins "to die is a momentous thing" when he pitched face forward onto the floor and died onstage.

"Did they stop the performance?" asked Rose.

"On the spot," said Margaret.

"Did they give everyone their money back?" asked Rose.

"I don't know," said Margaret.

"My husband pitched forward to the floor," said Rose, "but he wasn't performing in an opera. He was wiping the dog's feet."

Neither of them said anything for a moment. Then Rose said, "It would have been more tasteful, don't you think, if he had been onstage."

And they both cracked up.

They had strawberries and champagne between acts.

When it was over, Rose turned to Margaret and said, "That was wonderful."

"Yes," said Margaret. Margaret hadn't felt so excited, so happy, so complete for years.

They went to the Algonquin Hotel for supper. The next morning at ten o'clock there was a knock on Margaret's door. It was Rose. She was wearing jeans and a Cleveland Indians T-shirt. She was holding a baseball hat in her hand.

"I was wondering," she said. "I have two tickets for the Yankees game this afternoon. Ralph and I were supposed to go. I wondered if you would like to come. Instead."

They sat in the sun on the first-base line, and Margaret ate peanuts and a hot dog. After the third inning, Rose went out and bought Margaret a Yankees hat. Who would think that at eighty-three years old so many new things could be happening? Who would have guessed that at eighty-three years old Margaret would be up on her feet when Jason Giambi put one out of the park?

"That was a good one," said Margaret.

And it *was* good. But what was better, what was the most wonderful thing, was that in her purse Margaret had tickets for next year's opera. For *Turandot.* She had bought them the night before, during the second intermission. What was the most wonderful thing was that next autumn she and Rose had already agreed to meet in New York, to see *Turandot* and another baseball game. And once you had tickets you had to use them. At eighty-three, Margaret had just made a friend—a war bride who lived in Dayton, Ohio.

During the seventh-inning stretch, as they stood up together, Margaret turned to Rose, little beads of perspiration on her forehead.

She said, "It's hot in the sun. It hasn't been hot like this all summer at home. It's lovely."

TREE PLANTING

Late on a golden afternoon, in the dreamy late days of August, Dave's daughter, Stephanie, sat at a wooden picnic table at an outdoor café not far from her dad's record store. She was chewing on a pen, working on a letter that she had been labouring over for a good ten minutes. She had written two sentences. *I'm back in the city,* she had written. *What a summer!*

She poured herself a second cup of tea, spotted two girls walking toward her, and self-consciously tucked her left hand under the table. It was more than a month since Stephanie had come home. Her hand still hadn't returned to its natural shape. It remained swollen and stained, and that was after hours of scrubbing with soap and rubbing with creams.

Stephanie was back from a summer in the woods. She had been working as a tree planter.

She had thought it was going to be a ton of fun. She had heard you could make a load of money in no time flat planting trees. So she signed up and found herself on an old school bus, heading north out of Thunder Bay in the early days of May, full of hope.

She imagined she was heading into some sort of hippie commune—a world of tents, hammocks, and guitar-strumming nature-lovers. When the bus pulled into base camp, it turned out to be a burned and logged-out field of charred stumps, smudged by the smoke of a dozen camp-fires. It looked more like the battle of Passchendaele than a party: boys digging trenches, girls fighting with huge flapping blue tarps, dogs jumping around barking, and everyone smoking. A large guy with a ponytail was sitting on the back of a pickup, sharpening a shovel with a file while AC/DC's "Dirty Deeds Done Dirt Cheap" blared from a speaker nailed to the top of a portable toilet.

"Wow," said the boy who stepped off the bus behind her. "This is awesome."

No one said a word to Stephanie as she wrestled her tent up. She finished just as the supper bell sounded. Before heading for the cook tent, she struggled into her new tree-planting outfit. She had bought it at Mountain Equipment Co-op—an organic cotton long-sleeved boat-neck T-shirt (avocado green), over a white tank top and a pair of convertible pants, the kind where the bottoms zip off and they turn into shorts. At supper, a boy in a plaid wool jacket that smelled of wood smoke introduced himself. "I'm Scott," he said. "I'm your foreman."

There was a meeting after dinner. Scott stood on one of the picnic tables, his long hair brushing the cage of the work light that was swinging on a yellow electric cord from the tent ceiling. Stephanie and the rest of the crew had to huddle close to hear him over the generator.

"There are three million trees to plant on this block," said Scott. "The company is paying eight cents a tree. That means there is two hundred and forty thousand dollars up for grabs. There are a hundred planters in camp, and that means each of you *should* make twenty-four hundred dollars before we move to the next block." He looked at the fifteen kids around the picnic table. "That is if we're an *average* crew. You are in the North now. And the North is the land of hard work. I want everyone on this crew to do better than average. I want you guys to plant at least twenty-five hundred trees a day."

Everyone around the table was nodding. Stephanie too. She was determined to be better than average. She was bound for tree-planting glory.

"Make it happen, guys," said Scott as he jumped off the table.

A boy with blond curly hair, wearing a bright blue Gore-Tex jacket, smiled at Stephanie. The boy's name was Perry. It seemed he was the only guy in the camp who had come prepared. Everyone else was wearing ripped and dirty clothes. "Eddie Bauer," said Perry, pointing at his jacket.

THEY WERE SUPPOSED to be on the bus at 7:15 every morning. Before that, they were supposed to eat breakfast and make a bag lunch. By the time Stephanie got ready—no makeup (she *was*, after all, tree planting), just a good 30 SPF sunscreen, a bit of conditioning mousse to keep her flyaway hair in place, and, okay, a touch of mascara—and had made it to the cook tent, all the good lunch stuff—the cheese, the hummus, the cold cuts, and the bagels—was gone. She threw together a peanut butter sandwich on white bread and ran for the bus. She was five minutes late.

She sat beside a tall guy with a ponytail and a hemp necklace. His pants looked as if they were held together by duct tape. They *were*, in fact, held together by duct tape. The top half was beige. From the thighs down they were brown. He was wearing a white-collared dress shirt.

He looked like a loser. No, he looked like a totally *unprepared* loser.

Steph was wearing her new cargo pants.

Perry, the Eddie Bauer boy from the night before, was wearing orange Pumas, quick-dry pants, and a dark blue denim shirt. Perry looked like a pro.

After a half-hour ride, the bus rocked to a stop on the side of a logged-out clearing. The veteran planters headed out by themselves. Scott gathered the rookies around the end of the bus.

"This is the block," he said. He was pointing at the scarred slash in the forest. From the bus, it had looked like a field. Up close, Stephanie could see it was waist high in scrub and scattered with fallen logs.

Scott said, "You each get your own piece of land."

Twenty minutes later, Scott and Stephanie were standing by the side of the road, beside a stack of plastic trays. "White pine," said Scott, pointing at the foot-high saplings.

He pointed at the alder bushes and the deadfalls and the upturned rock. "That's yours," he said.

Then he said, "The first thing is to flag your boundary so no one creams your land." He pointed at a bag of orange ribbons. "Tie one of these off every ten feet, from here back to that small rock to the right of the tree."

It was all rocks and trees as far as Stephanie could see. Before she could ask, Which small rock? Which tree? Scott said, "Make it happen, man," and was gone.

Stephanie strapped on her hip belt and clipped on three canvas tree bags. Then she tied off the first orange flag, concentrating on staying straight, determined that her boundary was going to be perfect.

It took Stephanie less than ten minutes to rip her new beige pants. She tore them as she clambered over the trunk of a fallen pine. She swore out loud. Then she broke into tears, swore again, and stood there wondering what to do. There was nothing to do. Nothing but tie another flag, and then another, until suddenly and unexpectedly and mysteriously, she was back on the road. She had been concentrating so much on her perfectly tied flags that she had got herself turned around. Instead of walking in a straight line back into the bush, she had walked in the shape of a horseshoe.

It took her until eleven o'clock to flag her boundaries. By eleven, she had ripped her pants, flagged her land, and eaten her lunch. She was finally ready to plant her first tree. She plunged her shovel into what looked like a nice soft piece of ground. It struck the rock cap of the Canadian Shield about six inches below the surface, the vibration ricocheting through her body.

At lunch, Perry, the boy with the Eddie Bauer jacket, walked down the road and sat beside her.

"I already ate my lunch," she said morosely.

"I ripped my new jacket," said Perry.

They climbed onto the bus at five o'clock. Stephanie fell into her seat sweaty, exhausted, and starving. There was a rip in each leg of her pants. Her hands were cut and sore.

Perry fell into the seat beside her.

"I only planted five hundred," said Steph. "He must have been joking, right? No one could plant twenty-five hundred trees in a day."

"I did six hundred and fifty," said Perry. "I could have done more, but I hurt my wrist."

Stephanie didn't like that. She thought she should be able to plant as many trees as any other rookie—but surely not twenty-five hundred. Scott was exaggerating about that.

The guy with the ponytail and the white dress shirt was sitting across from them. His left hand was completely covered with duct tape, as if he were wearing a silver glove.

"How many did *you* plant?" asked Perry.

"Twenty-four hundred," said ponytail guy, unwinding the duct tape.

ALL STEPHANIE WANTED was a hot shower. But by the time they made it back to camp, she was too tired to shower, too tired to do anything but eat and fall into her sleeping bag. She slept for ten hours.

She woke up at six to the sound of rain hitting the roof of her tent.

She unpacked her yellow rain gear. It had cost her $179. She had been afraid she wouldn't get a chance to use it. Perry, who sat beside her on the bus again, was wearing the same rain outfit, except in blue.

Ponytail guy was wearing the same duct-tape pants and white dress shirt.

"You're going to get soaked," said Perry.

Ponytail guy shrugged.

"You're going to get wet too," he said. He pointed at Perry's rain suit. "That thing is going to make you sweat. And then you are going to get cold. I'll just get wet and then I'll come back to camp and I'll get dry. Rain gear is for wusses."

It rained all day. Stephanie planted six hundred and twenty trees—a hundred and twenty more than the day before. She also ripped both legs of her yellow rainpants.

Perry planted five hundred, down a hundred and fifty from the previous day. "I could have done more," said Perry, "but I sat in the bus for a couple of hours."

Ponytail guy planted twenty-five hundred.

THE REST OF that week was a complete blur. Every day was the same: up at six, stumble onto the bus and drive to the block. Every second day, the bus broke down and they had to get out and push it. One morning they had to repair a log bridge before they could cross it. Stephanie started to hate the bus and its fetid combination of sweat, abandoned sandwiches, and bug spray. Most of the planters hadn't taken off their clothes since they had arrived, not even for sleeping.

As week two began, Stephanie's cargo pants were festooned with duct-tape patches. She had built her total up over the first few days but then plateaued at around one thousand.

"I did eleven hundred today," she told Perry at the end of the first week.

"I did four fifty," said Perry. "But I could have done more. I played euchre last night until dawn. I took a nap after lunch on a bed of moss. Those little bags of saplings make good pillows."

The next afternoon, Stephanie came back to her cache of trees to fill up her bags, and the trays were thrown every which way.

"They are sprayed with pesticide," Scott explained later. "That's why they smell so skunky. It was probably a bear. Bears love the smell."

ONE AFTERNOON, THE sky turned ominously dark and the wind came up, howling through the trees, whipping everything around, even the foot-high seedlings. When stabs of lightning began to jump out of the sky, Stephanie was so determined to push her numbers up that she just kept on planting.

And then it started to rain.

It rained for a week solid.

It wasn't just that everything got *wet*, it was that it got wet and freezing. At night, Stephanie would crawl into her sleeping bag, and it would take her hours to warm up. It seemed that as soon as she was warm, it was time to get up and put on her damp boots and her damp clothes again. One morning she woke up and it had stopped raining, but her socks were frozen solid. She put them on and slogged across the camp to the bus.

And then, after seven days of rain, she woke up and didn't hear rain on the roof of her tent. She could tell the sun was out and she could hear a group of people singing in the cook tent. She struggled out of her bag and shimmied into her clothes, thinking, *At last*. She unzipped her tent door and the brightness almost blinded her. There was snow on the ground. At the same moment that she saw the snow, she recognized the tune they were singing in the cook tent. It was "Good King Wenceslas."

She thought that they would get the day off because of the snow, but Scott made them work. She planted all day, even though she could barely hold the little trees in her already swollen hand, never mind get her shovel into the earth, which was snow-covered and frozen.

People's resistance began to wear down. At night she would lie in her tent listening to people coughing.

And then it warmed up—and the blackflies came. Swarms of them, as if someone were pouring them out of a giant jar. All morning Stephanie could hear Perry swearing through the woods.

One morning Perry showed up with ski goggles and a hat with a bug net. His shirt cuffs were taped to his wrists with duct tape. Before he got off the bus he slathered himself in DEET.

"They're not getting me," he said.

But the swearing was even worse.

"What was going on?" asked Stephanie when she got back to the bus.

"They got under my goggles," said Perry, "and the DEET melted the cable on my iPod. Then it started dripping into my eyes with my sweat, and I couldn't see. I sat in the bus all afternoon."

The bugs got in your ears, up your nose, through your hair, and in your eyes. The mess tent was open on the sides, so they got in your food too. You couldn't get away from them. You breathed bugs, and you ate bugs, and there were bugs in your ears, so all you ever heard were bugs. Some kids tied bandanas around their ears so they couldn't hear them; some kids slathered themselves in olive oil.

The only person who didn't complain was ponytail guy.

"My name is Rob," he said.

"Why don't they bother you?" asked Stephanie.

"They do," he said. "I just don't complain."

The insides of Stephanie's arms were covered with sap, and the outsides with a rash, from constantly brushing against the trees. The pesticides on the saplings were drying out her skin, so when she opened and closed her fists, her knuckles would crack and bleed. But the thing that bothered her the most was her stubbornly low tree total. It didn't seem right that she couldn't do this—that she couldn't master something as simple as planting trees. She had always succeeded at anything if she wanted it badly enough, but she couldn't seem to crack tree planting.

She decided to try the visualization techniques she used to prepare herself for exams. She lay in her tent imagining herself planting trees really, really quickly. But when she fell asleep, she spent the night dreaming she was planting trees really, really quickly and then woke up exhausted.

Next she tried to speed herself up by listening to fast-paced dance songs on her iPod while she planted. The music made the day pass more quickly, but she suspected that her newly rhythmic movements were wasting precious tree-planting energy.

She attempted to achieve a Buddhist-like oneness with the earth, embracing the cycle of life she was helping to perpetuate. She chanted, "More trees, more trees" quietly under her breath all one morning.

When her voice gave out, she decided that she should focus on process. She was wasting too much time returning to the cache to bag up. She filled her hip bags with twice as many saplings as usual and staggered into her land. She got wedged between two trees in an unlogged section. She couldn't move backwards *or* forward. She screamed for help, over and over. What if a bear happened upon her? After half an hour, Rob showed up. He sat on the ground and laughed and laughed.

When he finally helped her get unstuck, she stormed off without a word.

STEPHANIE WAS GETTING nowhere fast. In fact, she was going backwards. At the end of week three, the evil tree-checker woman showed up. She marked off a two-metre circle in the middle of Stephanie's land and checked the spacing of her trees. There should have been fourteen trees, all seven feet apart. There were sixteen trees. The tree-checker told Stephanie she had to replant the entire area. And she wouldn't get paid for it.

Stephanie decided Scott was giving the highballers the best land.

"I'll switch with you," said Rob. So one day she worked Rob's land and he worked hers. It didn't make a difference.

"The bugs were crazy today," said Stephanie. "Look at my hands."

"You're right," said Rob, looking out the bus window. "There are always plenty of reasons to have a bad day."

"What does *that* mean?" said Stephanie.

Things were even worse on Perry's land. Perry couldn't sleep at night, but no sooner did he get off the bus in the mornings than he was hit by a potent wave of narcolepsy. Just the sight of a pine sapling had him yawning and woozy and sneaking off for a nap. That wouldn't have been so bad, except that the planters had to pay room and board. One night after dinner, Perry did the math. "Holy crap," he shouted. "I *owe* the company money!"

The next day he borrowed a handful of caffeine pills from another planter. When everyone got off the bus at the end of the day, Perry was still wide awake, twitchy and agitated. That night, he packed up and left camp without telling anyone. They woke up the next morning and he was gone. When they checked his land, they found he had planted two thousand trees on his last day—all of them upside down, their roots drying in the sun like hay.

THEY HAD A weekend off in Thunder Bay. Everyone spent the time showering in their motel rooms, eating in the fast-food joints, writing postcards in coffee shops, or just lying in the sun. Everyone except Stephanie. Stephanie had decided that if it wasn't her focus or her process that was letting her down, it had to be her tools. She tramped around town, looking for a garage mechanic who would cut down her shovel with a blowtorch to make it lighter, sharper.

When she eventually made it back to the hotel, everyone was heading out dancing. Stephanie stayed behind to clean up and hit the sack early. She was only minutes into her shower when she discovered that the drain was clogged solid with the accumulated grit and grime of her three roommates. She scooped handfuls of wood chips and sand out of the bottom of the bathtub and then headed to bed. But the motel mattress and the clean, dry sheets felt strangely uncomfortable. At a quarter to twelve, she was still awake, sitting on the edge of the bed, staring out the window into the dark and deserted street. She watched a solitary man walking down the sidewalk, moving in and out of the shadows of the streetlamps. His head was bowed slightly, and his pace was measured and steady.

He was carrying a metal lunch pail in one hand and a yellow hard hat in the other. He was heading off to work while the rest of the city slept. The North was the land of hard work, Scott had said. Suddenly Stephanie felt exhausted. She rolled back under the blankets and fell asleep.

She was the only one who caught up on her sleep that night. And so she was the only one awake when two provincial police officers arrived at the motel the next morning.

"There have been some problems at the golf course," said one of the cops. "We suspect two of your planters."

"Why do you suspect us?" asked Stephanie.

"Someone planted ninety baby spruce trees on the eighteenth green," said the cop.

BACK IN THE bush the next day, Stephanie still couldn't crack two thousand, even with her modified shovel.

She cornered Rob in the cook tent. "I know you aren't telling me something. There's a secret. Tell me the secret."

"Okay," he said. "I'll tell you the secret. But only if you are first on the bus in the morning."

Stephanie was on the bus ten minutes early for the first time all summer. Rob was sitting in the back seat—alone.

"Tell me," she said.

"You weren't first on the bus," he said. "I was."

She was ten minutes earlier the next morning and the same thing happened.

On the third morning, when she climbed on a half hour early and Rob grinned at her and said, "Morning," she had a tantrum.

"Okay," said Rob. "I'll tell you. The secret is . . . there isn't any secret."

"Of course there's a secret," said Stephanie, her voice almost hoarse with desperation. "Tell me."

"Okay," said Rob. "There is a secret. The secret to planting more trees is to plant more trees."

She thought he was making fun of her. She didn't understand he was serious.

He took her with him onto *his* land. "Watch," he said. So she sat on a huge rock, her knees drawn up to her chest, and she watched him. He took a tree from his bag with his left hand and drove his shovel into the ground. He bent over and fed the roots into the ground with the blade of his shovel. He kicked the hole shut, hardly standing up as he moved to the next spot. He didn't move fast, but he moved steadily, bobbing up and down as if he were eating the land instead of planting it. As if he were some sort of grazing animal.

She thought she had been working hard all along. Watching Rob, she wasn't so sure.

He didn't listen to music, and he didn't rest or talk to people when he bagged up. And he didn't take an hour at lunch.

He pulled a piece of paper out of his pocket and handed it to her. "I wrote this for the internet," he said. "I posted it on a tree-planting site."

She unfolded it.

"Read it," he said.

When it is time to plant, plant. When it is time to eat, eat. Whatever you are doing . . . just do it. If it's raining, you can worry about the rain all day or you can plant and make money. The rain will pass and then it will be dinner and then it will be time to go to sleep. And like the rain, the night will pass too, so better that you just shut up and sleep. As for tomorrow . . . Tomorrow, read Stephanie, *doesn't even enter into it.*

Stephanie said, "I don't think I can do that."

Rob looked at her and laughed. "That's your problem," he said. "You think too much."

There are moments in people's lives that change them forever. You go into the woods to plant trees for six weeks, and you come back and your life is never the same.

Stephanie hit nineteen hundred trees the next morning.

The morning after that she pounded in two thousand.

Two weeks would pass before she would break the magic twenty-five hundred mark. Before that would happen, the blackflies would return with a vengeance, and she would be bitten to bits, so swollen and scarred that everyone started to call her pizza-face. One morning she woke up and her right eye was swollen closed. She couldn't see out of it. She could have stayed in camp that day, but she used duct tape to hold her eye open and went out anyway. That was the day she pounded in twenty-six hundred trees—her personal best.

She sat on the bus at the end of that day, sweaty and tired, sore and stinky, her pants all ripped and repaired. Her hair was filthy, her hands swollen and cut and covered with duct tape.

"Twenty-six hundred," she said. "That was awesome."

And that's what she wrote about in her letter. About the day she hit twenty-six hundred. And about the afternoon she rammed her shovel into a wasps' nest. And about how, in June, her big toe went numb from kicking at the duff and stayed numb for the rest of the summer. *It's called Christmas toe,* she wrote, *because sometimes it stays numb until Christmas.* She wrote about all that, and about the afternoon she came upon the lake at the back of her land.

She came over a hill and saw the water sparkling in the sun. She couldn't believe it. She took off her clothes and jumped in, naked. Miles from nowhere. Alone in the great boreal forest. Amazed at herself. But most of all, amazed at life.

THE LAUNDRY CHUTE

S pring comes to the Cape Breton highlands later than it does to other parts of this country. It comes even later to Dave's hometown, the village of Big Narrows. When it comes, it comes on the sudden cry of a crow flapping over the hill behind the Macaulays' farm. The sound of the crow came on a Wednesday last year, and it brought Old Man Macaulay sprinting out of the barn. He stood in his muddy farmyard squinting into the pale sun, as sure a sign of spring as any crow, his dog beside him, tail wagging, head cocked, staring into the sky too.

Overnight the snow on all the hills turned granular, and little rivers began appearing everywhere. All the kids in town got wet, and pretty soon everything smelled of damp wool.

By the weekend, even the adults had joined in the festivities. On Saturday afternoon, it seemed everyone in the Narrows was out in their yard trying to hurry spring along—chipping away at stubborn piles of snow with shovels, hoes, and axes.

On Sunday, Dave's mother, Margaret, went to work on the snow along the north side of her garage. When she had

had enough, Margaret made a sandwich and sat in the back-yard with her shirtsleeves rolled up, the sun warming her skin for the first time in months. That night she sat in the parlour and listened to *Turandot*—Puccini's great operatic testament to love. She listened to the old vinyl albums her late husband, Charlie, had given her. "Why would I want a CD player?" she had said. "Is the music any different on CDs?"

"Exactly," said her son, Dave.

On Monday, Margaret, struck with the promise of spring, decided it was warm enough to walk downtown to get the mail.

She stopped at MacDonnell's Grocery and picked up a pint of milk for her tea. And that was when the most unexpected thing in the world happened. In a few days, Margaret's friend Rose will call from Dayton, Ohio, and Margaret will tell her the whole story, in minute detail, except for the moment when it all began—the moment in MacDonnell's Grocery. That part is a blank, like the moments before an accident.

Margaret was chatting with Julie Doucette about some-thing, for the life of her she can't remember what. Margaret and Julie were chatting about *something*—maybe the weather, maybe how nice it was to be warm again—when Margaret noticed the display table by the door. There was a sign taped to the table: BIG NARROWS VOLUNTEER FIRE DEPARTMENT: HOME SAFETY INSPECTIONS.

It wasn't, however, the sign that caught Margaret's atten-tion. It was the man sitting behind the table.

"He was adorable," said Margaret when she was telling the story to Rose.

He was the most adorable man Margaret had seen for years. He was wearing a soft plaid shirt—cotton—and a beige windbreaker. He had thin grey hair and large ears, and before Margaret knew what she was doing, she was talking to him.

His name was Smith Gardner. A widower, it turned out. He told Margaret he was new in town—used to be the fire chief in Port Hawkesbury. He had moved to the Narrows because his daughter and his grandchildren were there. Margaret, a dozen years widowed, signed up for a home inspection.

"I'll put you down for Thursday morning," said the adorable man.

Margaret went right home and started cleaning. *Deep* cleaning. She dragged the scatter rugs into the backyard, slung them over the clothesline, and beat them to within an inch of their lives. She mopped *and* waxed the kitchen floor. She vacuumed everything—even the drapes. She polished the silver. She attacked the linen closet and the upstairs bedrooms.

On Thursday morning, she was waiting in her kitchen when Angus McLeod pulled into her front yard in his red pickup and walked up to her front door carrying a clipboard.

"Hello, Margaret," said Angus. "They sent me over to do a safety inspection."

Margaret had been expecting the adorable man in the soft plaid shirt. She stared at Angus as if he had arrived from outer space. As if he didn't live two streets over.

"Angus McLeod," she heard herself say, "you are not inspecting *my* house. I want someone with a little more experience than you."

And then Margaret, who is known throughout the Narrows as one of the kindest and most sensitive women in the village, shut the door in Angus McLeod's face.

"Oh my," she said, her back to the door, her hand at her mouth.

She watched Angus through the kitchen curtains as he drove away.

Leonard Milton showed up two hours later. Margaret sent Leonard away too.

"Leonard Milton," she said, "not you."

On Friday afternoon, Arnie Gallagher called. Arnie the florist, the funeral-home director, the gift-store manager, and the travel agent. Arnie the fire chief and the mayor.

"Margaret," said Arnie, "is everything okay?"

"Everything is fine, Arnie," said Margaret.

"People have been saying that you are not yourself."

"People talk foolishness," said Margaret.

"People are worried," said Arnie.

"They shouldn't worry," said Margaret.

Arnie said, "Okay then," and hung up.

He phoned back an hour later.

"Margaret," said Arnie, "I have been thinking on things. I have been thinking that I have been sending you men who aren't as experienced as you might require. Margaret, there is a new gentleman in town. He used to be chief of the Port Hawkesbury Fire Department. I think he might have the sort of experience necessary to inspect a house like yours."

Margaret said, "That would be just fine, Arnie."

SMITH GARDNER ARRIVED at Margaret's house the following Tuesday, just after lunch. He was wearing a grey fisherman's sweater with a rolled neck. He said, "I'll start upstairs and work my way down." He smelled of Old Spice. Dave's father—Margaret's late husband, Charlie— was an Old Spice man.

The inspection took Smith twenty minutes. When he was finished, he walked into the kitchen.

"You need a smoke detector upstairs," he said. "The cord on the big lamp in the living room should be replaced. Otherwise you're in good shape. I'll write it up."

He didn't seem to be in a hurry to leave.

"Would you like a muffin?" said Margaret.

Smith sat down. He nodded at the baseball cap hanging by the back door. "Yankee fan?" he asked.

Margaret told him all about her trip to New York City.

"Charlie and I had always planned on going together," she said.

She told him about how she had gone by herself. How she had met Rose in the lobby of the Chelsea Hotel.

"Rose bought me the hat," she said. "I wear it in the garden." She was warming her hands on her mug of tea.

"Going to New York," she said, "meeting Rose, changed my life."

They sat silently for a few moments and then she said, "When your wife died . . . did people stop including you?"

Smith Gardner smiled and nodded slightly.

Then Margaret said, "My friends would only have me over on the nights their husbands went out. I was okay for girls' nights, but not for the nights people really got together."

"Like you would upset the balance," said Smith.

He stayed for two hours. Margaret told him about her grandchildren—Sam and Stephanie in Toronto, Margot in Halifax.

Smith had just finished telling Margaret about *his* grandchildren when she picked up a towel and wiped at the table absentmindedly. She stood and walked across the kitchen and opened a tiny door in the wainscotting of the kitchen wall. She threw the towel in and shut the door.

"Whoa," said Smith, rising out of his chair. "Is that a laundry chute?"

He was so alarmed, it scared Margaret.

"I'm sorry," he said. "It's a huge fire hazard. If you would like I could come back and seal it up."

He said he could fix the lamp cord too. And bring a smoke detector.

Margaret said, "That would be nice."

He said, "I better be going, then." But he didn't leave for another hour.

After he left Margaret picked up her New York Yankees baseball cap and fiddled with it. She put it on. She went into the bathroom and stared at her reflection in the mirror. She twirled the hat around so the peak was facing backwards.

"Play ball," said Margaret.

Then she phoned Rose.

"It sounds like you are falling in love," said Rose.

"Don't be ridiculous," said Margaret. "I'm too old to fall in love."

"How old are you?" said Rose, who had been dying to ask.

"There's an eight in it," said Margaret.

That afternoon Margaret wandered around her house aimlessly—walked between the parlour and the living room in a daze until she came to with her hand on the laundry-chute door, not at all sure how long she had been standing there.

She was thinking of the night the barn swallow got trapped in the chute—remembering how she and Charlie had tried everything to get the bird out. Eventually, Charlie had dropped one of Annie's toy umbrellas down the chute from the top floor. The tiny open umbrella floated down slowly, like in a René Magritte painting. The bird flew out into the basement. It took them another hour to wave it out a basement window.

Then she remembered the time Charlie left his painting tray at the base of the chute, and Annie's favourite plaid skirt landed in the paint.

And how Dave used to toss Annie's stuffed animals down it.

Margaret got a flashlight from under the kitchen sink. The batteries were dead. She ransacked the house, but she couldn't find batteries anywhere. She drove to MacDonnell's and bought some. When she got home, she peered up the chute with the flashlight. If Smith Gardner was going to board the chute up, she wanted to see the little piece of leather hanging up there one last time.

The scrap of leather got there in 1959, the year after the last big bump at Springhill. Dave was still a young boy, Annie even younger.

Margaret had gone out to take food up to her sister, who had lost her Donny when the mine went down.

She felt guilty about what had happened after she left her house, but it wasn't as if she hadn't told David a hundred times that the laundry chute wasn't a toy.

"It's not a toy, and it's not a slide."

"Don't drop your trucks down the chute, David. Don't drop anything down that chute except your clothes. Your *dirty* clothes. And for heaven's sake, don't lean into it like that."

What could she do? She couldn't be home all the time. Margaret was taking a roast chicken to her poor lost sister.

And Dave, nine years old, alone at home with *his* little sister, was playing "Springhill Mining Disaster."

THEY BEGAN TO mine for coal in Springhill, Nova Scotia, in the 1800s. By 1958, the coal mine in Springhill was one of the deepest mines in the world. The number-two colliery—the colliery that collapsed—was a labyrinth of tunnels and caverns. At the face of the mine it was more than fourteen thousand feet deep.

It was a couple of hours after supper on a Thursday evening near the end of October when the mine face collapsed. People who lived in Springhill knew what had happened right away. It was like an earthquake when it went. Phones bounced off tables. Pictures fell off walls. Off-duty coal men dropped what they were doing and ran to the mine.

One hundred seventy-four men were trapped underground.

By dawn they had seventy-five of them on the surface. That's when the real work began. Soon men were heading for Springhill from all over Nova Scotia to help. Dave's dad, Charlie, drove five miners from Glace Bay.

It was one of the biggest disasters in North American mining history, and the first disaster to be broadcast live on television. The story went all over the States. But there were no TVs to watch in the Narrows. Dave listened on the radio.

On the next Thursday, a week after the collapse, they brought twelve miners up alive.

On Friday, with men still missing, Prince Philip, the Duke of Edinburgh, who had been in Ottawa, visited the site with Premier Stanfield.

They brought the last living men up on Sunday.

Seventy-five men didn't make it—including Dave's uncle Donny.

A group of the rescued miners went to New York City and appeared on *The Ed Sullivan Show*. Another group was offered a free vacation on Jekyll Island by Marvin Griffin, the segregationist governor of Georgia. It was a publicity stunt that didn't turn out the way Governor Griffin had hoped—there was a miner from Africville in the group.

IT WAS ON a night about a year after the bump that Margaret said, "I am taking this roast chicken up to your aunt Elizabeth."

It was about twenty minutes after she left that Dave called Annie.

"I need your help," he said earnestly. "I am pretending this is a mine shaft. I have to climb to the bottom of the shaft."

"You can't do that," said Annie. "You aren't allowed."

"I have to," said Dave.

"Why do you have to?" asked Annie.

"There are men trapped down there," said Dave.

Annie frowned. She was only five years old. She wasn't tall enough to see into the chute, but she was pretty sure there weren't men down there.

"I don't hear them," she said.

Dave went into her bedroom and came back with an armful of stuffed animals. He threw the animals into the laundry chute.

"There," he said.

Dave was wearing a windbreaker and a toque. He had a flashlight stuck in his belt. He pushed a chair under the laundry-chute door.

"You aren't allowed," said Annie.

Dave looked at his little sister earnestly. "Look," he said. "Mom doesn't know everything. We do lots of things we aren't supposed to do. We aren't supposed to stand up on toboggans, and we aren't supposed to ride cows. We aren't supposed to play in the creek with our clothes on."

"I don't do any of that stuff," said Annie.

"We aren't supposed to go outside in the winter with wet hair," said Dave. "You do that."

"That's because I like the way it freezes," said Annie.

"You aren't supposed to do it," said Dave. "I have to rescue the men at the bottom of this shaft," said Dave. "I need you to hold the rope."

Dave handed his sister the end of the rope that was tied around his waist. He climbed onto the chair and then pushed his leg through the chute opening. Then, holding on to the sides of the chute, he hoisted his other leg through the hole. He began to lower himself into the laundry chute, bracing himself by pushing his feet and his arms into the wall in front of him and his back into the wall behind. It was harder than he had imagined. He had wormed his way about eight feet down before he realized he wasn't going to be strong enough to make it all the way to the bottom.

There and then, doubt seized him, and then, as doubt always does to the weary, it overtook him, and Dave felt a rush of fear. He called his sister's name.

"Annie," he called.

Before she could answer, Dave was dropping down the chute like a stone. The rope burned through Annie's hands. And then it jerked to a stop.

"Ow," said Annie, looking at her hands.

Then she said, "Dave?"

There was no answer. Annie put the rope down and climbed up onto the chair. She peered into the chute. Her brother was about halfway down.

"I'm stuck," he said.

"It serves you right," said Annie. She got off the chair and disappeared.

The wall was squeezing Dave around his waist. His left arm was jammed down by his thigh. He couldn't pull it free. His right arm was okay, though, and he tried to use it to pull himself up. He kicked his feet. He called his sister.

"Pull on the rope," he called.

Annie's face appeared at the top of the chute.

"Mom's going to kill you," said Annie. Then she threw her end of the rope into the chute and said, "Pull on the rope yourself," and disappeared again. Dave winced as the rope coiled around his shoulders.

He could hear Annie walking down the stairs.

Then everything went deadly quiet.

"What are you doing?" called Dave.

There was no answer. It was black in the chute. Annie had closed the door upstairs, and Dave had dropped his flashlight. He held his hand out in front of his face and wiggled his fingers. He couldn't see them. He couldn't see anything. He was all alone and he was afraid.

Suddenly there were beams of light shooting from below him. Annie had opened the door in the kitchen.

"What are you doing?" said Dave.

"I am making chocolate milk," said Annie.

"You're not allowed," said Dave.

"If you're not nice to me," said Annie, "I am not going to talk to you."

She closed the door and the chute went black again.

"Annie," he called.

She ignored him. She sat in the kitchen and drank her chocolate milk. She left him alone for five minutes.

Now, under most circumstances five minutes is not a long time. But when you are wedged in a laundry chute halfway between where you started and where you were heading and it is black as night and you can't move one of your arms, a lot can go through your mind in a few short minutes.

Like what would happen if there were rats in the chute with you. Or if the house caught fire. Or if your mother never came home. Or worse . . . if she did. Dave banged on the wall with his free hand.

"Annie," he called.

No answer.

Five long minutes passed before she appeared at the top again.

When she did, she could hear a strange snuffly sound coming from the chute. She peered down. Her older brother was crying.

"Don't cry, Davy," she said, surprised. "Mom and Dad are coming home soon. They'll get you out."

"But what if they don't?" sniffled Dave. "What if they can't rescue me?"

"They'll save you," said Annie, this time with less certainty. Then she said, "Just wait a minute. I'll be right back."

And her head disappeared from the chute. A few minutes later, the door opened again and Annie lowered a little brown lump of something down the chute, attached to a string.

"What is it?" asked Dave.

"It's the ears from my chocolate Easter bunny. I hid them in the bottom of my toy box so you wouldn't eat them."

Dave grabbed the chocolate with his free hand. It was covered with lint and grit. He brushed it off as best he could and took a bite.

"Eat as much of it as you want," said Annie.

After a few minutes, however, Annie could hear her brother sniffling again.

"Dave," she said, "remember when Auntie Brenda sat on the birthday cake?"

"Yeah?" said Dave. He sounded a bit more cheerful.

"And remember," said Annie, "when Mommy dropped the watermelon?"

She went on like that for an hour and twenty minutes.

"Remember when Daddy barfed in the car?"

Annie reminded Dave of all the funny things that she could think of. And when she ran out of stories, she told him every knock-knock joke she knew. Then she launched into the tale of Hansel and Gretel, the way their father told it, where the witch's house was made of Cape Breton shortbread and raisin scones. When she could think of nothing more to say, Annie started to sing. She sang "Jesus Loves Me, This I Know," "Diana," and her favourite, "Splish Splash, I Was Taking a Bath."

When Charlie and Margaret finally walked in the door, Dave was humming along to the theme from the radio show *The Shadow*.

HALF AN HOUR later, Charlie was standing in the basement, peering up the chute and poking at his son's small bottom with a broom handle. It was Charlie who guessed that Dave's belt was snagged on some rough piece of the wooden chute. It was Margaret who carefully lowered Dave her pair of sewing scissors and told him how to cut the belt loops of his pants. And it was Charlie, standing at the bottom of the chute, with his arms outstretched, who caught his crying son and held him tight to his chest when it was all over.

LATER THAT NIGHT, as Margaret was tucking Dave into bed and kissing him good night, he asked his mother about the Springhill miners.

"Do you think they talked to each other when they were trapped down there?" he said quietly.

"Yes, I do," said Margaret.

"Do you think. . ." asked Dave, hugging his pillow. "Do you think they sang?"

Margaret brushed the hair back from Dave's face and smiled gently. "Yes, Davy," she said. "I'm *quite* sure they sang."

And now, some forty-odd years later, Margaret was standing in the basement, shining her flashlight up the dark chute and telling Smith Gardner her rescue story.

"What's the matter with me?" she said. "I'm getting all choked up about a laundry chute."

She dropped the flashlight to her side but didn't move.

"Anyway," she said, "that's the whole story."

Smith Gardner didn't say anything. Instead, he reached out and took Margaret's hand. They stood there for several minutes more, looking up at the small bit of leather belt still hanging in the chute. Then Smith moved over to his toolbox.

"Are you sure it's okay that I start?" he said.

Margaret smiled at him and nodded. "You get going," she said. "I'll go upstairs and make tea and fix a snack for when you're finished."

Friends—Two— and Four-Legged

DAVE THE DOG WALKER

It began on one of those glorious spring days, a day full of sun and hope, one of those days that arrive with promises of resurrection and rebirth. Of redemption, and, well, if we are going to keep the Rs rolling. . .

"Relief," said Dave. "A feeling of relief that we made it through another winter."

"It's not over yet," said Dave's neighbour Bert Turlington as he stepped onto the porch, his breath puffy under the night sky. He looked around and then ducked back into his house and grabbed a toque.

"But we are on the downhill side of it," said Dave. "Have you noticed the light?"

There was no doubt about it, the sun was lingering longer each day. But there was also no doubt about the chill of the night. Bert pulled his toque on.

Ever since the Turlingtons got their dog, a teacup Pomeranian named Tissue—Mary's idea, not Bert's—it has been Bert's habit to join Dave and his dog, Arthur, on their nightly walk.

They walk over to the park and when the weather is agreeable, circle it endlessly, around and around like a never-ending sentence, talking, or not talking, allowing the dogs to insert the punctuation. Which instead of commas and colons comes as fence posts and fire hydrants, or, as was the case on this evening, a shrub, which Dave's dog, Arthur, was sniffing with great intensity.

Bert was watching and vaguely wishing he had worn his gloves.

"I know," said Dave. "But it was such a great day."

Suddenly Arthur stopped and looked up at Bert and barked, more a grunt than a bark really, a soft grunt that came from deep in his throat. Bert squinted at Arthur.

Bert said, "You sure?"

Arthur's tail started to wag.

Bert shrugged and said, "Okay."

He unzipped his jacket, reached in, and pulled out a little white ball of fluff. Bert was carrying Tissue in a baby sling.

Tissue tires easily.

Bert set Tissue down. She shook herself, yapped, ran over to Arthur, sniffed the shrub, walked in a circle three times, and prepared herself for business. When she was done, Bert bent over, scooped her up, and gave Arthur a pat.

"How does he know that?" said Bert. "Every night. How does he do that?"

It was on their way home that Dave offered to take care of Tissue during March break.

Bert and Mary were taking the twins to Costa Rica. Well actually they were taking the whole family. Last year they left Adam home alone. That was a mistake. And although Adam got the house more or less back together for their return, there were things he had to leave until his parents got home—the hallway banister for one. And things he overlooked—most unfortunately, a frat-house tower of empties in the garage.

Mary wasn't prepared to leave Adam home alone this year. Adam was coming with them, no discussion. Tissue was going to get a dog sitter.

"We can look after Tissue," said Dave. "Honestly. It wouldn't be a big deal. It wouldn't be a problem."

And so it was agreed. And once it was, how could Dave say no when word got around, as word always does.

Carl Lowbeer asked about Preston.

"I heard you were looking after Tissue," said Carl. "We just hate the idea of a kennel. And we were wondering. . ."

"No problem," said Dave.

Preston, a Labradoodle, would be more of a handful than Tissue, no doubt about that, but Tissue was so small and eager, that . . . well, like Dave said, she hardly counted.

"That's what I thought," said Carl.

By the time March break arrived, Dave had agreed to look after *four* dogs. So when Polly Anderson called, really what difference did a fifth make?

"Five dogs," said Morley.

"Six if you count Arthur," said Dave. "But you can't count Arthur. He lives here anyway. And Tissue hardly counts either . . . so four dogs, technically."

"Living here," said Morley.

"Only for a week," said Dave.

"A week," said Morley.

"Well," said Dave. "Ten days, technically. But that's if you count weekends."

SIX DOGS. NUMBER one being Arthur. Dave's dog. A mutt of sorts, a sort of Lab-retriever, longhair-shorthair combo. Kind of a biggish dog in a smallish way. Sleeps on the heat vents. Likes ice cream. Has control issues.

Two: Tissue. The Turlingtons' Pomeranian. Bert had been agitating for a dog for years. Bert was thinking chocolate Lab. Tissue is no Lab. In fact she is not much bigger than a squirrel. Tissue is a purebred princess. Pink leather collar. The baby carrier.

The day they left for the south, Mary brought Tissue over with a crate-load of stuff. Blankets, bowls, stuffed toys, and a collection of little outfits.

"I want her to feel at home," she said. "I wish she could stay at our house in more . . . comfortable surroundings."

"Comfortable?" said Dave, looking around his house.

"I mean, familiar," said Mary.

She pulled a jar of hand cream out of her purse.

"It's made from caviar oil. It keeps her paws soft. Massage

some in before bed, after you shampoo her, when you do her nails, and if you are leaving her alone for more than fifteen minutes. It helps with her anxiety."

Then she handed Dave a toothbrush and a tube of toothpaste. Beef flavoured.

Mary said, "Here are some Q-tips for her ears. She is allergic to dust. Keep her out of the basement."

Dave nodded earnestly.

"She'll be fine," he said.

He walked Mary to the door. He wanted her to leave. He wanted to be alone so he could try the beef-flavoured toothpaste.

Mary was almost out the door when she stopped and turned.

"I almost forgot," she said. "Remember when we had those birds flying into our living-room window? I ordered these." She pulled a life-size sticker of a bird out of her purse. A hawk. "I put one on the glass, and it seems to keep the birds away. I thought you might want one." And she was gone.

"Come on, Tissue," said Dave. "Let's go brush our teeth."

Arthur padded along behind them. He seemed pleased to have Tissue there, like it was a grade-five sleepover or something.

So that's how it started. With one—Arthur, and two—Tissue.

Three was Summer. A Portuguese Water Dog. Afraid of actual water. Summer came with a little coat and booties. A garbage hound.

"She'll eat anything," said Brian when he dropped Summer off.

Four was Preston. A Labradoodle. Bird crazy. Although what exactly Preston loved about birds Carl didn't make clear.

"Just be careful," said Carl, ominously, ". . . around birds."

And NuNu. Polly Anderson's cocker spaniel. Who pees when she gets excited.

"But all cockers do that," said Polly.

"And what would she possibly get excited about?" said Morley.

"Exactly," said Dave. "How many is that?"

"That's five," said Morley.

"There's another," said Dave. "The one with the leather chews."

"Leather?"

"Rawhide," said Dave.

"Rawhide chews," said Morley, sounding relieved.

"No, Rawhide is his name," said Dave. "The chews are leather."

"I have never even *heard* of Rawhide," said Morley.

"They're new people."

"I have never met them?" said Morley. "And we have their dog?"

"Just for a week," said Dave.

Morley stared.

"Well, ten days," said Dave.

AS THE DOGS arrived Arthur became increasingly anxious. His tail stopped wagging each time the doorbell rang. By suppertime, Arthur had holed up in the downstairs bathroom and wouldn't come out.

It's understandable. You put six dogs who don't know each other in a house together, any six dogs, any house, and there are going to be moments. And there were, no doubt about it.

The first walk. Just getting out the door was fearsome.

Dave picked up a leash, one of the six leashes in the basket by the door. Preston, who was sound asleep on the living-room couch, lifted his head. Both his ears flicked up. But he didn't budge. He was waiting for one more jingle. And there it was. With the second, confirming jingle, Preston went from sound sleep to full-speed running and barking. It happened in the blink of an eye. Preston was asleep and then he wasn't. The Labradoodle was running to the door as if he had been running for hours. Preston had one thing on his mind.

Birds.

And he wanted to tell everyone.

Birds! Preston barked.

Birds! Birds! Birds!

Preston passed Summer on his way to the door. Summer jumped up too. *Garbage!* barked Summer.

Garbage! Garbage! Garbage!

The two of them barked past NuNu, asleep in the corner, and NuNu joined in. Although she wasn't sure why or what was going on. She was just running. But by the time she made it to the hall she was so excited she had stopped twice to pee.

In the blink of an eye all five dogs were at the front door, jumping and barking, and Dave was standing there in the middle of them like a puppeteer who had lost control of his puppets. Arthur, however, was nowhere to be seen. Dave finally found him hiding in the bathroom. He had to drag Arthur out and put his leash on before he could deal with the others.

The first walk was a disaster. It took them forty-five minutes to make it a block and a half. It took longer to get home.

THE SECOND ONE wasn't much better. Arthur managed to slip loose in the park. He settled under a tree. Dave couldn't budge him. He had to come back to get him once he'd brought the other dogs home.

On walk number three, Dave had hardly been gone five minutes when he came pounding home again. He burst through the front door.

"I've lost a dog," he said desperately. "I'm a dog short."

Morley looked at him calmly. Morley said, "You mean Rawhide?"

Who, it turns out, was happily tucked behind the couch gnawing on his shoe. Not Dave's shoe. Rawhide's owners had left a carton of shoes when they dropped him off.

"We get them at the thrift store," they said. "He goes through one or two a week."

No doubt about it, those first few days were difficult. But Dave wasn't going to give up.

He went shopping. He bought himself a belt at a surplus store. A mountaineering belt, with hooks. Before the next walk he cinched the belt around his waist and clipped each dog to a separate hook.

"Look at me," said Dave. "I'm hands-free!"

Which seemed to be a good idea—until he wore the belt on a walk. Until he had to lean over to scoop up after one of his dogs. As he leaned over, a pigeon fluttered by. Preston barked. Then he lunged. And everyone else joined in for fun. Preston in the lead, the other five fighting for it, Dave being pulled behind them like he was a sled.

It took Morley thirty minutes and a pair of tweezers to get all the gravel out of his palms.

Yeah, there were moments.

But Dave wasn't about to admit defeat. That night he lined the dogs up in the kitchen. Determined to get control.

"Sit!" Three of them went down like good little soldiers. Summer, NuNu, and Rawhide. Arthur went down too. But he went reluctantly.

Preston didn't budge. Preston stood there staring at Dave.

Dave dropped to his hands and knees and put his face right in Preston's face.

"Grrr!" said Dave.

Preston dropped like a rock.

"I have to establish dominance," said Dave to Morley, who was watching.

In a way she never would have expected, Morley was enjoying this. The whole thing had given Dave a sense of responsibility, a sense of seriousness, and a focus that she had never seen before. Her only real concern was Arthur, who had developed an uncharacteristic sulkiness.

Dave was standing at the far end of the kitchen. The dogs lined up by the stove.

"Come," he said.

This time they came. All of them. A grand scrabbling over the kitchen floor, a scrabbling and a sliding stop at his feet.

"Good dogs," said Dave, slipping each one a treat.

"*Yap*," said Tissue from the baby sling.

"You too," said Dave.

"They are pack animals," he explained smugly to Morley as he got them ready for a walk. "I'm the pack leader."

By mid-week they would come bounding from all over the house, skidding to a stop at his feet, their tails thumping like a little dog orchestra.

Morley had to admit she found it a little bit sexy.

Dave sensed this, and one morning when he saw Morley watching, he walked over to her, looked her right in the eye, and said, "Who's your alpha dog?"

EVERYTHING WAS SURPRISINGLY fine for a few days. Oh, NuNu had the odd accident. Preston was a handful in the park. And Arthur seemed a little out of sorts with it all. But it was all good until the end of the week. When suddenly it wasn't. By the end of the week, it was pretty clear something was wrong with Tissue.

Tissue's eyes were red and runny, and so was her nose. She spent all Thursday on the couch, uninterested in anyone or anything.

"She's allergic to dust," said Dave.

"Our house isn't clean enough for a dog?" said Morley.

"Not Mary's dog," said Dave.

They decided the best thing to do would be for Dave to take the dogs over to Mary's house and spend the last two nights there.

"I don't want Tissue sick when they come home," said Dave.

It was sort of fun. Dave got to do stuff he would never get away with at home. On the first night, he grilled a huge steak on the Turlingtons' barbecue, and they sat in front of the television. Dave and his six dogs. Everyone with their own plate of steak.

He found another tube of the beef-flavoured toothpaste.

"It's delicious," he said to Kenny Wong the next day. "It tastes like hot dogs."

Best of all, Tissue recovered. So everything was ship-shape for Bert and Mary's return.

They were due home just before supper.

Dave spent the afternoon tidying up. He did the dishes. There were dog prints on the kitchen floor. He found a mop and mopped the kitchen. He watered Mary's plants. Things were better than shipshape. They were perfect. Dave glanced at his watch.

His plan was to take everyone back to his place. But not Tissue. His plan was to leave Tissue to welcome Bert and Mary. They would be home in about half an hour.

He felt a flush of pride. He had done well.

And then Summer knocked over a dining-room chair. It crashed into the wall and left a long scratch in the paint.

There was just no way he was going to leave *that* for Mary to find. Not when he was so close to perfection. He went down to the basement and found a stack of paint cans, and, in the middle of the stack, one marked DINING-ROOM WALLS. There was a shelf nearby with an assortment of brushes, hung neatly on hooks. He grabbed a brush and the can of paint and went back upstairs. He pried open the lid with a kitchen knife.

Dave picked up the brush and then put it down again.

"Better safe than sorry," he said to Tissue, who was sitting in the dining room, watching him.

Dave began to move through the house, looking for the other dogs. When he found each one, he put on a leash. Then he led them all into the living room and tied them to Mary's potted palm.

"Stay!" he said.

When Dave returned to the dining room, he laid out a

couple of sheets of newspaper on the floor and set the lid down on the newspaper. It was worth taking a little extra time. It was worth being careful.

He touched up the wall. The mark disappeared in no time flat. Excellent. He glanced at his watch. He ran upstairs and found a hair dryer. Ten minutes later, you couldn't tell there had ever been a mark. Or you could barely tell.

He grinned at Tissue.

"Good dog," he said.

He was looking for the lid.

"Good dog," he said again, but he said it absentmindedly. Where *was* the lid?

Tissue barked and stood up. *There* was the lid. Tissue had been sitting on it. Her entire back end was soaked in paint.

"Tissue!" said Dave.

At the sound of her name Tissue's tail began to wag. Flecks of paint were flying everywhere.

"Tissue," said Dave again.

Tissue thought Dave wanted to play. Her whole back end started to twitch.

Tissue jumped. Dave lurched. He caught her as she was heading for the kitchen. Dave held her tight and looked around.

Mary's dining-room floor and furniture looked like they had been decorated by Jackson Pollock. *Huh*, thought Dave. *Nice effect.* Then he came to his senses. How was he going to clean *this* up before Mary got home?

He searched for a place to put Tissue. The breadbox was empty. He grabbed some paper towel, patted her bum, and dropped her in the empty breadbox.

Dave ran downstairs and grabbed a jug of turpentine. When he got back into the kitchen, he opened it and emptied it into a saucepan.

Then he rushed around wiping the furniture, walls, and floor. He was running out of time.

Sure enough, when he peeked through the living-room curtains and glanced out the window he thought he spotted the Turlingtons' car at the far end of the street.

He was so close. He raced back into the kitchen, opened the breadbox, and looked at the paint-soaked Tissue.

"Sorry," he said. He picked Tissue up and lowered her bum into the saucepan.

A number of things happened, quickly.

Dave put the turpentine-soaked Tissue down on the counter and said, "Stay."

Then he ran over to the living-room windows and pulled open the curtains to check again for the Turlingtons' car.

Preston looked up and spotted the silhouette of the hawk Mary had stuck on the living-room window. And when he saw it, Preston did what Preston does. Preston howled and jumped.

The four other dogs began barking too. And then all of them, all five, still tied to the palm, joined Preston as he strained toward the window. The five dogs, caught up in the excitement, pulling like a seasoned team now, managed to drag the palm straight across the living room. A trail of dirt spread in their wake. Moistened by a little stream from NuNu. In no time, the dogs were at the window, Preston bounding at the hawk.

Outside, a tan and relaxed Mary Turlington stepped out of the car and smiled at her husband.

"It's good to be home," she said.

And that's when the living-room window exploded.

And one–two–three–four–five dogs sailed through it, one after another like a circus act, NuNu spraying everyone as she flew by.

Mary staggered back and brought her hand up to wipe her face.

As she did, the front door burst open and her little dog, Tissue, came running out and leapt into her arms. Tissue's rear end was smoking. And Dave was right behind her with a fire extinguisher.

IT WAS TWO days later, nearly midnight. Dave and Morley were in bed. Everyone was in bed. All the dogs safely home. The Turlingtons' house back together.

Dave put his book down and said, "Well, anyway, no harm done."

Morley, who was still reading, didn't say anything.

Dave said, "I mean Tissue's fine. No one died."

"No," said Morley. "No one died."

And then she said, "What's that noise?"

It was a far-away sort of noise. A moist, sloppy sort of far-away noise. Dave propped himself up on his elbow. And frowned.

"Is it in the wall?" he said.

"I don't know," said Morley. "Maybe the closet."

Dave got out of bed and stood in the middle of the bedroom listening. He walked over to Morley's closet.

Before he opened the door, Morley said, "The other one, I think. Try yours."

They say you can't teach an old dog new tricks. Well, they say lots of things. And not all of those things are true.

Dave opened his bedroom closet and there was his old dog, Arthur. Arthur was lying in Dave's closet amid a pile of sodden leather. Arthur, looking for all the world like a gourmand in a fancy restaurant. Dave recognized one of his brand-new leather slippers between Arthur's paws. Arthur looked up at Dave and burped.

Later, when Dave would tell this story, he'd swear that Arthur had smiled before that burp, and then given Dave a long reproachful look. As if he was saying, *You owe me, buddy.* And Dave had nodded and closed the closet door gently. He couldn't argue with that.

MARY TURLINGTON HAS LICE

The best time to share bad news is almost always *never*. The best thing to do when you are sitting on something that you would like to sit on for the rest of your life is almost always to sit a little longer. That's the way it feels, anyway. There are all sorts of things that might happen if you do.

The thing could go away on its own—things do that from time to time. The impulse to share could depart of its own accord. Or the person you should be sharing with might depart themselves, and you can quietly bury whatever it was, and carry on, as if nothing had ever happened.

Yet as you consider the probability of *any* of these prayed-for possibilities, you know, deep in your sorry little heart, that that's just not the way things work out for you, is it? And you know you *should* deal with the situation. You know you *have* to deal with the situation. Although maybe right now is not the right time. Today, I mean. Maybe *tonight* would be better. When things are quieter. Or even better—*tomorrow*. Tomorrow would be good.

The problem was Morley didn't have the luxury of tomorrow. The problem was Morley had made a promise.

"If this ever happens again, you will tell me?" said Dave.

"I promise," said Morley.

Though, that was—what? That was a decade ago. At least. Surely there was a statute of limitations on promises.

IT WAS NOW, or it was never.

Dave and Morley were in the kitchen. It was Saturday night. Five o'clock. Good Lord. It was almost five-thirty.

The clock, as they say, was ticking. Bert and Mary Turlington were coming to dinner. They would be there within the hour.

"I have something to tell you," said Morley.

There is never a good time for bad news.

Dave stopped what he was doing. He stared at his wife.

Morley closed her eyes and threw her head back. When she said it, she said it in a bit of a rush.

Three little words.

"Mary-has-lice."

Mary Turlington.

I think we should press the pause button for a moment. I think I should tell you a few things before we go any further. In the few minutes we have before Bert and poor, louse-plagued Mary arrive for dinner, I think I should fill in a little of what the big-time Hollywood writers would call "the back story." I want you to be able to appreciate the *significance* of this disclosure. This uncomfortable moment—Dave and Morley standing in the kitchen staring at each other, intently.

They have, you see, a certain history with lice.

THE FIRST TIME those nasty little creatures crawled into their lives was when Stephanie, their daughter and only child at the time, was in daycare.

Which means, we are talking—well, we are talking almost two decades ago. Stephanie is maybe three, four, possibly five years old, and Dave comes home from his store, on a beautiful autumn afternoon, and there is Morley sitting on the porch, with Steph in her lap, and Morley is combing through her daughter's hair. When Stephanie spots Dave, she waves the Popsicle Morley is using to distract her and announces proudly, "I have bugs. I'm disgusting."

"Lice," says Morley. "Head lice, not bugs. And it is not disgusting."

Then she looks up at Dave, shrugs, and says, "Okay. It's a little disgusting."

Believe me, Morley handled it differently the next time. But it was too late for "handling" on that late September afternoon. The cat was out of the bag.

And the shock of it—his wife picking through his daughter's hair, the shouted greeting—it overwhelmed Dave.

His daughter had *lice*. His own flesh and blood was having *her* flesh and blood sucked on by microscopic vampires that, at any moment—Good Lord, were they contagious? He didn't know anything about lice.

He was already itchy.

"Don't panic," he said.

No one was close to panic. Except him, of course.

He wasn't only panicked. He was impossible. He was frantic. He was . . . irrational.

"I am not irrational," said Dave.

He certainly looked irrational. This is an hour or so later. He is sitting at the kitchen table, wearing one of Morley's shower caps.

"We are talking about parasites," he said. "Not only *in* our house. But *on* our daughter."

Oh yeah. He was frantic, standing up now, waving his hands around.

"You are thinking of them all wrong," he said. "Imagine them like a microscopic mob of mice. Crawling all over her—nibbling at her flesh and blood."

Morley said, "If you say flesh and blood one more time, I am leaving you."

It wasn't his fault. Whoever owned the old Savoy Theatre in Glace Bay back when Dave was a boy had a thing for parasite movies. *Invasion of the Body Snatchers, The Brain Eaters, Attack of the Giant Leeches, The Tingler.*

"*The Tingler?*" said Morley.

"The one about the thing with the pincers that lives on your spine and grows bigger the more afraid you are," said Dave.

"You do realize that wasn't a documentary, right?" said Morley.

Morley tried her best. She sat him down after supper and ran through everything the nurse had run by her.

"They are not dangerous. They don't spread disease. They prefer clean hair. They can't get a grip on dirty hair. They are actually a sign of cleanliness."

Dave stared at her blankly. "Are you trying to say we are happy they've dropped by?"

It wasn't hard to figure out he was as concerned for himself as he was for his daughter.

Yet as freaked out as he clearly was, he wouldn't let Morley call in the big dogs.

"No way. No cancer-causing, chemical shampoos."

So they soaked Stephanie's head in tea tree oil and shampooed her with vinegar. Every morning they laundered her bedclothes. And Morley combed, and she combed, and she combed.

"I am nitpicking," she said, never having thought about the derivation of the phrase before.

And while she combed, Dave fretted.

"Where is my bear, Daddy?" Steph asked one night. She was upstairs in bed.

Steph's stuffed Pooh Bear.

Dave had taken it, along with all her stuffed animals and the sofa cushions, sealed them in plastic, and deposited them in Kenny Wong's giant walk-in freezer.

He had to phone Kenny and get him to open the café so he could retrieve the toy.

"Listen," he said later that night. Dave was lying on the edge of the bed. He was as far away from Morley's half as he could get. He hadn't washed his hair in three days.

"They *say* they are not dangerous. Maybe they aren't. But they say lots of things. Can you imagine the panic if they said anything else?"

"A lice conspiracy?" said Morley, picking up her pillow and heading to the guest room.

"Hey," said Dave, "where did that pillow come from?"

EVENTUALLY, STEPHANIE WAS lice-free.

Eventually, Dave retrieved the rest of the stuff he had squirrelled away in Kenny's cooler and a semblance of normality returned. Although there was scar tissue, no doubt about it. It wasn't something they came to laugh about. There was nothing funny about it. Instead they packed it up and put it away. Filed it away under bad experiences. Sometimes that's the best you can do.

Over a decade passed before they returned. The lice, I mean.

Sam was in grade two. Who got it first was anyone's guess. Because this time, the whole family was infested.

"This is disgusting," said Stephanie, who, at fifteen, was denying ever having had lice before.

They were at the kitchen table. Stephanie, Sam, and Morley—and Morley was laying down the law.

"This is going to be our little secret," she was saying. "We are not telling Dad."

Why?

"Because you know how your father worries. I don't want to worry your father."

By then there were services that came to your house to deal with these . . . situations. Morley had called one.

It was a Saturday morning. Dave was at work. The woman from the service shampooed them with a chemical shampoo. Then she went through their heads one by one.

The woman gave Morley a written guarantee.

"You're nit-free," she said. "And if *they* come back, *we'll* come back."

Of course that left Morley to deal with Dave. She had to be sure he was nit-free too.

"It's unlikely he is infested," said the woman. "They don't favour men."

But Morley had to be sure. And screening him without his knowledge was not going to be as easy as it sounds.

It was not her finest moment.

She got the sleeping pills from her mother. She drugged Dave that night, at supper. In the mashed potatoes if you must know. She doubled the dosage to be sure.

And, yes, it was wrong. She would agree with that if she were here, but before you judge, you weren't there for round one.

You try being married to Dave.

Morley and Dave were on the couch, watching the television news. But Morley was watching Dave more than the television.

He started to list ever so slowly. And then he wilted. Like an asparagus. Before long he was staring at his shoes rather than the television. And he didn't seem to have noticed the difference.

It actually scared her a little.

"Dave?" she said. "What are we watching?"

He pulled himself up. Not fully erect, but to a forty-five-degree angle. He stared at her from under his heavy eyelids, like an afternoon drunk in some seedy tavern. Then carefully and deliberately, he said, "We are watching exactly what we were watching a minute ago."

He smiled at her. Clearly proud of his answer. As if he had outfoxed her.

Morley said, "Let's go to bed."

He didn't argue.

When they got upstairs, she propped him against the headboard and started in on him.

Of course he was infested too.

"Hi-yo, Silver," muttered Morley, who was hovering over him with a flashlight in her mouth.

She wasn't strong enough to wrestle him into the shower and use the shampoo. She wouldn't have risked it anyway.

The lady from the company had said she had heard people had some success with mayonnaise. Morley slopped a complete jar through Dave's hair and covered the gooey mess with her mother's old aquamarine bathing cap. The idea was she would smother the little buggers overnight.

She set her alarm for six A.M. and collapsed beside him. Her plan was to clean him up before he came to.

She hadn't counted on the dog. Arthur. Arthur had a thing for mayonnaise.

Dave woke in the depths of the night with Arthur's tongue in his ear.

Well, "woke" is overstating it. He shifted from deep slumber to some drug-addled, semi-conscious stupor. It was in this state that he stumbled from his bed into the bathroom, and it is while he was standing there, in the utter darkness, that he ran his hand through what he expected was his hair and his heart stopped.

All his hair had fallen out.

He staggered over to the mirror and peered at himself, and there, in the dim twilight of not-yet-morning, he saw that not only had he gone bald—his scalp had turned a strange shade of greeny-blue.

Through the haze of the medication, he had a brief moment of lucidity. He was able to put it all together. It was obvious what had happened. There had been a nuclear disaster.

It was clear to him what he had to do. He had to get his family away from the radioactive dust that had obviously settled on their house.

He stumbled down the hall, bellowing.

"Everyone up. Everyone down to the basement."

Morley got to him before the kids woke. They ran into each other in the hall.

She said, "There hasn't been a disaster."

"But what happened to my hair," said Dave.

Morley's heart started to race. Her eyes darted around the room wildly. She searched for something to say.

"You have cancer," said Morley.

"Oh," said Dave. "That's a relief. Am I going to be okay?"

"Yes," said Morley. "But you need to get some more rest."

She waited until he was asleep again and then worked the cap off. She called Arthur to deal with the mayonnaise.

Dave slept through it all.

He didn't come downstairs until ten o'clock the next morning.

"I had the oddest dream," he said.

Then he said, "What's for breakfast? I have this incredible craving for tuna salad."

She had to tell him what she had done. What had happened.

"I've called someone to help," she said.

By the time the lice lady arrived, Dave had shaved his head.

"I didn't want to take any chances," he said.

It wasn't a flattering look on Dave. And his hair took longer to grow in than you would imagine.

Hence the promise.

If lice ever returned to their life, Morley would tell him. Right away.

SO HERE WE are then, back in the kitchen, back at a place they never should have returned to, ever. The two of them staring at each other intently.

Dave said, "Mary has lice."

Morley nodded.

"That's what I said. Well, *had* lice. From her sister's children, I think."

Then she said, "I thought you might find it . . . amusing. I mean, of all the people in the world. And I'm sure she's got it all under control by now."

"And she and Bert are going to be here," said Dave, looking up at the kitchen clock, "in less than an hour."

As they stood there in the kitchen, Morley watched the fear overtake Dave. It was like that scene in *Lawrence of Arabia*, when Omar Sharif appears like a mirage on that flea-bitten camel—out of the shimmering desert, a dot on the screen at first, then a moving thing in the distance, the camera lingering on him forever and forever as he gets closer and closer and closer. That's what it was like.

She watched as Dave slowly went bug-eyed and twitchy. Watched as he began to scratch.

She said two words.

She said, "Don't panic."

And then she sat him down and said, "Listen."

Mary, Morley explained, had been beside herself for a week. She had had professionals in to treat the entire family. She had spent a fortune steam-cleaning the furniture and spraying the beds. She had washed everything there was to wash and thrown out things she couldn't. She had barely left the house. For days.

Morley hadn't invited Mary to dinner. She had coaxed her.

Mary was coming and Morley expected Dave to step up.

Dave murmured a weak acknowledgement and disappeared. It seemed as if he had accepted the situation.

He hadn't, of course. What he had accepted was that he had half an hour to figure out how he was going to evade Mary without attracting attention.

Half an hour to figure out what he could get away with.

Would anyone notice if he put out a washable kitchen chair in the living room? What if she brought a purse or, worse, a coat? Could he sneak her things downstairs and slip them into a plastic bag and store the bag in the freezer? Could he get them back upstairs when it was time for her to leave?

Should he put something in his hair? Vaseline? Mayonnaise? Was there time to spray the sofa with tea tree oil?

BERT AND MARY—WHO live closer than anyone else, save for old Eugene and Maria—use the front door and always ring the doorbell.

And they rang that bell at exactly six-thirty.

Morley said, "You get it."

Dave headed to the door.

On the way he slipped into the bathroom.

When he was there he pulled one of Morley's shower caps out of his pocket. He tugged it over his hair and quickly slipped on a ball cap. He stared at himself in the bathroom mirror. There were bits of shower cap showing, so he worked on that for a few seconds. The problem was when he tucked in one bit, another bit poked out. He got it the best he could and sprinted for the door.

The first thing that struck him was *Mary's* hair. She had been oiling it, blow-drying it, and heating it with a straightening iron all week. Anything that might deter lice. It looked dry and straw-like. Yet greasy too. She had big bags under her eyes. Her arms were covered in scratches.

And in that moment Dave realized something. This all happened in a flash, mind you, this part at the door. It happened before anyone had a chance to say anything, in that instant when the door swung open and Dave and Mary came face to face.

Dave looked at his neighbour, his friend, his nemesis, and he recognized himself.

And in that moment, that brief smashing second, Dave understood Mary more than he had ever understood anyone in his life.

And his heart went out to her in a rush. He actually felt it happen.

"Come in, come in," he said. As he said it, he stepped back slightly behind the open door. While he was momentarily out of sight, he reached up and pulled off the ball cap and shower cap and stuffed them in his back pocket.

He closed the door behind Mary. And then he leaned over, hugged her, and said, "Morley is in the kitchen. We're so glad you could come over."

As they walked down the hall, he left his hand resting on her back. And just before they got to the kitchen, Dave felt Mary do something that she doesn't often do. He felt Mary relax. Felt it first, then saw her shoulders loosen and drop. A moment later she sighed and stopped. She turned toward him and said quietly, "We almost didn't. Come, I mean. Morley convinced me."

It is not often that we are our best selves. We are, so often, too preoccupied, too afraid, too busy, or too taken up with whatever it is that has taken us up, too something, anyway, to allow ourselves to be our best selves.

Every once in a while, however, we step up to the plate, and we hit the ball out of the park. And every once in a while, if we are very lucky, *when* we connect, we have the sweet, lovely knowledge of *what* we have done.

And we get to stand there at home plate and watch the ball sail over the stands and disappear into the dreamy night. This was one of those rare moments. Dave had not only done good, *he knew he had.*

Of course hitting the ball over the stands is always sweeter when there is someone in the stands to see it.

When Dave and Mary walked into the kitchen, Morley was standing by the sink.

"Look who's here," said Dave, his hand now resting on Mary's shoulder.

The look on Morley's face. The smile. Well, that is all he has ever wanted from her. Looks like that. It is all he has ever needed.

THE LOST CHORDS

It was noon on a summer afternoon. Dave, alone in his car, reached out and flicked off the radio. Whatever list they were playing from wasn't working, for him at least. They hadn't played a decent song since he had left home. The exit ahead said NIAGARA FALLS—43 KILOMETRES. He glanced at his watch. He had plenty of time. He took the exit.

Dave was on his way to Cleveland. He had decided to drive by the falls for old times' sake, but when he got to Clifton Hill, just north of the falls, he parked and went into a place across from the wax museum and had a grilled cheese sandwich and a vanilla shake. When he finished he walked along the edge of the river, mesmerized by the power of the black water. Right before the lip of the falls, it seemed to both gather speed and slow down at the same time. He leaned against the green railing lost in melancholy. And indecision.

Dave was going to Cleveland to see his old friend and roommate, Scamp Gordon. It was so long since he had seen him. Dave should have been feeling happy. But he was dreading the visit. Partly it was the profiles of Scamp he had read online. But mostly it was the piece of cardboard beside him on the passenger seat of his car. Chord changes for a song written—well, it had to be over twenty-five years ago. It was before he opened his record store. And Dave had been running the Vinyl Cafe for a good twenty years.

You wouldn't think a guy could actually make a go of a second-hand record store in these unpredictable and impatient times. But Dave does. It helps, of course, that his aspirations have always been modest. His store's war cry, which you can see hanging on the wall over the cash register, sums things up as well as anything. WE MAY NOT BE BIG . . . BUT WE'RE SMALL.

A modest motto, there is no denying that, but spend a moment deconstructing it and you can't deny the whiff of determination. You might even say, defiance.

Dave, born and bred in the Age of Aquarius, isn't a *total* deadhead. He owns the building that houses his store. And the building next door. He bought them both years ago, after his touring days, when he was flush and real estate wasn't. Then there's his collection of music memorabilia on the second floor, the flotsam and jetsam of a rock-and-roll beachcomber, assembled over twenty vagabond years.

The store pays its way—carries a few modest salaries, his included—and in good years turns a profit. If Dave has an unusual expense, or needs cash for something, he goes up to the second floor, sifts through his collection, and sends something to one of those big British music auctions. The people at Christie's know him. He owns a few items they have been after for years. Dylan's set list from the 1965

Newport Folk Festival. A vest Jimi Hendrix wore at Maple Leaf Gardens.

Dave turned away from the waterfalls. He opened a stick of gum and tossed the wrapper at a garbage can. It bounced off the rim and landed at the feet of a lady wearing a sweatshirt that said *Michigan Is for Lovers*. She shot him a dirty look. He sighed, picked up the wrapper, and headed for his car. He wanted to be in Cleveland for sound check.

The trip was unexpected. It had come together a few weeks before. Dave had been putting some new albums on the shelves at the back of the store, and Scott was poking around behind the cash. Scott was one of his part-time employees.

"Who is this dude anyhow?" said Scott.

When Dave turned around, Scott was holding an old album. It normally leaned on the shelf behind the cash register. It is one of the albums in the store that is not for sale. There are a number of them. Truth be told, if Dave had his way *none* of the things in his store would be for sale. But a man has to make compromises to make his way in this world. This album, the one Scott was looking at, was recorded in 1969 by his pal Scamp Gordon. The man Dave was driving to see.

"You've never heard of Scamp?" said Dave.

Scott was only a teenager, but he knew a lot about music and he knew a lot about musicians, even musicians from back in Dave's day. The fact that Scamp was a complete mystery to him made Dave sad.

"He wasn't one of those weird polka guys, was he?" said Scott.

"Not quite," said Dave with a sigh.

DAVE WAS NOT totally surprised that Scott had not heard of Scamp Gordon. Dave has always argued that Scamp is one of the best guitar players this country has ever produced. Better even than Amos Garrett. Or any of those guys. But Scamp has never been a frontman. That record is the only *solo* album Scamp has recorded. And that was over thirty years ago—when Scamp tried out the folk thing. Scamp never released the album on CD.

Scamp was born and raised in Sault Ste. Marie. He was still a kid when he showed up in Yorkville. He said sixteen years old, but people who were there say he was younger for sure. He was in a band that had played around northern Ontario for a couple of years. They had come down to the city because they had been promised a gig as the house band at a club in Yorkville called the Parrot's Patch.

They had been told the place to stay was the Warwick Hotel. When they got there, disappointment descended on all of them. They had one room for the six of them, which was normal, but the "big city" luxury they were hoping for was nowhere to be found. The bathroom was just a rusty toilet and a chipped porcelain sink. The hems of the faded curtains looked as if they had been chewed by mice. The sloped hardwood floor, where most of them were going to be camping out, was seamed with dirt. Scamp noticed a bucket of sand on a rope by the window. There was a note attached to it, explaining it was the fire escape. If they smelled smoke, they were supposed to throw the bucket out the window and climb down the rope.

And then, the next morning when they got to the Parrot's Patch, the club was no longer there. The building was. But it wasn't a club any more. It was a doughnut shop. So they went for a coffee at a little place a couple of doors down called the Mouse Hole, and they took a vote. Scamp was the only one who voted to stay.

Scott said, "Did you say you lived with him?"

Dave said, "Yeah, but that was years later. Yorkville was pretty much over by then. We lived in the Annex. On Lowther, or maybe Kendal. We had a room with a hot plate. Scamp used to make up recipes from song titles. Like Booker T. and the M.G.'s had a song called 'Red Beans and Rice.' Scamp was famous for his red beans and rice."

"Were you guys hippies?" said Scott.

"Scamp was never a hippie," said Dave. "He was a musician. He was always working. Me too. I always had a job."

Those were good years. Dave and Scamp buying records, hanging out at Long & McQuade music store, staying up all night. They were like brothers. And now Dave couldn't remember the last time they had talked. It had been years for sure.

That night, after dinner, Dave made a pot of tea and went upstairs. He typed Scamp Gordon's name into Google.

Dave had always felt Scamp never caught the break he deserved.

Scamp had hung around the village for years. But eventually, like everyone else, like Joni and Zal and Neil, Scamp had left too. Instead of heading for the States like the others, however, Scamp headed for England. He played with Peter Quaife for a while, after Peter left the Kinks; and later with Bruce Palmer and Dewey Martin in a resurrected Buffalo Springfield. Without Neil and Stephen Stills, but with their blessings.

Dave thought he would find more entries about Scamp online than he did. He read an interview Scamp had done with *Rolling Stone* back in the 1970s, and a page in *Mojo*. The most recent clipping was seven years old—a one-page profile in *Uncut*, a feature called "We Thought You Were Dead." The three articles spanned almost thirty years. Scamp told the same story in each one.

Dave told Scott the story the next morning.

He paced around his store, agitated, while he spoke.

"He says that one night back then he wrote a song..."

"Back when?" said Scott, interrupting.

"Then," said Dave. "Back then. He was playing with Muddy Waters and—"

"Excuse me," said Scott. "This guy played with Muddy Waters?"

"Scamp played with everyone," said Dave. "That happened all the time. Someone comes to town, and they need a band. Scamp always ended up in the band."

"How come I've never heard of him?" said Scott.

"Probably because you keep interrupting people," said Dave.

"He was playing with Muddy. And when the night was over, he had a song in his head, and he scribbled it down on the back of the set list. He forgot the set list in the club. He says he remembers vague bits of the song. The main riff and certain other parts, or he thinks he remembers certain other parts. He is not sure. He has tried everything to bring the song back. Even hypnosis. Because he is certain in his mind of one thing."

"What's that?" said Scott.

"That it is the greatest piece of rock and roll ever written. He says since he lost it, he hasn't been able to write anything."

"That sucks," said Scott.

"I have it," said Dave.

"What?" said Scott.

"I have the set list," said Dave. "It wasn't Muddy Waters. It was John Lee Hooker. And I have the set list upstairs. It's what I used to do. Save that sort of stuff. I have a whole attic full of that sort of stuff."

And so Dave disappeared for three days. Upstairs into the room over the record store. He spent those days digging into boxes and crates. Looking for the lost song. He kept lugging things downstairs. A sheet of paper with handwritten lyrics by Stu Sutcliffe, the fifth Beatle, on one side and Stu's drawing of his mother on the other. A $6 ticket stub from the 1969 Toronto Rock and Roll Revival, where John Lennon's *Live Peace in Toronto* album was recorded. A set list from The Who's appearance in the city in 1975.

"Keith Moon's final North American show," said Dave, waving it at Scott.

He was making Scott crazy.

On one of his last trips upstairs, Dave returned pulling something from a long cardboard tube.

"Look at this," he said.

"Do I have to?" said Scott.

Dave was holding up a poster.

Two girls and one boy. It was hard to tell them apart.

"Ohmigod," said Scott. "Is that you?"

"There was this place called the Blow Up," said Dave. "It was the first poster store in the city. You could take your pictures there and get them, uh..."

"Let me guess," said Scott. "Blown up?"

"Right," said Dave. "How did you know?"

He eventually found what he was looking for, on the afternoon of the third day. A piece of brown cardboard. Both he and Scamp were wrong. It was neither Muddy Waters nor John Lee Hooker. It was John Hammond. But it was there.

"This is it," said Dave. "This is what Scamp has been talking about for thirty years." He dropped the cardboard on the counter. He was running his hand through his hair. "I never understood why he stopped writing. This is amazing."

It took him a day and a half to find Scamp.

"Hey," said Scamp. "I'm playing in Cleveland on Thursday night. Could you bring it here?"

"I could send it by courier," said Dave. "You could have it tomorrow."

"It's been thirty years," said Scamp. "If you brought it yourself, I could see you. It would be good to see you."

There was a pause. "I don't want to lose it," said Dave.

"You won't lose it," said Scamp.

Dave put the cardboard in a file folder. He put the file folder on his desk by the cash register.

Scott picked it up the next morning.

He sat down in the chair beside the counter and began to play the song on his guitar.

When he finished, Dave and Scott stared at each other.

"That's it?" said Dave. "That's not it. Play it again."

Scott played it again.

Dave said, "It's sort of. . ."

Scott finished his sentence: "It's sort of . . . vapid?"

"No. Not exactly vapid," said Dave. "Not *that* good."

Dave said, "Maybe you have the tempo wrong. Maybe if you. . ."

"You want me to slow it down?" said Scott.

"Please, no," said Dave. "It will last longer that way. I was thinking, speed it up."

There was something about the tune and the lyrics and the weird syncopation that made the song grating and annoying. And like all grating and annoying tunes . . . unforgettable.

"You're doing it again," said Scott later that afternoon.

Dave was humming the song.

"I can't get it out of my head," said Dave. "It's stuck in my brain right between "God Didn't Make Little Green Apples" and "Honey, I Miss You." It's going to be there for the rest of my life. I am not sure what to do about this. I am not sure how Scamp is going to take it."

Scott had picked up the piece of cardboard, was studying it once more.

Scott said, "I am not sure about this, but I think this is the same chord progression as 'The Chicken Dance.'"

AND SO IT was with a sense of foreboding that Dave left for Cleveland. As he drove along the grey highway, he kept glancing at the file on the seat beside him. For thirty years, Scamp had been held prisoner by the song. Or his memory of it. And now it seemed, as it so often does, that Scamp had mixed up his memories with his dreams.

When Dave passed the sign that said NIAGARA FALLS—43 KILOMETRES, he pulled off the highway and went into the little café by the wax museum and ordered the grilled cheese sandwich and the vanilla shake. He was trying to kill time. When he was finished his lunch, he walked along the edge of the river, lost in his memories. Mesmerized by the water. He unwrapped his last stick of gum, threw the paper at the garbage can, and missed. He picked it up.

It was early evening by the time he got to Cleveland. The sun was down and the city was hazy. He parked behind the club, beside the big tour bus. He sat in the car for a minute.

There were two stagehands smoking by the back door.

Dave hadn't smoked in years. Maybe he could bum a smoke. *That is the first good idea I've had all day*, he thought. Then he gave his head a little shake.

"Hey," said Dave as he walked by the stagehands. "You guys got any gum?" *One day at a time*, he told himself as he walked into the theatre empty-handed.

There was no one there, so he settled in the back by himself. The smoking guys came in and started tweaking the lights. Dave sat watching. Just like the old days. Scamp noticed him first.

Dave got up and they hugged.

Scamp had put on weight. Maybe ten or twenty pounds. It looked good on him though. Smoothed him out.

"You look good," said Dave. Then he said, "You don't have any gum, do you?"

"Come on," said Scamp. "Meet the guys."

He knew the bass player, Dennis. He had never met the lead singer, Keith. But he knew Keith's stuff. "I saw you years ago," said Dave. "I love your music."

And then he and Scamp were alone.

Scamp said, "Do you have it?"

Dave nodded. Dave said, "It's in the car."

Scamp said, "Well?"

Dave didn't move. He knew what he was going to do. Dave said, "Listen. We can go get that song out of the car if you want. But for what it's worth I suggest we don't do that."

Scamp said, "You're kidding, right? I have been waiting thirty years for this."

Dave said, "Well. That's the point. That's all you've been doing. That song isn't you any more. It's you thirty years ago. I always thought you could be a lot better writer than you ever thought. Don't you think it's time for us to find out which one of us is right? If I'm wrong, you can call me and I'll send you the song."

DAVE FIGURED HE was going to hear from Scamp in a week. He figured wrong. It was almost a year.

He got an email.

"We're playing in your neck of the woods. Some place called Guelph. Some crazy hippy thing on the side of a hill."

Dave went to the show of course. He stood on the edge of the stage like the old days.

As Scamp walked on Dave grabbed him by the arm and said, "This is nice."

Scamp laughed. Standing there on the edge of the stage with his guitar on his shoulder.

"Yeah," he said. "It's nice."

Then he said, "I've been writing, eh. I've got a record coming. In the fall. New songs."

It was one of those shows Dave knew he would always remember. Dennis on bass, leaving plenty of space between his notes. And the drummer, all snapping and syncopated and all over the offbeats. Keith? Keith rocked as always. But Scamp took a lot of the vocals. Scamp at the mic. Singing his new songs.

There was a moment halfway through the set when they were doing a bluesy kind of thing, but uptempo and rocky, locked in a groove, and the drummer did this totally joyful thing that caught Dennis by surprise. He laughed out loud. Scamp turned and they all smiled at each other. Then Scamp looked into the wings and beamed at Dave, and Dave thought, *It will never get any better than this. Some people have God, and some people have money, and some people don't have anything at all. I have this. I have the beat and the back beat. I have the Beatles and I have the Rolling Stones. I have Leonard Cohen singing "I'm Your Man" and Bob Dylan singing "Positively 4th Street" and, God bless her, I have Aretha Franklin.* That's when he started dancing.

JIM'S TOBOGGAN

It was after eleven. Eleven at night. And it was snowing again—for the third night in a row. Fifteen centimetres on Tuesday. The same Wednesday. And there had been more than fifteen centimetres already this night.

It was coming down relentlessly, although not unpleasantly. It was the agreeable sort of snow. Soft and almost dreamy.

The kind of snow that makes you stick out your tongue rather than hunch up your shoulders. The kind of snow that draws you to the bedroom window and imbues you with the tranquility of winter.

Which is where Dave was, by the window, lost in the snow, when he spotted his neighbour Jim Scoffield slipping out his side door.

Again. Third night in a row. And, for the third night in a row, Jim had something tucked under his arm.

"Come. Come. Come," called Dave. "Look. Look. Look."

Of course, by the time Morley got there, by the time Morley was out of bed and at the bedroom window, Jim was not out of sight exactly, but well down the street.

"What's he carrying?" said Dave.

"It's hard to tell," said Morley. She had her hands cupped on the cold windowpane. She had her face pressed to the glass.

It looked like a board or something.

"An ironing board?" said Morley. "He is doing some midnight ironing?"

"Jim?" said Dave. "Ironing?"

Dave had *his* faced pressed beside hers. The two of them staring out like little kids.

"If he goes tomorrow night," said Dave, "I'm following him."

Morley said, "What are you . . . ten years old?"

Jim was gone now, and Dave was too, staring wistfully at the half-buried snowman that the kids down the street had built.

The next night, Dave was back at the window. His coat beside him. His boots by the side door.

And precisely at eleven, like the night before and the night before that, there was Jim again, slipping outside.

"Don't wait up," said Dave. And he was slipping out his door too.

It was not unpleasant out. It was warmer than it had been for the last couple of days. Or it felt warmer, although it always felt warmer when the city was blanketed with snow.

Everything seemed softer. Even the light. The lights of the city reflecting on the low clouds and on the blanket of snow made the neighbourhood glow.

It might seem odd to you, for Dave to be out there. Following his neighbour the way he was. But the truth is, he was being driven by concern as much as by curiosity. Dave was worried about his neighbour. Jim had been different the last few months. Out of sorts. Not exactly depressed—it was hard to find the right word—just, not himself.

And here he was, again, heading out into the middle of the night. Something was up.

Dave stood in the shadows of his driveway and watched as Jim headed west. The sidewalks hadn't been ploughed. Jim was walking in the street, following the packed tire tracks.

Dave stepped out onto the road to follow. It was pretty clear where they were heading. They were heading for the park.

When they got there, Dave held back. He watched Jim from the far side of the street, watched Jim as he settled on one of the benches at the top of the north-end hill. The benches where the old Italian guys sit in the summer with their little dogs and their cigarettes.

Jim sat—slumped really, his shoulders sagging. And then . . . absolutely nothing. He just sat.

Dave felt weird to be standing there, watching his friend like that. A little creepy. He had no explanation for what he was doing, nothing to say if Jim spotted him. Dave decided that rather than stand around he would do a lap of the park. It would take fifteen minutes. If Jim was still there when he got back, he could just pretend he was out for a walk.

If Jim was gone—well, it was none of his business anyway.

Jim was still on the bench when Dave returned, still staring down the hill. Still so preoccupied that Dave could have walked right by and Jim wouldn't have noticed.

Dave almost did. Walk by. But the part of Dave that wanted to know what was going on seemed to be the part that was in charge.

"Hey," he said, acting surprised. "Jim. What are you doing here?"

Jim looked up and blinked. There was an uncomfortable moment while Jim reeled himself back from wherever he was. Dave could almost hear the gears grinding.

He could now see the thing that Jim had been carrying under his arm. It was leaning on the bench beside him.

A toboggan.

Jim still hadn't said anything. Instead he glanced at the toboggan and then back at Dave with a look of utter embarrassment. Then Jim shrugged, slid over, and patted the bench beside him. He said, "You want some tea?"

Dave hadn't noticed the thermos. The empty lid upside down beside it. Dave sat down.

Jim picked up the thermos and refilled the lid.

He handed Dave the little cup of tea and then he began to talk.

JIM GREW UP in Nova Scotia, in one of the pretty little towns strung along the floor of the Annapolis Valley.

"Winter was always my favourite season," he began. "We used to skate on the river, play shinny. And toboggan."

And then, as Dave and Jim sat on that bench, in the middle of the city, in the middle of the biggest snowfall of the winter, Jim told Dave about the greatest toboggan ride he had ever had.

"It was the winter I was eleven," said Jim. "On Bugdens' Hill."

"Who were the Bugdens?" said Dave.

"They had a house on the north mountain," said Jim. "Overlooking the valley."

And every winter, the Bugdens built a toboggan run.

"The greatest toboggan run ever," said Jim.

But not just a toboggan run. They had a skating rink, and a firepit, and a wood-fired hot tub. Maybe the first one in the country.

Mrs. Bugden was from Norway, you see. Despite her Nordic roots, she found the winter months long, sometimes dreary. So Mrs. Bugden decided to turn her backyard into a place where people would gather, and laugh, and play. A place that would ring with happy voices during the short chilly days and the deep frosty nights. A place everyone wanted to be. When she was finished the work, her backyard was a winter paradise. And the toboggan run was the highlight.

The run started on the back porch, right beside the hot tub. Mrs. Bugden would shovel all the snow off the top of the tub and pile it against the porch railing; then she would add to the pile, using snow she had shovelled from the roof. And that's where the toboggan run started. At the top of the pile by the railing, maybe five, six feet from the ground.

"It was like a launch pad," said Jim.

The run followed the contours of the Bugdens' yard, and the Bugdens' yard was made for tobogganing—filled with slopes and swales and trees.

And Mrs. Bugden didn't just pile snow on the porch; she built sides to the run that followed the curving rises and valleys, and banked around the trees.

"Like a bobsled run," said Dave.

"Exactly," said Jim.

It ran. . .

"It ran toward the river," said Jim.

But it didn't end on the river. It ended before the river.

There was a ravine before the river, and the run stopped short just before the ravine. In a sort of bowl. You would slide *into* the bowl and then go round, and round, and round it, until you slowed down.

Sometimes kids would toboggan in their bathing suits.

"Come on," said Dave.

"It's true," said Jim.

They would pile into the hot tub and when they were really hot, when they couldn't stand it any longer, they would jump out and take a run on a toboggan.

"In your bathing suit?" said Dave.

"That's right," said Jim.

They would fly down the hill with steam rising off their skinny pink bodies, like they were on fire. Of course when they got to the bottom, they had to climb back up the hill.

"In our bare feet." Jim smiled. "Those were the days."

THE TWENTY-FIRST OF February of that winter, the winter that Jim was eleven, was pretty much a perfect day for tobogganing.

"You remember the date?" said Dave.

"I remember it all," said Jim.

Over a foot of snow had fallen at the beginning of the week. It had been cold, so the snow had come down dry and powdery. At the week's end, however, it had warmed up, so Mrs. Bugden had been able to work on the banks of the toboggan run, sculpting and carving the sides. By the time Friday night arrived, the sky was clear and starry, and the toboggan run was packed and smooth.

"Just like this," said Jim. And he pointed at a band of slick snow that started in front of his feet and plunged down the side of the hill.

"There were a lot of people there," said Jim.

It was Fraser MacFayden who issued the dare.

"I dare you," he said.

"What?" said Dave.

"To use the old wood toboggan," said Jim.

No one ever used the wood toboggan on the Bugdens' Hill. It was against the rules.

"Why?" said Dave.

"Because Mrs. Bugden didn't think we could turn a wood toboggan," said Jim. "A wood toboggan wants to go straight. And the Bugdens' Hill had curves and bends, and if you didn't make the curves you were going to hit a tree."

"I dare you," said Fraser.

They were hanging around the fire. Four of them: Jim, Fraser, Lydia Bugden, and Sheri White.

"I dare you," said Fraser, "to get the wood toboggan out of the shed. Running start. From the swings."

Kids were always issuing dares. Like if they were in the hot tub, someone might dare everyone else to get out of the tub, run across the yard, and see who could sit on the rink the longest without moving.

"Don't," said Sheri.

"And I wasn't," said Jim. "I wasn't going to do it."

Until Fraser MacFayden said, "Double dare."

And then someone standing on the edge of the circle started counting, "One . . . two . . ." Well, on "three," Jim headed for the shed.

A group of parents were gathered around the firepit. One of them turned and smiled. They had no idea what was about to happen.

Jim got the toboggan out of the shed and over to the porch without an adult seeing. He balanced it on top of the snow pile, and then Candace Thomas came over to hold it in place for him. And Jim jogged across the yard so he could get a running start.

He stood for a moment staring at the porch and then, then he started running.

"Don't," said Sheri again.

It was too late to back out now. He sprinted across the yard and leapt onto the toboggan and Candace let go.

The first part of the run was dead straight. Straight off the porch and over the stone wall. There was a flat-tish bit and then, after the flattish bit, a dip. Jim had been concentrating so hard on getting going that he hadn't considered *where* he was going. So when he hit the flat part he took a moment to collect himself. He tucked his feet under the curved front of the toboggan. He gathered up the rope so there was no slack. And just in time, too, because when the toboggan hit the first dip it left the ground slightly. Jim's stomach lurched. And then it was just him and the hill and no time to think about his stom-ach, or the kids around the firepit, or anything else. The first turn was coming, and he had to be ready or he would be in trouble.

He leaned hard to the right and pulled on the left rope, like he was trying to turn a horse. He was drawing the toboggan up and right but he was climbing the left wall of the run, and it felt as if he was going to go right over the edge. He pulled even harder and leaned so his shoulder was almost touching the ground.

And now he was picking up speed as he slid back down the wall into the centre of the run, heading for the second curve. He had made it.

And he got around the second bend too, everything a blur because he was flying down the straight part, the trees a flash of grey on either side. He could hear people yelling but he had no idea what they were saying.

Another dip and he was in the air again.

And there! Right in front of him was the big curve into the bowl. He made the turn and went down into the bowl.

But instead of going round and round and slowing down the way you were supposed to, the rigid wooden toboggan flew straight into the centre. Jim could feel the wood bend ever so slightly as it hit the narrow well at the bottom. And then the front was lifting again, heading up the other side of the bowl.

Suddenly . . . time stood still. Suddenly everything went into slow motion.

He had jumped the bowl.

No one had ever done that.

Dave was sitting on the park bench listening in rapt attention. He had forgotten where they were or what the point of this was. He didn't *care* about the point of this any more—only that Jim had jumped the bowl and was suspended in mid-air. Somewhere above the snow and below the stars.

"Floating," said Jim. "I was floating . . . it was like I was floating."

Trees to the left of him and trees to the right—flying through the trees like he was Peter Pan. Flying through the trees and heading toward the ravine.

"Smack!"

"What's that?" said Dave.

"I landed," said Jim. "With a wallop. And I was off again."

Now speeding across the ground once more, breaking a trail through the white drifts, snow billowing in front of him like he was a train burning through the night. And straight ahead of him—the ravine.

He should have bailed of course.

"But I was going too fast," said Jim. So he shut his eyes, and he rode that toboggan over the edge of the ravine like he was riding a roller coaster.

"What happened?" said Dave.

"I had to navigate my way down the ravine, through the trees," said Jim, "but by then I had figured out how to turn the toboggan so it wasn't too hard."

"I thought you said the toboggan didn't turn," said Dave.

"That's what everyone thought," said Jim. "But it turned, if you knew how."

And so he steered through the trees, down the side of the ravine, and right out onto the flat, frozen river. Until he came to a stop.

Jim sat on the ice for a minute, stunned by what he had done. When the shock left him, pride and a sense of diamond-bright joy took its place.

Every once in a while you have a moment like this. A moment *so* good that, even when it's happening, it feels nostalgic. You know this is something you'll remember for the rest of your life.

Jim turned around to look at the way he had come. And the way he had to return. Uphill. On foot. Dragging a wooden toboggan.

He should have felt daunted. But he didn't. Not remotely.

"I don't even remember the climb," Jim said. "The next thing I remember is coming over the rise, and there was everyone, standing in the Bugdens' backyard, cheering."

No one ever attempted the wood-toboggan run again. Not before or since. And when Jim gets together with his childhood friends, when he's back, visiting his mother, they often return to that evening at the Bugdens'. "The greatest toboggan ride ever" is how they all describe it.

Jim picked up his thermos cup and took a sip. "I talked to Mrs. Bugden about it years later," he said. "I was home and I ran into her at the grocery store. I hadn't seen her in decades. When I was a kid I stayed clear of her after that night. I thought she'd be upset with me for breaking her rule about the wood toboggan. But she told me she never was. She said she built the run for moments like that. 'Winters are hard on me,' she told me. 'You kids always breathed a little life into them.'"

Dave and Jim stared straight ahead.

Then Jim said he'd been watching the kids heading to the park all week. And he'd been coming at night, when no one would see him, trying to build up the nerve to go down the hill himself.

"You can hurt yourself on a toboggan," said Jim. "People hurt themselves. Break their backs even."

He looked over at Dave and shrugged.

Jim, who is north of sixty now. Never married. Never had kids. Hadn't tobogganed in years.

Dave stood up and picked up the toboggan and said, "Come on."

Jim said, "I don't know."

And Dave said, "I dare you."

Jim laughed and said, "Well. If you put it that way."

And the two of them sat down on the hard length of wood. Dave in the front. Jim in the back.

WE LIVE OUR lives so cautiously, playing by the rules, driving between the lines, staying out of the passing lanes unless we have to pass. And all the cautious little while, it is the reckless moments we hold close to our hearts. The day we told the girl we loved her and would love her until the day we died. The night we stayed up and waited for the sun to come. The year we changed direction in mid-flight and walked away from the safe thing. Those times and this one too.

This night in the park when they should have been in bed. Two men who should have known better, climbing onto an old wooden toboggan.

Jim says, "Here goes nothing."

And he pushes off, dragging his mittened hands on the ground at first, partly to steer, but mostly to slow them down. And then he picks them up and puts them around Dave and says, "Aw, who cares."

It's a long way from the top to the bottom of that park hill. A lot longer and a lot steeper than you would think looking at it on some summer evening.

Halfway down Dave and Jim hit a patch of ice and started spinning. Backwards, frontwards, sideways. Jim holding on as tight as he could. The two of them hollering at the top of their lungs. Screaming in the middle of a winter night. In the middle of their lives. Halfway between the top and the bottom, between fear and joy, between the beginning and the end.

Their lives suspended. And all the moments that had come and gone, and all the ones left, were a blur; all that mattered was the snow in their faces, and the stars above them.

For they were boys again. Their hearts were young. And anything was possible.

LE MORTE D'ARTHUR

It was a summer evening—the heat of the day was done, but night was nowhere in sight. It was that lovely time *between* time. It was dusk. Everything was faded—as if the world had been stonewashed.

Dave was driving through the countryside—around the long corners, over the low hills.

"Corn's up nice," he said.

No one said anything in reply. No one had said anything for half an hour.

The silent ones were Stephanie, sitting in the front seat beside Dave but staring out the window, away from him, and Sam, sitting in the back.

Dave shrugged and fumbled with the button on the arm-rest of his door. His window slid down. He stuck his left arm out and let it ride on the current.

A convertible passed them going in the opposite direction. Dave said, "The problem with convertibles is there is only fifteen minutes a year when you would want to have the roof down. The rest of the time is either too hot or too cold."

Still not a word.

"I think this," said Dave, not giving up, "this moment, right now, is this year's fifteen minutes."

Still silence.

"Right now," said Dave, again.

Finally, Sam said, "When I get a car, it's going to be a convertible. And I am *always* going to have the roof down."

Dave said, "Yeah? What kind of convertible are you going to get?"

"I dunno," said Sam.

It got quiet again. Five minutes quiet. Ten. . .

Dave started to sing. "Twilight Time."

Louder than one should.

"Dad," said Stephanie, dragging it over two syllables.

Dave said, "That was a big hit for the Platters."

Stephanie let out a long sigh.

She said, "I don't care."

At least they were talking.

Then Stephanie said, ". . . I can't stop thinking about Arthur."

"Me too," said Dave. "Me too."

ARTHUR, THE DOG, was sick. They weren't sure how sick.

"Is he going to die?" asked Sam.

"We don't know," said Dave. "We don't know."

"If we don't *know*," said Stephanie, "why did you come and get me?"

Good question, thought Dave.

They had driven . . . what? Two and a half hours that afternoon, Dave and Sam, to pick her up. They had eaten supper along the way, at a little place by the river. And now they were driving home—the three of them.

"I just thought you should see him," he said.

"So he *is* going to die," said Stephanie.

"We don't know that," said Dave.

But he was going to die. If not now, soon. They all knew that. That's why all the quiet. Arthur was old. And now he was old and sick.

They rolled along, quietly. Until a little while later when Dave said something under his breath.

"What?" said Sam.

Dave said, "Oh. I was just thinking of *my* old dog."

Sam asked, "How did *he* die?"

Dave said, "I wasn't there. I was away."

SCOUT. A MUTT. Black and white coat, strong legs, built for running. There was probably some Border Collie in him: he had the loyalty and the focus, but not the brains. Definitely not the brains. Scout was one dumb dog.

"He was one dumb dog," said Dave.

This was back when Dave was a boy and living in Big Narrows. Back when people built their own homes. You'd start with the basement and live in the basement until you could afford to go higher. Scout, born in some basement, always stayed close to the ground. Scout *hated* water.

It drove Dave's dad, Charlie, a duck hunter, to distraction.

"A dog should know how to swim," he'd say every year as duck season approached.

One spring Charlie decided to do something about that. They drove to town. Charlie threw Scout off the government pier.

Scout sank like a stone. He didn't even try. He went straight down, until he reached a point of stasis about three feet below the surface, and he hovered there, looking up at them. Sorrowfully.

"Oh no," said Charlie, down on his knees, peering into the water, calling the dog.

Scout's mouth appeared to be opening and closing. It looked as if he was barking, underwater.

"Oh no," said Charlie again.

Dave and his sister, Annie, were both there, standing beside their dad, pointing and crying.

There was nothing for Charlie to do but yank off his jacket and jump in. This was Mother's Day weekend. Bras d'Or Lake in May. Not even the teenagers were thinking of swimming.

When Charlie hit the water, he gasped. He almost sank himself. When he told the story later, that's the part he would start with: "It was close, I'll tell you."

And that's just when he *hit* the water. He knew it was going to be colder *below* the surface.

But he couldn't let the dog drown, not with the kids standing there bawling their eyes out. Not with witnesses.

So Charlie sucked in a lungful of air, ducked under, grabbed Scout by the tail, and swam him over to the beach.

"So, he saved him," said Sam.

THE SUN WAS pretty much gone now; night was settling around the car. The darkness that was obscuring the world was working them together. This was the way Dave had hoped it would be. The three of them, driving along, talking as they went.

He said, "Hand me the thermos."

Stephanie opened the silver thermos and poured milky tea into the black lid and held it out for him.

"Thanks," he said.

Then he said, "Scout was never taken on a walk in his life."

"What do you mean?" asked Sam.

"He used to walk *us*," said Dave.

When the weather was good, Scout walked to school with Dave and Annie. He would drop them off and then meet them at the end of the day.

"He was always waiting in the wings," said Dave. "I have no idea what he did in between."

There was plenty for him to do. Scout was a small-town dog. He had a full life. Mostly he hung out with the other dogs and barked. Mostly they did that back of Kerrigan's grocery store. On a good day, the butcher would slip someone a bone. And then there would be a fight to see who got it.

Sometimes one of them would slip *into* the store and grab meat right off the counter. Not Scout. But there were dogs in town who would do that. They were dogs, after all—they believed in invisibility. They figured if they were fast enough, even if they were seen, no one would recognize them.

"Did I ever tell you about the day he went to church?" asked Dave.

Stephanie rolled her eyes.

Dave wasn't fussed by that. He knew he had told them before. He knew what he was doing. You *have* to tell stories over and over. It is the creation of myth. The only road to immortality.

"Tell it," said Sam.

"Of all the things he did," said Dave, "this was probably the best."

By *the best* he meant *the worst*.

"It was summer," said Dave. "We were driving our mother crazy."

"Who?" said Sam.

"Me and Annie," said Dave. "Your aunt, Annie.

"So my mother decided that on Sundays, everyone was going to go to church. Except her. So she could have some time alone."

So Sunday mornings, they'd all set off. Charlie took his truck, but Dave and Annie walked. They followed the railway tracks into town, where they would pool their money and buy a pop or a box of potato chips, then head out of town over the bridge and up the hill to church.

"We would head out around nine for the eleven o'clock service," said Dave.

The Sunday he was telling them about, the famous Sunday, they got to town, and there was Scout in front of the Maple Leaf Restaurant. He had his nose in a french fry box. He was *covered* in ketchup.

The moment he spotted Dave and Annie, Scout decided he was going to go with them—wherever it was they were going. The church was in the same general direction as the trout pond, and you never knew—there could be fish heads involved.

Dave and Annie knew letting Scout follow them to church was not a good idea.

"So we stood there," said Dave, "and told Scout to go home."

"And did he go?" said Sam.

"Of course not," said Dave.

"He followed them," said Stephanie.

"But not on the road," said Dave. "In the woods, *paralleling* the road. He had been hanging around bad company. He figured we couldn't see him.

"When we got to the bridge," said Dave, "we stopped and called him: 'Come here, boy. Come on.'"

"And then what?" asked Sam.

"We threw stuff at him," said Dave. "Sand."

They made it up the church hill just in time—the church bell ringing, and no Scout in sight.

"Though I did have a bad feeling," said Dave.

Charlie was already there. They slipped into the pew beside him.

Now, Charlie went to church for the same reason they did—because Margaret told him to. He made no bones about it. He would cut articles out of the *Reader's Digest* and slip them in the hymnal and read for most of the service. He would look up occasionally and mutter unhelpful things like, "Father O'Neill is climbing new heights on Mount Monotony today."

"Anyway," said Dave. "The three of us were sitting right near the front."

When they heard a murmur from the back of the church, Annie, who was on the aisle, turned around.

Annie said, "Don't look now."

"It was Scout," said Sam.

"That's right," said Dave. "But I couldn't see him."

Scout, who had finally arrived at church, had decided he would sneak up to the front to join Dave and Annie. So he had slid under the back pew and was worming his way forward row by row—invisibly. Or so he thought.

Sadly, on his way through the woods, Scout had managed to pick up a stick. The stick was attached to his undercarriage, dragging behind him. There were some other things attached to his belly—some coral-coloured muck that he had rolled in and was matted in his fur, and something horrible and foul smelling.

It was hot in the church that July afternoon and a heavy sense of torpor had settled on the congregation. Father

O'Neill, who was about to begin his homily, sensed he was losing everyone. He had been watching Valentine Kavanagh. Valentine had been fighting off sleep for a good ten minutes—his head drifting toward his chest and then snapping back as if he had been shot. But he had finally given in. Valentine's head was hanging lifelessly from his neck. He was snoring softly.

Father O'Neill was just coming to the part where the Israelites are punished for speaking out against God and Moses.

In an attempt to rouse Valentine from his siesta, and to get the attention of everyone else, Father O'Neill slammed his hand down on the pulpit and bellowed, "The Lord sent fiery serpents among the people and they bit the people and many died!"

And that is when Scout popped up under Valentine's pew and nuzzled old Valentine's hand with his ketchup-covered snout. Valentine, who had been dreaming about biting serpents, blinked one eye open. And there was Scout grinning up at him.

He had no doubt that Scout was a serpent. When Scout licked his hand, Valentine lurched out of his seat and screamed, "Jesus save me!"

Scout dove under the next pew, and came up between Lillian McAllister's outstretched legs. She saw him and fainted. It was Pearl McCoy who stood up and called out, "There are serpents among us."

Father O'Neill leaned forward to see the serpents for himself. He knocked the pulpit over.

As it went down, he caught a glimpse of Scout and said, "Dear God, serpents," and that was more or less the end of the service.

"Scout came right up to us," said Dave. "His tail wagging, as if to say, 'Isn't church great?'"

"BUT HOW DID he die?" asked Sam.

"Oh," said Dave.

And now it was his turn to be silent.

"I was away," he said finally. "He was hit by a car."

"And he was killed," said Sam.

"No," said Dave. "He made it home. He died a couple of days later. I have always felt bad that I didn't go home and, you know, see him."

"Why didn't you?" asked Stephanie.

"I was working, and I figured if he made it home, he was going to be all right."

Then he said, "No one said I should. Go home, I mean."

FIFTEEN MINUTES LATER, Dave pulled into a general store in the middle of nowhere—the only store on a country corner. They parked beside a phone booth, under the yellow glow of a street lamp. They got Popsicles and a bag of chips.

While they were walking back to the car, Dave looked at his daughter. "You want to drive?"

She shook her head.

When they got back on the highway, they were quiet again, but it was a different kind of quiet, a together sort of quiet, not an apart one.

Sam said, "Tell the one about Arthur and the potatoes."

"There's not much to tell," said Dave.

"Just tell it," said Sam.

"He used to sit on potatoes," said Dave.

"Like he was trying to hatch them," said Sam.

"If we wanted to cook potatoes, we had to pull them out from under him," said Dave.

Stephanie said, "That is so gross."

"And sleeping on the vent," said Sam.

"In our bedroom," said Dave. "Mom and I froze one whole winter. Because he was sucking up all the heat."

"And you couldn't figure it out," said Sam.

"We brought the furnace guy in," said Dave.

"Twice," said Sam. "It was me who figured it out."

"That's right," said Dave.

"And the ice cream," said Sam.

"He was crazy for ice cream," said Dave.

"*Is*," said Stephanie. "He *is* crazy for ice cream."

IT WAS AFTER ten when they got to town. They drove by the vet's, but the vet was closed. So they went home. Morley was in the kitchen. When she saw Stephanie, she smiled, but only for a second. She smiled, and Stephanie smiled, and then one of them started to cry, and pretty soon, they were all crying.

"The vet called," said Morley. "He didn't make it. He went to sleep and didn't wake up."

And they stood there, the four of them in the kitchen. Arthur's empty basket by the back door.

WE DO THIS thing. We open our hearts to the world around us. And the more we do that, the more we allow ourselves to love, the more we are bound to find ourselves one day—like Dave, and Morley, and Sam, and Stephanie—standing in the kitchen of our life, surrounded by the ones we love, and feeling empty, and alone, and sad, and lost for words, because one of our loved ones, who should be there, is missing. Mother or father, brother or sister, wife or husband, or a dog or cat. It doesn't really matter. After a while, each death feels like all the deaths, and you stand there like everyone else has stood there before you, while the big wind of sadness blows around and through you.

"He was a great dog," said Dave.

"Yes," said Morley. "He was a great dog."

WHEN HE WAS a puppy, Arthur was allowed to sleep on Dave and Morley's bed. When he got bigger, they tried to move him onto the floor and found they had a battle on their hands. No dog in the world was as determined, or skilled, at insinuating himself onto a bed as Arthur.

They bought him a basket and put it in the hall just outside the bedroom door. Arthur would make a big deal of climbing into his basket every night—circling it neurotically, sighing and grunting as he worried his blanket into a pleasing hump. But as soon as Dave and Morley were breathing rhythmically, Arthur's head would rise like a periscope, and he would slide over the edge of his basket and work his way into the bedroom, keeping low to the ground—as if he were hunting. He would stop a foot short of the bed and cock an ear. If he didn't like the way one of them was breathing, he would bring his face close to theirs and listen, sometimes for five or ten minutes, staring at them like a priest taking confession, his wet nose only inches away from their faces.

One night Dave woke up when Arthur was in the middle of a reconnaissance. When he opened his eyes, all he could see were two huge eyeballs glaring back at him. Dave had no idea these were Arthur's eyeballs he was looking into. Then Arthur exhaled. Dave was enveloped by the sour smell of his dog's breath. It was like the breath of death, and he jerked upright. He woke Morley with his gasp. Arthur bounded back to his basket.

When Morley opened her eyes, Dave was pointing at the bedroom door.

"A serpent," he said.

Arthur was in his basket snoring. Pretending to snore.

If, however, when he crept into their bedroom, Arthur was satisfied that Dave and Morley were sound asleep, he would lift one paw slowly onto the bed and place it there without moving another muscle. If neither of them stirred, the other paw would go up just as slowly. Then rising, like a mummy rising from a crypt, Arthur would pull his body onto the bed and settle near their feet with a sigh, taking, at first, as little space as possible, but slowly unfolding, expanding as the night wore on—as if he were being inflated. He liked to work his body between theirs on his way toward the pillows.

"He stole my heart," said Dave. "Over and over. I'm so glad we had him with us."

"Have," said Sam. "*Have* him with us."

And Sam got up and went to the cupboard and got a potato, and without a word walked over and dropped it into Arthur's basket.

"He's still here," he said. "He always will be."

THE VINYL CAFE CELEBRATES

Marriage

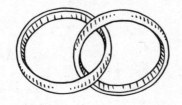

LABOUR PAINS

There was a Saturday a few summers ago you might remember—so smudged and feverish that you might have thought, like Dave, that the city was about to ignite, that any moment the temperature would soar through a critical flashpoint and all the front lawns in sight would begin to smoulder.

It was the Saturday Dave staggered into his basement in search of his children's inflatable swimming pool. Not for the children. For him. When he found the pool, Dave lugged it onto the front lawn, inflated it, filled it with water, flopped down beside it, and sat there in his shorts and his T-shirt, with his bare feet in the pool, holding, for dear life, on to the shards of his sanity.

He was sitting there looking as if he had been hit on the head with a rubber mallet when Amy Lane and her husband, Jim, walked by. Jim was wearing their week-old infant on his chest in a corduroy Snugli. It was the first time Dave had seen Amy and Jim since the birth of their baby.

"Congratulations," he croaked, barely summoning the strength to wave. He fully expected them to continue down the street. He had forgotten that Jim Lane was a first-time father.

Ten minutes later, Jim and Amy were sitting beside him with their feet in the pool. Dave was holding their daughter, and Jim Lane was well into the story of her birth.

"It was an amazing day," Jim was saying.

"Two days," said his wife pointedly.

"Thirty-six hours, *actually*," said Jim, smiling at Dave, "of *actual* labour. But the pain wasn't that bad."

"Thirty-six and a half hours, *actually*," said Amy.

"And we didn't take any drugs," Jim said proudly. "We did the breathing thing. I was the coach."

If he hadn't been so hot, Dave might have let that go by. If he hadn't felt so sticky and utterly exhausted, Dave probably wouldn't have said a thing.

But he was hot beyond belief. And feeling cranky. So instead of letting it go, Dave said, "I understand the breathing thing can be very helpful. I hear a lot of women recommend it to their husbands for root canal work."

IT HAS ALMOST been twenty years since Morley was first pregnant, with Stephanie. It wasn't the easiest of pregnancies. On Dave, that is. It was hard on Dave right from the start.

When Morley learned she was pregnant, she phoned Dave at work, at the record store. She called from a phone booth outside her doctor's office.

She said, "It's me. I have something to tell you."

She was feeling so tender and sentimental, so full of hope and fear and great love, so full of so much emotion that she burst into tears.

She cried for five minutes.

Dave was holding on to the phone imagining horrible things—all the worst things. She was incurably ill. She had fallen in love with someone else. She was leaving him.

When she stopped sobbing, he said, "For God's sake, what's the matter?"

She said, "I have something to tell you," and then she burst into tears again.

When she finally blurted it out, when she finally said it—"I'm going to have a baby"—he was completely overwhelmed. He couldn't believe this was happening to him. It was too momentous, too God-like, to be part of the creation of life. Something bigger than him must have been involved.

She said, "I'm going to have a baby."

And Dave blurted out, "I didn't do it."

He closed the store and went right home.

They both cried.

FOR A WEEK, Dave was buffeted by waves of anxiety. How could he, of all people, be a father? Then something clicked. He went to bed one night worried and woke up the next morning feeling oddly pleased with himself.

He also woke up with a new and dramatic aversion to chicken. Suddenly, he couldn't stand the smell, the texture, or the taste of chicken. He couldn't stand the sight of chicken. He couldn't stand the idea of chicken.

He would break into a cold sweat driving past the Swiss Chalet.

Morley agreed to cut chicken from their diet.

By the end of the first trimester, Dave had put on twelve pounds. He'd gained the weight because the same morning the chicken thing happened, Dave developed a king-size yearning for dill pickle potato chips. By the end of the thirteenth week of Morley's pregnancy, Dave was eating a family-size package of dill pickle potato chips every day. He carried them around with him like a blankie.

Morley, however, was okay.

Morley had gained only eight pounds.

And it didn't really show.

Not like Dave.

AT THE BEGINNING of the fourth month, Dave forgot to pay the Hydro bill for the record store.

"I'm worn out," he said to Morley. "I'm all fuzzy. I'm finding it hard to concentrate."

Everything seemed less important to him than the impending birth.

Morley began to worry. He was so wound up. She wanted to calm him down. She decided to cook a special meal—a romantic meal for just the two of them. She roasted a chicken. She'd completely forgotten.

When Dave came home from work, she sat him down at the kitchen table. There were candles flickering as she poured him a glass of red wine. Everything was beautiful. Until she produced the chicken and Dave started to cry.

This happened on and off for the next two months. Dave would be happy one moment and crying the next. He barked at her for the first time since they had been married.

She said, "You just barked at me."

He said, "You don't understand. What if there's something wrong with the baby? What if I'm a bad father? What if the baby doesn't like me? What if I lose my job?"

Morley said, "You own the business. Who is going to fire you?"

It didn't help.

She put her hand on his head. She said, "Dave, I love you."

He said, "What if you love the baby more?"

WHEN THEY WERE six months pregnant Dave and Morley went, with their pregnancy class, on a tour of the hospital birthing rooms.

Like most men, Dave was pretty ignorant about his wife's reproductive system. He thought he understood in the broadest of terms what was going on, but he really didn't have a clue. It had all been explained to him once, but he had never got it clear.

It was as though someone had registered him in a book-of-the-month club without going over the rules. Dave was aware that there was a monthly mailing—but he wasn't at all certain what was sent. Or where it was sent from. Or, for that matter, where it went. Whenever he tried to remember any details, all he could summon up were disconnected words. Mostly nouns. Mostly place names, places that sounded like stops on the Paris Métro: the Oviduct; the Fallopian Tubes.

And the truth was he had belonged to this club for so long it seemed a little late to be asking about the rules. It would be like meeting someone on the street you don't recognize. There is that brief moment when you can say, "I am sorry, I have forgotten your name." But if you let that brief moment pass, there is no turning back. You have to fake it. Dave had been faking it for too long.

Taking everything into consideration, it was probably better he didn't know all the details of this book club.

The only trouble was he liked reading so much.

And so it was that, while Dave was navigating this foggy sea of uncertainty, he sailed into the hospital for his tour of the birthing centre.

It was all blue water until he nosed into the sterile field and fetched up in front of the stainless-steel table, face to face with the forceps and stirrups, face to face with the moment of truth. He made a weak signal and tried to paddle backwards, feeling dehumanized, feeling embarrassed, feeling seasick, but mostly . . . feeling faint.

As the class began to troop out of the room after the instructor, Dave went white and ghosted against the delivery room wall. Morley spotted him just before he pitched over. She leaned into him and pinned him to the pale-green wall until three of the other fathers came to her rescue. They picked Dave up and laid him on the birthing table. Before he came round, Ron, the class clown, tenderly placed Dave's feet in the stirrups. Then they scooted out, leaving him with Morley—shipwrecked.

When he came to, he made her promise she wouldn't tell anyone what had happened, especially the other fathers.

She never told him how he had ended up on the table.

IT WAS A week later, at a regular meeting of their birthing class, that the nurse in charge asked the women to divide themselves into two groups.

"Everyone who is planning on a natural childbirth stay here," she said. "With me.

"Anyone who thinks they are going to have to take a chemical painkiller go to the far end of the room." As if they were being banished.

The husbands scuffed to the side while their wives guessed their way to either end of the room.

Morley was well aware that, if there was any truth in statistics, most women in this class would take something during their birth. She resented the nurse standing there, setting everyone up to feel bad. Morley didn't want to take painkillers during the birth, but she didn't want to disappoint herself either. She joined the one other woman at the painkiller end of the classroom. When the room was finally sorted, there were just the two of them facing the ten women standing beside the nurse.

The fathers were all looking on anxiously. All except one. Only Dave had misunderstood the instructions. Only Dave among the men had moved numbly into the non-painkiller group. He was standing there amid the other mothers, staring bleakly at Morley, who was at the opposite end of the room glaring back.

THE MALE AND the female mourning dove are both involved in nest building. The male collects grass, weeds, twigs, and pine needles and brings them to the female at the nest site. They both arrange the materials, and the nest is completed in one to six days.

Dave began to nest during Morley's eighth month. The nesting began unexpectedly at five o'clock one Saturday morning. It began when Dave sat up in the darkness and said, "I can't sleep. I'm going out to the garage to organize stuff."

Morley, who had spent the hours between midnight and four thrashing around, muttered, "Good idea." At three-thirty she had become convinced that this child she was carrying had a firm grip on her left kidney and was trying to stuff it over to the right side of her body so it would be more comfortable. She had been so sure this was happening that she had stumbled out of bed and checked the index of the book that was guiding her along this strange journey—a journey she had begun to call "the Watermelon Highway."

Morley, who had finally fallen into a restless sleep at four, muttered, "Good idea," but she had no memory of that moment when Dave appeared before lunch and told her proudly that he had sorted every last nut, nail, and screw into little glass jars.

"I'm glad we got that done before the baby," he said.

"Me too," said Morley as she slumped in a kitchen chair and stared vacantly at a pile of laundry. She had been sitting there for forty-five minutes. She had been struck by the certainty that she was going to have twins and was wondering how the ultrasound could have missed this most obvious fact.

THAT WAS THE weekend they bought the crib—a task they sailed forth to accomplish in high spirits only to flounder in the showroom, only to come aground on the rocky shore of choice.

"Would that be a traditional crib or something a little more contemporary?" said the saleswoman as they stood at the door of a place called Rock-a-Bye Baby. "Or perhaps a contemporary rendering of a traditional design?" she added before they could get away. "Or," she said as she put her arm around Morley's shoulder and chivvied her into the store, "perhaps something altogether different. Perhaps . . . a rocking crib."

Morley had a weepy moment in front of an Amish Sleigh crib and the woman quickly turned to Dave and said, "We have it in pecan or mahogany."

Dave stared at her dumbly so she continued, "Well? What colours are the nursery?"

Dave gestured helplessly toward Morley.

"We don't have a nursery," he said. "Do we?"

WRESTLING WITH THE profusion of choice there in the showroom turned out to be nothing compared to the mountain of misery they had to scale when they got home and Dave headed upstairs to assemble the crib.

"It shouldn't take long," he said.

He laid the pieces out on the floor and stared at them in mounting horror.

After an hour and a half he had all but given up hope— there was, as far as he could see, no visible way of attaching the bottom to the sides.

But even sure of this fact about this crib, he pushed on.

Three hours later he went downstairs and got Morley.

"I'm finished," he said.

And then, as they stood in the bedroom doorway, their arms around each other, admiring what they had done, the cat purred past them and glided to the middle of the room. She stopped there and flicked her tail. When the air current she had disturbed hit the far side of the room, the crib shuddered, the sides folded in, and it collapsed into a heap.

It was another two hours before Dave called Morley upstairs for the second time. He was standing beside the crib, his arm resting on the headboard.

"See?" he said, shaking it. "Solid."

Solid, certainly, but now the side went up instead of down, so if you wanted to take a baby in and out of the crib you would have to slide it in and out—the way you would slide a turkey in and out of an oven.

They didn't get it right until the next day. Not until Dave had phoned the crib helpline.

"I bet you get a lot of calls like this," he said.

"Not really," said the earnest young woman who had walked him through the instructions.

All he could think was, *If I can't even assemble a crib, how will I cope with being a father?*

LATER THAT WEEK Morley walked by the baby's bedroom and caught Dave bending over the crib. At first she thought he was admiring his handiwork. She stopped and watched him from the hall. As she watched, he bent over and fumbled with the latch and slid the crib side down. It was only then that she saw he was cradling the cat in his other arm. It was only then that she realized what he was doing. He was practising. She sneaked away without saying anything. She sneaked away filled with love.

It wasn't until the next morning that she realized the cat smelled of talcum. It wasn't until the next afternoon that she found the diapers in the garbage covered in cat hair.

SHE BOUGHT A breast pump and left it on the baby's changing table. Dave found it and thought it was a development toy. He suspended it over the crib.

"I put the mobile up," he said at supper.

THEY TALKED ENDLESSLY about how they were going to handle things. Dave didn't want the baby sharing their bed with them. He was adamant about this.

"What about the middle of the night?" asked Morley. "What if the baby is sick or crying? What if I fall asleep feeding her?"

"Her?" said Dave.

He wouldn't budge. He finally told her what he was afraid of. He was terrified he might roll over and smother his own child.

"But there is an instinct to stop you from doing that," said Morley.

"How can you be sure I have it?" he asked. "They might have missed me."

He filled a white plastic bag with five pounds of margarine, sealed it tightly, and drew a stick-picture baby on it with a black marker. He set the bag down between them one night.

"I didn't say anything about a margarine instinct," said Morley. "I said a baby instinct."

"We'll see," he said.

Morley woke up at three in the morning to find Dave beside her, holding his hands out like Lady Macbeth. He was covered in margarine.

"I killed her," he said. "I killed her."

It was only the second time in four years that Morley had serious doubts about their marriage.

THE NIGHT BEFORE she went into labour, Dave woke up and found Morley sitting up in bed staring out the window.

He reached out and patted her head and said, "It's pretty, the moon."

She said, "Have you ever wondered what those Milk-Bone dog biscuits taste like?"

As Dave tried to imagine what the right answer to this could possibly be, Morley sighed, lay back down, and fell immediately asleep.

AFTER MONTHS OF anxiety and doubt, Dave was now ready to have this baby. Not, that is, because he had overcome his nervousness, but rather because he couldn't bear the pregnancy any longer. The extra weight he had gained was making his back ache. His feet had begun to swell at the end of the day. He had to pee all the time. And lately he had been having trouble sleeping. Maybe, he thought, it would just be easier to have the baby now and be done with it.

Morley began her labour the next morning—a week earlier than anyone had expected.

She waited until after lunch and then phoned Dave at work. She said, "We have to go to the hospital."

Dave felt a surge of panic. He had changed his mind. He said, "Not today. I'm not ready. Give me one more day."

By the time they arrived at the hospital Morley's contractions were five minutes apart. Everything was a rush and a panic—there was a nurse taking Morley's blood pressure and temperature and someone else listening to her tummy. Dave was standing apart from the flurry hoping this was a normal kind of flurry, and then they were alone and everything ground to a halt.

Dave leaned the bag of fruit and the tapes he had recorded in the corner. He and Morley sat on the edge of the bed and chose a spot on the ceiling that would be their spot. They stared at the spot and began breathing through the contractions, which were still pretty mild (although they didn't know that then).

Dave held Morley and said, "That's our spot. That spot is going to get us through this night."

It was five hours later, when they were well into it, that Morley gripped Dave's arm with a ferocious strength—a strength he had never suspected her of possessing. It was five and a half hours later, while she was huffing and puffing

and the contractions were coming in powerful waves, that
she gripped his arm just above the elbow and stared wide-
eyed at him and said, "What is it?"

Dave, who would have done anything for her at that
moment, had no idea what *it* was. He looked around to see
if it was something he could see, and when it wasn't, all he
could say was, "What is what?"

"The spot," said Morley, through her clenched teeth. "I
need to know what the spot is."

Dave, who had his face almost pressed into hers—Dave,
who was staring right into her wide, white eyes—said triumphantly, "It's *our* spot."

And that was when Morley's eyes got even wider. When
she moved even closer and said, "*My* spot! Not *our* spot, *my*
spot, Dave. I'm the one having this baby! I want you to tell
me what *my* spot is!"

Dave nodded at her earnestly, prying her hand off his
arm. He pushed a chair to the middle of the room and stood
on the chair. While Morley huffed and puffed he peered at
the spot on the ceiling and said, "I think it's a squished fly."

Their nurse winced.

There was the briefest moment of silence.

Then Morley began. She said many things, most of them
mercifully forgotten and never repeated. The gist of what
she said was that she was not about to focus all her life-
producing energies—all her God-like, child-producing
strength—on a dead fly. You idiot. The gist of what she said
was that Dave had to find another spot or he might as well

forget about fatherhood. But Dave couldn't see another spot. He had never heard her speak like that. He was terrified.

Then Morley wasn't talking to him any more. She was talking to the doctor, she was telling the doctor (in what might be described as an assertive tone) that it would be a good idea if he gave her something for the pain.

Dave thought to himself, *This is the moment I am supposed to step up to the plate.* They had agreed that Dave—the birth coach—was, at this moment, to dissuade Morley from taking painkillers, to encourage her to keep at the breathing, to focus and visualize away the "discomfort."

Dave faced the doctor and said, "We aren't going to take anything for the pain."

The doctor looked at Dave and then glanced at Morley, who had just been hit with a contraction so powerful that she was moaning like a wounded beast. Dave turned to the doctor and, in a small, faraway voice, said, "On the other hand, could I maybe have something for the pain too?"

The book had said there might be moments like this. Moments when he would feel uncomfortable and queasy, and he had thought he understood that, but nothing he had read had prepared him for this. There were sounds coming out of his wife that were making him afraid.

Sounds so frightening that he didn't want to hear them. She was bathed in sweat and making extraordinary sounds. He was sitting in the corner of the room now, and that's when he realized what the breathing was for. The breathing they had learned in class and had practised together wasn't for Morley. What she was doing now was beyond breath.

The breathing was for him. He was breathing in and out, in and out, and while he breathed, she was bringing life into the world. All he could think was, *In and out, in and out.*

He looked at the pathetic bag of fresh fruit he had brought. Offering his wife a kiwi fruit at this moment would be as ridiculous as trying to tame a mythological beast with a plate of olives. The doo-wop tape he had made seemed so ludicrous. Why hadn't anyone told him what this would be like? Why hadn't they told him he should have been wearing mountain-climbing gear? Next time he would be ready. Next time he would wear a helmet and crampons. This wasn't a breathing thing, this was an Everest thing. This was a survival thing. A life-or-death thing. The next time he would bring rope. Lots of rope so they could tie themselves together. And maybe a large mallet. He would bring a large rubber mallet for the pain. This is what he was thinking as his daughter's head crowned. He was thinking about rope, and then he remembered he had to keep breathing—in and out. Just as long as he didn't have to do anything but breathe in and out the way they had taught him in class, he would be all right. He closed his eyes and concentrated on his breath. He didn't feel uncomfortable and queasy; he felt terrified. He was involved with something much too big for him. And suddenly there was another cry and the doctor was holding a baby in his arms.

Suddenly the two of them were three. Dave felt a rush of wonder. The doctor was holding their baby. Their daughter. Their Stephanie. He took her in his arms and the very first thing that came into his mind was *One day this girl is going to break my heart*. And he began to cry.

THIS IS WHAT Dave was thinking about as Amy and Jim continued to talk about the gory details of their daughter's birth. He realized he had missed some of their story, but now he had no urge to rush them along, to hurry them through their own Everest tale. He peered down into the baby's remarkable, tranquil face and smiled.

"What happened next?" he said. "What happened next?"

THE CANOE TRIP

Dave has already started planning next year's wedding anniversary celebration. He has been pawing through brochures about hiking trips in Banff, boat tours of the Great Lakes. Even a train excursion to the North.

"You get a certificate," he said, "when you cross the Arctic Circle."

"I beg your pardon?" said Morley.

"It's suitable for framing," said Dave.

Dave and Morley got married in the summer, over twenty years ago. And Dave, you might be surprised to learn, has been planning all of their wedding anniversary celebrations for the last few years. Morley, if she had her way, might have let each anniversary slide by unannounced.

I should be clear about this. Morley still loves Dave. She is happy in her marriage.

But as the years add up, the sheer numbers give Morley pause for thought. There is nothing like a twentieth wedding anniversary to drive home the point that you are no longer twenty years old.

Dave, by contrast, *loves* to mark each passing year—loves to tell everyone about the longevity of his marriage. It makes Dave feel rejuvenated. And hopeful.

Twenty years. *Over* twenty years.

And all is still well. Twenty years gone by and he is still as happy as he was when he first married. It makes Dave feel as if he has managed to stop time, as if he has discovered the fountain of youth.

It was *this* notion—this notion that he and Morley have hardly changed—that led Dave to this year's idea. The idea that this summer, he and Morley should spend their anniversary the same way they spent their honeymoon. In a canoe. It would be the first canoe trip since their honeymoon.

"What do you think?" said Dave to Morley as they got ready for bed one night in early June. They had the time. Stephanie would be tree planting. Sam would be at camp.

Morley thought back to that summer they were married. She was in her mid-twenties. They had gone to Algonquin Park. She remembered blue-skied days on the lakes and rivers, the heat of the sun penetrating her skin, the cool water splashing her hand as she dipped her paddle. The call of loons, the rippling leaves, the two of them, alone, lying in their sleeping bags, outside their tent, staring up at a sky of crowded stars.

"That would be . . . perfect," said Morley.

On their honeymoon, young and fit and with time on their hands, they had spent six full days in the park.

"Six days?" said Morley.

They settled on three days and two nights. The wolf of ambition not as restless as it was when they were young. It had all fallen together nicely. They would drop Sam off at camp, spend a week at a friend's cottage, and then they would head to Algonquin Park. After their canoe trip, they would pick up Sam and head back to the city.

Dave found a route they could do in the few days they had. And one night late in June, he and Morley descended into the basement to look for their camping stuff. Morley sorted through the pots and pans, checked out the propane stove, inspected the backpacks. She headed to the sporting goods store to fill in the holes that twenty years had made in their camping gear.

Dave . . . well, Dave was in charge of the tent.

THEIR FIRST MORNING in Algonquin Park was gloriously sunny and warm. Dave and Morley paddled gently along the shoreline talking about the kids, reconnecting with one another. When the sun was high in the sky, they found a little spot where a shelf of smooth rock slipped from a piney island into deep water. They paddled the canoe until its bottom scraped the rock, then Dave jumped out and held the bobbing boat while Morley crawled out. The food was in an old green canvas backpack with a leather tumpline—a Woods Tripper.

Morley unpacked cheese and crackers, raisins and almonds. Dave popped some freeze-dried turkey hash into his mouth.

"You're supposed to add water to that," said Morley.

"I know," said Dave, who was chewing energetically. "But you'd be surprised how good it is like this."

After almost an hour on the rock, they climbed back in the canoe. They spent the rest of the afternoon on the water, paddling steadily. It took longer to reach their campsite than Dave had predicted. By the time they dragged the canoe up on shore, the sun was dipping and the sky was a dusty orange.

The campsite couldn't have been nicer. A flat clearing under the trees for their tent, a flat rock for cooking. There was a fire bowl, and the last camper had left a little pile of dry split wood. Dave stretched and squinted up at the trees.

He was thinking they would have to get an early start in the morning if they wanted to make the next campsite any earlier. He didn't say this to Morley. Instead he pointed at the fire bowl and said, "Won't it be great to cook over a fire again?"

Morley was rubbing her back. Morley was thinking take-out pizza would be nice. But she didn't say it.

They set up camp. Dave took his backpack out of the canoe. Morley had bought them two new hiking packs for the trip. Dave had left his at home. Instead, he'd hauled out the pack he'd used on their honeymoon. He wanted everything to feel the same as it had their first time in the park together. Morley pulled the camping pots from the canoe, and Dave headed over to the edge of the clearing to put up the tent. He had packed the same two-man tent they had used all those years ago. But not without checking it first.

"Checking it" included pulling the tent from the bag, confirming that there were still poles and pegs—and that the fly was there too. Checking it did not, however, include unfolding the nylon tent, or fitting the poles together, or doing a trial run by putting the tent up in the backyard. If Dave had done any of that he would have remembered how monstrously difficult this little tent had been to set up— the stubborn refusal of the poles to stay together, the trickiness of getting the thick steel tubes through the flimsy fabric loops. If he had, Dave would have also realized that even that miracle fibre "nylon" changes over twenty years.

In the forty-five minutes that it took Dave to wrestle their tent up, he had plenty of time to take in the rotting seams, the cracked fabric, and the rusty zippers. Crouching inside to unroll the mats and put down the sleeping bags, he watched the last fiery rays of the sun seep through the yawning gaps of their only shelter.

SUPPER THAT NIGHT was steak and potatoes, cooked over the fire. Dave and Morley ate by the light of their lantern. At the end of the meal, Dave gathered all of their food into the green pack and tied a rope around the top. He flung the rope over a high branch of a maple tree some distance from the tent. Then he hauled the food high into the air.

"There," he said. "If the bears want a snack, they'll have to do a bit of climbing."

Morley fell asleep almost immediately. Dave lay there grateful that she was so exhausted she didn't notice the bumpy ground poking through the foam mats, the mouldy smell of his pack, or the mosquitoes that moved in and out of the zipped-up tent with impunity.

Then he fell asleep too.

THEY BOTH WOKE up again at more or less the same time. About two in the morning. Morley's back ached. Dave couldn't get the drone of mosquitoes out of his head.

"If we don't get back to sleep soon," said Dave to Morley two and a half hours later, "we'll just get going. Get an early start."

The next thing Dave knew, Galway the cat was on the bed. She had been doing this a lot lately. Climbing up there before the alarm, rubbing around the pillow, tickling Dave with her whiskers, walking on his hair—making sleep impossible. She wanted Dave to feed her. And he half thought of batting her away, but it was probably time to get up anyway. So he said, "Okay, Galway," and he opened his eyes.

Like many people, Dave has, in idle moments, wondered how he might react if he ever found himself in the thick of a crisis. If he was, say, a customer at a bank during a holdup, or a hostage in a hostage taking. Largely he wonders these things in bed at night—lying in the darkness, working out the steps he would take if his parachute was twisted when it opened. Not that he has any plans of jumping out of a plane. But these are important questions, and they are things that occupy Dave's mind when sleep won't.

He has considered many things, worked through many scenarios, though never what he should do if he woke up in a tent, eyeball to eyeball with a skunk.

He said, "Okay, Galway," and he opened his eyes. And there was a beat and then another, and what he did was he gasped and sat bolt upright.

The skunk scampered to the bottom of his sleeping bag.

And lifted its tail.

And stood there with its eyes tight on Dave's face.

Dave tried to look friendly. He smiled and nodded.

The skunk twitched its tail.

Dave froze.

The skunk, which was outside of the sleeping bag, was actually standing on Dave's feet, which were inside the bag.

The skunk seemed undecided.

The two of them stared at each other for what felt like a long time and actually *was* a long time given the circumstances.

Five minutes passed.

And during those five minutes Dave had only one thought: *Don't move your feet. Don't. Move. Your. Feet.*

FIVE MINUTES PASSED, though it felt much longer, and then the skunk, who seemed to have taken Dave's smile as an invitation to stay a while, sat down.

Then it got up again and ambled over to Morley's backpack. The bag was lying in the corner of the tent, the zipper open. Dave watched as the skunk poked its nose into the pack.

And that's when the squirrel leapt out.

A blur of brown fur catapulted across the tent and both the skunk and Dave jumped simultaneously. The skunk landed in Dave's lap, and Dave screamed, and Morley, who had been asleep, shouted.

And there was a flurry of flying fur and the sound of nylon ripping, and Morley and Dave burst from the tent gasping for breath.

And as they stood there beside what was left of their tent, Dave glanced at his watch.

9:30?

It couldn't be.

"Oh my God. Hurry up. Hurry up," he said.

"We've got to pack up." He was shoving things into his backpack. "Pack up, pack up, we've got to get going."

"What about coffee?" said Morley, staring at the heap of nylon that was once their tent. "For the love of God, let's make some coffee."

"There's no time," said Dave. "We've gotta go now, or we won't make the next campsite."

Twenty minutes later, they were floating along the shoreline again.

By 12:30, Morley had gone as far as she could go without food. They decided to have a picnic on the water.

At just about that time, another considerably less frazzled pair of paddlers were getting ready to take a break too. They were floating down the same shoreline Morley and Dave had left behind. And at just about that time, they spotted the campsite Dave and Morley had vacated a few hours earlier. It wasn't the easy access or the small clearing that drew their attention. Nor was it the obvious swimming spot, or the pretty gathering of small spruce trees where Dave had set their tent. What caught their attention was the large green backpack hanging from the branch of the tree.

"WHAT DO YOU mean you forgot the food?" said Morley weakly. She wasn't as angry as you might imagine. Her right eye was swelling from a mosquito bite and her back ached—Morley felt too beaten up, too weak, and too hungry to be angry.

"We'll go back and get it," said Dave, feathering his paddle on the water. "It'll only take a few hours."

But they couldn't go back. They were supposed to pick up Sam the following afternoon at five. They were two days' paddle away from the park entrance, from their car, from phone service, or from any way to reach their son.

Morley could imagine the scene. A deserted camp parking lot, the last car pulling out, Sam standing small and alone, waiting sadly for the parents who had clearly forgotten him. A steely, mother-bear look crossed Morley's face.

"Paddle!" she said. "Just paddle!"

AS LUCK WOULD have it, they were not entirely without food. After half an hour of paddling, Morley remembered that she had shoved some snacks into her pack and had forgotten to move them into the food bag the night before. There was a one-pound bag of red licorice, a small Swiss chocolate bar, and two packs of sugarless gum. Dave watched in amazement as Morley pulled it from her knapsack.

No wonder there was so much activity in their tent.

He thought that. He didn't say that. Instead of saying that, he took a big bite of red licorice.

After the licorice stop, Morley and Dave fell into a rhythm. Their strokes steady and even. Across the lake Dave spotted a young couple paddling. They were the only people they had seen since entering the park.

"I wonder if they are on their honeymoon?" said Dave.

"If they get a little closer," said Morley, "I have some advice I'd like to give them."

BY LATE AFTERNOON they had entered the river. They were supposed to paddle several miles downstream, then portage past a set of rapids, and continue on for another mile to that night's campsite. Dave manoeuvred to the left side of the river. He wanted to stay good and close to the bank so he could see the clearing where the portage began.

An hour later he looked at his watch for the fifth time. He was getting nervous. It was later than he had planned. He had expected to see the portage entrance some time ago. Morley, who was paddling robotically, was quiet. Dave decided not to say anything. Twenty minutes later, however, Morley pulled her paddle from the water.

She said, "I hear something."

Dave could hear it too. And as he heard it, he could feel fear putting its big icy hand around his heart, because what he was hearing was the rumbling of thousands of gallons of water cascading down huge, hard, sharp rocks. What he was hearing was the rapids.

"Where's the portage?" said Morley.

IT SHOULD HAVE been right there. Dave was gesturing at the riverbank. The bank was not so much a bank but a bog—a stretch of wet, marshy land, bulrushes, water lilies, and rotting logs. The bank was more a bayou than a bank.

Morley said, "Paddle to the other side." Her voice had raised several octaves, her neck muscles were dancing.

Dave was waving the map in front of him like a flag.

Dave said, "The map says it's this side."

Morley reached over to take the paper from him, but as soon as she grabbed it, the map fell into two pieces. Morley peered at the piece she had. It was faded green. It was covered with coffee rings and water stains. The ugly truth had begun to whine around like a hungry mosquito.

"Dave," she said slowly, "where did you get this map?"

Morley recognized the look passing over her husband's face. It was the "I thought it was a reasonable thing to do" look. The look that suggested that what others might think was reasonable didn't even come into the picture.

Morley said, "Where did you get the map?"

Dave said, "From our honeymoon album."

The map was over twenty years old. They had stopped paddling. The current, which was picking up, was carrying them into the middle of the river.

Energized by panic, Morley and Dave paddled to the far side of the river. It was just as soggy. "The trail must be back there," said Dave, pointing up the river. "We must have passed it."

He spun the canoe around and they began to paddle back to the left shore, trying to move the boat upstream at the same time.

Eventually they reached the other side, but after twenty minutes, their paddles digging into the water with every-thing they could give to them, Morley realized that they were beside the same rotting log. They were getting nowhere. Slowly.

They were going to have to get out of the river and

portage—trail or no trail. Dave wedged the canoe between two fallen logs, as close to dry land as he could. Then he and Morley jumped out, into the knee-deep water. They muscled the boat toward the shore. When they got to higher ground, there appeared to be a path of sorts, narrow and overgrown. They put the canoe down and rested. Dave looked over at Morley, who was sitting in the dirt, her back against the side of the canoe. He gave a little gasp. Her hair was tangled and matted and sticking out at odd angles. She was gritty and sweaty. Her face sunburnt and spotty.

"What?" said Morley.

"I didn't say anything," said Dave nervously.

They set off down the path with the canoe hoisted over their heads. And as they trudged along, the sun began to dip below the trees. Fifteen minutes into their hike, Dave felt a tug on his back, heard a little sound, like cloth tearing. The right strap of his backpack had given way. The bag landed right in front of Morley, sending an arc of mud smacking against her thighs.

"Sorry," said Dave in a small voice.

They stopped and put the canoe down. Dave lifted the slimy bag out of the mud and jammed it under the seat of the canoe. But as soon as they lifted the boat again, it slid out. Dave had left his only rope behind at the campsite, with the food. He grabbed a spare pair of tube socks and used them to tie the backpack to the centre yoke. They hadn't been walking for more than five minutes when the knot gave way. Dave twisted around, trying to catch the pack, but instead knocked it backwards, straight into Morley. As Dave would describe it later to Kenny Wong, it was as if the pack had a mind of its own. "Like it *knew* it shouldn't go any further." Or not with them in any case.

They stopped again. It pained him to do it, but he decided to put his old friend out of its misery. He took the lantern out and left everything else—the pack, the ripped tent, his sleeping bag—abandoned at the side of the path.

It was no longer dusk. It was getting dark. Night was settling on the forest path. With Morley's pack on his back, Dave held the lantern in his teeth and the two of them lurched along, like two soaked donkeys, the canoe balanced awkwardly over their heads.

Morley was up to her ankles in mud, and she was sinking deeper with each step. Pretty soon she was wet up to her thighs, covered in muck and mosquito bites. She could only see out of one eye. Her arms ached and her head hurt. Before long the mud was sloshing around her knees and Morley was thinking that she was about as uncomfortable as a person could be.

Unfortunately, she was wrong.

A minute later her foot settled deep into the oozing, slippery muck. When she pulled it out her shoe was missing.

That's when Morley said a few words that Dave didn't think he'd ever heard her say in their twenty years of marriage. He prayed it was just the licorice talking.

THE SUN HAD completely disappeared by the time Morley and Dave stumbled into the clearing at the end of the old portage trail. As they stood on the riverbank, they could hear the crashing rapids above them. Then the lantern battery gave up. The light dimmed and then flickered out.

Dave said, "I guess this is the end of the road for us."

And Morley said, "Yup."

"I meant," said Dave nervously, "for tonight."

They settled the boat into muddy ground beside the river. Dave put Morley's soggy sleeping bag in the bottom and crawled in. He had his feet under one seat and was leaning against the other. Morley got into the canoe and sat between Dave's legs. She covered herself with a rubber ground sheet. It started to drizzle.

If anyone could have seen them, they would have thought it was an odd but romantic scene—Morley with her head on Dave's chest, Dave with his arms wrapped around his wife. But Dave wasn't thinking about Morley; he was thinking about bears. And Morley was leaning into Dave, not as the love of her life, but as the only heat source available.

Eventually, somehow—who can explain these things—Morley fell asleep. She was actually dreaming that she was sleeping, or rather just waking up in her own soft queen-size bed. In her dream she opened her eyes and then closed them again, savouring the delicious smell of coffee that was wafting into the bedroom. She was warm, and comfortable, and thinking about going back to sleep, but Dave was nudging her.

"Wake up," he was saying. "There's something you should see."

Morley opened her eyes, and when she did, she was in the wet canoe again. It had stopped drizzling and the clouds had blown away. The sky was glowing—flashing streaks of pale blue and green filling the sky like sheet lightning. It looked as if someone had draped the horizon with some sort of huge shimmering veil. It was the northern lights.

"Remember?" said Dave. They had seen them on their honeymoon too.

Dave and Morley sat in the middle of the canoe, in the middle of that night under that most spectacular of light shows—the aurora borealis. They were together and totally alone. Dave's arms were still around Morley. She moved her head onto her husband's chest. She heard his heart slowing down, beating a gentle, steady rhythm beneath his sweater. A loon called out across the water. And the lights continued to dance.

Morley sighed. She was cold. She was hungry. She was bug bitten. But she was right where she should be. She was with Dave. And he was doing what he is always so good at doing: finding light in the darkness.

DAVE HAS STARTED planning next year's anniversary already. He hasn't given up the idea of taking another canoe trip, some time, but next year, he is thinking he will try something different. He has been looking at a brochure for a place called the Albion Resort. The brochure is pretty slick. It says: "The inn where *we* take care of everything."

After twenty years of marriage, Dave knows good advice when he reads it.

ODD JOBS

I t was on a Saturday afternoon in September, five years ago, that Dave and Morley sat in their backyard and had one of those conversations that married couples have from time to time, about where they had been and where they were going. It was during that conversation that they decided, once again, that they would, without fail, start saving money. They agreed to put away two hundred dollars a month in an account they would never touch, never, not ever. And for the last five years they have been doing that, making those monthly deposits—to their own amazement, without missing one month. They did, however, miss one step because it seemed so self-evident: they never hammered out *why* they were saving. This was not a problem when they were beginning and there was no money in the account, but after five years Dave and Morley had accumulated a significant nest egg, and nest eggs have a habit of hatching.

What had hatched in Dave's mind was a duck-egg-blue 1969 Austin-Healey 3000, with a cream scallop inlet, a red leather interior, fifty-two-spoke wire wheels, and Lucas fog lights mounted on a shiny chrome bar.

Ted Bescher, a retired schoolteacher who lives across the lane from Dave and Morley, owns a bright yellow TR6 that Dave has admired ever since Ted, and his car, moved into the neighbourhood. Ted's car hardly ever leaves the garage, but it is there calling out to Dave whenever he walks by. And sometime after his forty-fifth birthday Dave realized that under certain circumstances, just to be able to say that you owned an Austin-Healey would make your world a better place. He wouldn't *have* to drive it. In fact, he wasn't entirely sure he *could* drive an Austin-Healey without worrying what people were saying behind his back. But just to have one in his garage would make life better.

Morley, of course, had *her* own plans for the money, which had nothing to do with little blue cars. When Morley thought about the savings account she imagined a new second-floor bathroom, where there would always be clean towels and a dry toilet seat.

These were not things they talked about, however, until one summer morning when they were eating breakfast, and Morley looked at the toaster and said, "It would work so much better if we could plug it in at the table. So we wouldn't have to get up and walk across the kitchen every time someone wanted toast."

It was just an idle thought, but it struck her as a good one. She considered it for a moment and said, "Maybe we should take some of the money from the savings account and get someone to put in another outlet."

This sent a chill through Dave's heart.

The next morning, a Saturday morning, Dave was sitting alone at the breakfast table looking at the toaster on the other side of the kitchen. He was thinking, *I should install the outlet myself.* It had nothing to do with toast. It was a defensive manoeuvre. It had everything to do with the Austin-Healey.

Morley was already at work—they were opening a new play. As she left, she said she wouldn't be back until after the curtain came down.

The kids were still asleep—Dave wouldn't see *them* for hours. Sometime in July their body clocks had slipped into the Pacific time zone. Dave had the whole day stretched out before him like a white line running down the centre of a highway. How complicated could it be for an old roadie to run some wires through a wall and install an outlet?

The more he thought about it the more he liked the idea. What he liked best of all was that he would get to knock holes in the kitchen wall. It felt good just *thinking* about that. Without thinking about it any further, without letting coffee or the morning paper waylay him, Dave fetched a hammer from the basement. He returned to the kitchen and stared at the bare white wall beside the table, tapping the hammer anxiously on his thigh.

Like a Spanish conquistador sealing the fate of his troops by burning his ship as soon as his last man stepped on shore, Dave raised the hammer over his head and swung it at the wall with all his might. *Hiii-yah.*

The hammer sank into the plaster with a pleasing crack.

Dave pulled it out. *Take no prisoners! No turning back!* Three more whacks, and he was staring at a hole the size of a cantaloupe.

What a glorious feeling of destructive accomplishment. Not as good perhaps as changing the oil of a small blue Austin-Healey, but good nevertheless. Dave gave the edges of his hole a few prods with the butt of the hammer and bits of plaster flaked onto the floor. Then he reluctantly put the hammer down. He went upstairs to look for the big *Reader's Digest Book of Home Repairs* to see where he should find the wire that he was going to run to his hole. To his new outlet. It would have to come from somewhere.

He rooted around the bedroom for a while and decided he must have lent the book to a neighbour. He went downstairs and stared at his hole and decided to clean it up a bit. By the time he had finished tinkering, the hole was more symmetrical, neater, and considerably larger. More the size of a pizza than a melon. A largish pizza, thought Dave.

He wondered if Jim Scoffield had his repair book. He didn't really need it, but it would be good to see what the *Reader's Digest* had to say before he went too far. He glanced at the kitchen clock. Jim was the kind of neighbour you visited rather than phoned.

"I don't have your book," said Jim, "but I have a new mallet. I can't believe you started without me. Let me get it."

Jim and Dave stared at the hole where Dave wanted to put the new outlet.

"Where's the wire going to come from?" asked Jim.

"That's what I was wondering," said Dave.

Jim pointed at a light switch by the back door. "There'd be wire over there we could patch into," he said.

Then he smiled. "Of course, we'll have to punch a hole in the wall to pick it up."

He was fiddling with his new mallet.

"Be my guest," said Dave.

"Are you sure?" said Jim, moving toward the back wall, not waiting for the answer.

Two satisfying swings and Jim was through the plaster. Dave pushed forward to peer into the hole. Jim pushed him back. "Maybe," said Jim, "I should tidy that up a bit."

There *were* wires there. In fact, when Jim stepped back and they both peeked in his hole, wires were about all they *could* see—all sorts of wires. Black shiny wires, grey cloth-covered wires, wires snaking through the wall like. . .

"Like spaghetti," said Jim.

"We're not wanting for wire," said Dave.

Jim pointed at a grey wire running through a porcelain insulator.

"Knob and tube," said Jim. "I didn't think that stuff was legal any more."

"Those aren't live," said Dave. "I had an electrician in to replace all that a couple of years ago."

Dave reached into the hole with his screwdriver and jiggled the old wire. There was a sudden puff of smoke. Dave gasped and the right side of his body jerked spastically. A deep alien-like moan rolled out of him as the screwdriver flew across the kitchen, end over end like a tomahawk, ricocheting off the kitchen sink and disappearing through the window.

There was a moment of stunned silence. Jim and Dave both stared at the broken window as shards of glass tinkled to the floor.

"Could you do that again?" said Jim. "I especially enjoyed the way the chip of porcelain from the sink followed the screwdriver through the window."

A minute later Bert Turlington was standing on the stoop. He had Dave's screwdriver in his hand. "This yours?" he asked, standing a little close, talking a little loud.

Dave nodded. Yes.

"Are you out of your mind?" said Bert, even louder now.

Dave shrugged his shoulders. No.

"I opened the back door," said Bert, "and this is flying across my yard like. . ."

"A tomahawk?" said Dave helpfully.

"It stuck in the door frame about a foot from my head," said Bert.

"We're moving some wires," said Dave. "I got a shock."

"You're moving wires?" says Bert, stepping back, his fists unclenching, his voice softening. "I got a new drill for my birthday. One of the cordless ones. Maybe I should bring it over."

Something inexplicable happens when a man picks up a tool to do home repairs. Some force, as yet undescribed by science, but nevertheless well known to women, is set loose. It's a force that lures men away from their families and the things they are supposed to be doing to the place where hammers are being swung.

Maybe the act of a hammer moving through the air sets off a cosmic thrumming only men can hear. Or maybe when a man picks up a screwdriver, he releases an odour only men with tools can smell—a musty, yeasty sort of smell, with a hint of leather and WD40. Men in their backyards raking leaves and men in their basements listening to ball games on portable radios are seized by this odour the way the urge to migrate seizes lesser species. Suddenly they're thinking, *I don't belong here any more. I belong in another place. I should be doing something else, and I should take my coping saw with me just in case.*

Men can sense when a wall is coming down, and they can't help the fact that they have to be there to watch it fall, or better yet, help push it over.

It has been argued that the fall of the Berlin Wall had nothing whatsoever to do with the collapse of communism: it was just a weekend project that got out of control—thousands of German guys satisfying their undeniable urge to fix things up.

CARL LOWBEER, HIMSELF of German descent, was the next neighbour to arrive at Dave's house on this Saturday morning.

He burst through the front door without knocking. Dave and Jim looked up to see him standing in the kitchen.

"Hi," said Carl, trying to slow himself down, trying to act nonchalant.

"Need any help?"

He was carrying a bright yellow thing about the size of an electric drill (except more dangerous-looking). It looked like a cross between an Uzi and a woodpecker. It was his reciprocal saw.

Carl got the saw last Christmas. It is his pride and joy. But there are only so many holes a man can cut in his own house before he is told to stop. The saw spent most of the summer on Carl's worktable in the basement—calling to him.

One day, when Carl's wife, Gerta, went downstairs with a load of laundry and found him cutting random holes in a sheet of plywood, she took the saw away from him. She said he could have it back if he stood in front of the house on Saturday mornings with a sign around his neck that read NEED HOLES CUT?

By noon there were seven men in Dave's kitchen. Two of them friends of Jim Scoffield's whom Dave had never met—guys with tools.

Carl was in the living room, huddled on the sofa beside Bert Turlington. Bert was demonstrating his new electric drill. The drill had more gears than a Maserati. Bert was revving the motor and explaining what it could do. He handed the drill to Carl, who didn't expect it to be so light.

"Oops," said Carl, holding it too close to Morley's Brazilian hardwood coffee table. The drill skidded across the table leaving a long white streak in the dark finish, such as a skater might leave on a freshly flooded rink.

"That's okay—don't worry, don't worry," said Bert, spitting on the table and rubbing the gouge with the palm of his hand. "I have something at home that will cover that."

Things were lurching along at about the same pace in the kitchen. There were now a series of twelve melon-sized holes punched in the kitchen wall at two-foot intervals, leading from the light switch by the back door to the hole where Dave intended to install the plug for the toaster.

Twelve holes and seven busy men.

Jim and Dave were routering putty out of the broken window. Phil Harrison was sucking up plaster dust with Carl Lowbeer's Shop Vac. The two men Dave didn't know were racing a pair of belt sanders along a couple of two by fours they had set on the floor. Everyone was productively occupied—except for Carl Lowbeer, who was sitting at the kitchen table, morosely cradling his unused reciprocal saw and watching the belt sanders shudder along.

Counting Bert Turlington's electric drill, there were, at noon on that Saturday, six power tools operating in Dave's house.

And noon on Saturday was the moment when Sam arrived downstairs, rubbing his eyes, taking in the chaos of his kitchen and asking the most reasonable question.

"What's for breakfast?"

"Toast," said Dave. He said this without turning the router off or even turning around. Sam stared at his father's back for a moment, then shrugged and dropped a couple of slices of bread in the toaster. As soon as he pushed the handle down, the toaster began a loud and peculiar buzzing. No one could hear it over the din of the tools. Except Sam, who said, "What's that?"

No one heard Sam either.

Then the lights went out.

And the tools died.

In the sudden silence someone, perhaps Bert Turlington, said, "Do you smell that?"

It was an elusive odour, but it was there.

Somewhere.

"I think it's coming from behind this wall," said Jim Scoffield.

"*This* wall," said Carl Lowbeer.

Sam watched the men, some of them bent over at the waist, some standing on their toes, all of them sniffing the walls, the ceiling, the cupboards.

And then there was smoke hanging in the air like wisps of fog.

Someone said, "We overloaded the wires. The wires are burning—cut the wall open over here."

And Carl Lowbeer jumped up and said, "My saw works on batteries." And he lurched toward the wall, revving his reciprocal saw in front of him. Before anyone could stop him, Carl had cut a hole in the wall the size of a loaf of bread.

"Not there," said Bert Turlington. "Here."

"Coming. Coming," said Carl, moving around the kitchen like a mass murderer. He cut a second hole five feet down the wall.

Sam's eyes were as wide as saucers.

"I've got a fire extinguisher in the truck," said one of the men Dave didn't know.

They found the remnants of the fire with the third hole. A mouse nest leaning against the overheated wires. It had burned itself out. The man with the fire extinguisher gave it a blast.

"Just in case," he said.

At twelve-fifteen Dave took stock of what they had accomplished: the broken window, the chipped sink, fifteen holes, the sodden plaster where they had used the extinguisher.

Bernie Schellenberger looked at Dave and said, "Uh, Dave, when's Morley coming home?"

Dave said, "Not until tonight, not until ten, eleven."

Arnie said, "There's an electrician I know from the plant. He might come over. If you did the window he could do the wiring and we could patch the holes by"—he looked at his wrist—"ten?"

The electrician, Ted—black jeans, black jean jacket, earring—arrived at five. He looked around the kitchen and pointed at the knob-and-tube wiring and crossed his arms.

"I can't repair that. It's the law. Whatever you've exposed I have to replace."

He looked at the expression of horror on Dave's face.

"You need this done tonight. Right?"

Dave nodded.

The electrician looked around. "You guys got a reciprocal saw?"

Carl Lowbeer's hand shot into the air like a schoolchild's. "I do. I do," he said way too fast and about an octave too high. Everyone turned and stared at him. Carl looked down and said it again, this time slower and a register lower. "I do," he said.

The electrician pointed at the back wall of Dave's kitchen. "We're going to pop out the drywall," he said. "Take the wall down to the studs. That way I can get at everything at once."

Dave was frowning.

"It's the fastest way," said the electrician.

He looked at Carl.

"Cut around the top by the ceiling and along the base-board. We'll pop it out, nice and simple."

Carl was beaming.

He was about to sink the saw into the wall when the electrician held up his arm.

"You guys turned the electricity off. Right?"

Everybody stopped and looked at each other.

MORLEY CAME HOME soon after nine.

When she turned onto their street, she noticed her house looked strangely dark.

She pulled into the driveway and parked the car and gathered an armful of junk, her purse, a sweater, some files. She headed toward the back door. She was exhausted. She dropped a file and stooped to pick it up. It was only then that she noticed the warm glow of candles flickering through the back window. She felt a wave of affection wash over her.

Dave had made a romantic meal.

She had barely eaten all day. She was smiling as she opened the back door. She put her purse down and called, "Hello." She stopped dead in her tracks.

Sometimes you are confronted by things that are so far from what you expect that your brain is unable to process what it is looking at. There is a momentary disconnect between what you think you are looking at and what you are actually looking at. Morley looked around her kitchen. There were candles everywhere. And flashlights and snake lights. And men. There were four men in the kitchen. All of them on their hands and knees.

The four strangers on their hands and knees were staring at her the way a family of raccoons might stare at her from the back deck. She thought, *This is not my house. This is not my kitchen. This is a frat house. This is a fraternity party.*

As her eyes adjusted to the light, she took in more details. The men were holding tools. There was a pile of pizza boxes on the floor. And an empty case of beer. Sam, her son Sam, was sprawled beside the pizza boxes. Asleep.

What was he doing in a frat house? This couldn't be her kitchen—two of the walls were missing. She looked at the men again.

One of them stood up.

"Hi. I'm Ted," he said, "the electrician. We'll have this cleared up in just a minute or two."

And then she saw Dave, her husband, crawling toward her. He stopped about ten feet away. "Hi," he said.

He waved his arm around the room—at the broken window, the holes in the wall, the back wall that had completely disappeared—and he said, "We're fixing the toaster."

This *was* her kitchen.

Morley's mouth opened, but no words came out. It closed, then it opened again. She *seemed* to be trying to say something. Dave nodded, trying to encourage her, as if they were playing charades. Her mouth kept opening and closing, opening and closing, but no sound came out.

Then without saying anything—not one word—Morley turned around and walked out of the house. She got in her car and backed out of the driveway.

Dave said, "She'll be back in a minute."

Bert said, "I think I should be going."

Carl said, "Me too."

Dave said, "Maybe if we could just get the power on before she comes back."

Morley wasn't back in a minute. She wasn't back for nearly an hour.

When she did return, she walked across the kitchen and opened the freezer door. About a cup of water trickled onto the floor. She let out a muffled sob.

Dave helped her empty the freezer. They deposited plastic bags of food in an assortment of neighbourhood fridges. "They're all within easy walking distance," Dave pointed out helpfully.

When they had finished unloading the fridge, Morley went into the living room and met Jim Scoffield's two friends. They were still sitting at her coffee table. They had a naphtha-gas camping lantern resting on the arm of a chair and were playing cards in its garish light. When Morley came in the room, one of the men looked up and said, "Are there any subs left?"

THE RENOVATION TOOK six weeks to finish.

Dave worked on it alone until the middle of the next week. He reconnected the electricity on Tuesday, but when Morley came home she got a shock when she tried to open the refrigerator, which, unfortunately, was the first thing she tried to do. So he shut the power off again and rechecked everything and turned it on the next morning. Everything seemed to be working fine until Sam came home from school and showed them how he could turn the microwave on with the TV remote.

There was a thunderstorm that night. Morley became increasingly agitated with each lightning flash. She had read stories about women washing dishes at the kitchen sink and WHAMMO! they get hit by lightning. Cows, golfers, people in boats—why not her kitchen? She didn't trust the wiring.

They called an electrician to finish the job: a methodical and trustworthy man. It was the electrician who spotted the lead pipes running into the upstairs bathroom, and he said, "If you want to have them replaced you might as well do it while you have the walls down."

So they had the plumbers in and had the entire upstairs bathroom redone, and downstairs, where the back wall was, Morley had one of those bay windows put in, which is something she has always wanted. She has a herb garden going in the window space.

It was six difficult weeks and they had to get a new vacuum because the old one got clogged with plaster dust, but the upstairs bathroom is lovely and so is the bay window with the plants in it.

Dave was admiring the plants two weeks later, standing in front of the window and looking out into the yard, enjoying the new view. You can just see the alley over the back fence. He was standing there staring out the new window and into the alley when Ted Bescher drove by in his TR6.

But it is a beautiful window ... and Dave likes it, especially in the evening when the light is soft. In the morning too, especially Saturday mornings, when the kids are still in bed. It's lovely to sit in the kitchen together—the sun drifting down on the coriander, Morley and Dave sipping coffee and reading the paper. They were sitting there one Saturday morning in October, a month after the renovation was finished, when Morley stood up and walked over to the counter to make some toast. She turned and smiled at Dave and said, "Don't you think it would work better if we could plug it in at the table? So we wouldn't have to get up and walk across the kitchen every time someone wanted toast?"

LOVE NEVER ENDS

There are people you meet when you are a child—school teachers, coaches, store owners—people whom you orbit when you are small and without much gravity, people who influence the way you travel for the rest of your life. Art Gillespie was such a person for Dave.

Whenever Dave thinks about Art Gillespie, the thing he inevitably returns to is a baseball game on a Sunday afternoon in 1966. Sometimes he starts thinking about that ball game, and it is the ball game that leads him to Art, rather than the other way around.

Big Narrows Miners versus the Baddeck Junior All-Stars. Dave playing left field. Art Gillespie coaching. Kevin Campbell, sliding into third base, is called out, and Art is exploding off the bench—storming toward the third base umpire, Scotty Leblanc. Art, looking for all the world as though he is going to slug Scotty—which would have had all sorts of unfortunate repercussions, considering that Scotty, who owned and operated Scotty Leblanc's Academy of Music, happened to be teaching Art's daughter, Milly, the clarinet that spring. Milly was counting on playing in the Elks' Music Festival in Antigonish, big time.

Scotty almost fainted when he saw Art steaming toward him, his face all red and pushed forward, his fists clenched. It did look bad. Until Art abruptly drew up not six feet from where Scotty was standing. He looked down at his fists and up at Scotty, and then he shook his head as if he was trying to clear it, as if *he* was just as surprised to find himself halfway to third base, and abruptly spun and walked back to the bench without saying a word.

He dropped down beside Dave and said, "You don't have a chocolate bar, do you, Davy?"

It was a most un-Art-like moment. Art never got angry. Art never raised his voice. Dave, his mouth hanging open, his eyes wide with surprise, looked up at his coach and shook his head. "No," he said, "I don't have any chocolate, Art."

Art spat on the ground. "Don't worry. It don't matter."

ART GILLESPIE, THIRD-GENERATION owner-operator of the Big Narrows Ice Company. Born in March of 1917 on the farm where he spent his boyhood and all his adult life, the farm nestled in the maple bush at the base of Macaulay's hill.

Art Gillespie. Son of Norm, who ran the ice company before Art took it on. Norm, who used to drink with the great pilot Johnny McCurdy.

In fact, eight years before Art was born, Norm used the Big Narrows ice sleigh to drag the Silver Dart—the biplane that made the first powered flight in the British Empire—onto the ice of Baddeck Bay. Norm was, in fact, standing beside Graham Bell the moment the airplane bounced twice and lifted off the ice. He heard the great man mutter "Goddamn" under his breath when the rickety flying machine, or aerodrome as Bell liked to call it, took flight.

Art kept the sleigh in the back of the barn long after his father had passed on, long after they had stopped cutting lake ice, and he would show it to anyone who asked. He would stand by the barn door, tugging on his ears, which were as big and spotty as portobello mushrooms, enjoying them enjoying it.

Art Gillespie actually flew with John McCurdy when he was a boy. He was five years old. It was 1922. McCurdy took Art up the day Art's father took him and his brother to Baddeck for Bell's funeral.

Art Gillespie, who everyone said could have played ball in the big leagues. He had a tryout with Boston and was offered a contract, but he didn't sign. A month after he came home, they even sent someone, a scout or someone, all the way to the Narrows from Boston to try to talk him into changing his mind.

"It was just a minor-league contract," said Art, when Dave asked him about it that spring Kevin Campbell was called out sliding into third base and Art asked Dave for the chocolate bar.

Dave never saw Art play ball, but he saw him play golf. Art hit the ball long and straight and easy just as you would have thought.

Art and his plaid shirts. Art and his suspenders. Art and his dog.

Art always travelled with a dog at his knees. He had one, a Sheltie, who used to chew tobacco. Kept chewing even after Art himself quit.

Art, who moved around town as if he was connected to it by a big elastic band. You couldn't imagine Art leaving the Narrows—he would be snapped back if he went too far. In some ways, he *was* the town. You got the feeling that if *he* left, everyone would have to go.

Art, who started delivering ice when he was thirteen years old, in the days when everyone in town depended on the Gillespies. They had a team of blind horses that pulled the ice wagon in those days—two old pit ponies who knew the route so clean that Art and his brother would jog along beside the wagon working either side of the street as the horses stopped where they were supposed to, without anyone telling them. Norm would ride in the back of the wagon and cut ice—and keep the books. The father had taught his boys a series of hand signals that *his* father had taught him, and as they peeled out of a house, they would either wiggle their hand in the air the way you signal a waiter for a bill (that meant a charge) or they'd swing their whole arm out, like an umpire calling a man safe at home, which meant they had been paid. Twenty-five cents for fifty pounds.

Art, who worked with the horses and could show you a photo of a clipper ship loading ice that his grandfather had cut out of Bras d'Or Lake, bound for Europe. Cape Breton ice, boy. Going to Paris.

Art, who had kept the ice business going. Bought an ice-making machine when refrigeration came and delivered bags of Big Narrows ice cubes as far away as Sydney. He kept harvesting a few hundred pounds of ice out of the lake every January—just because—but he wasn't sentimental about it. He loved the new machine. He would reach into the freezer and pull out a handful of ice cubes, holding them the way a grain farmer might hold a handful of prize seed. He would pop a cube in his mouth, suck on it, and then pull it out, saying, "Now that's beautiful ice . . . you put that in a glass of water and it would just shimmer. It's so clear it would disappear."

When he got the ice machine, he bought a storefront on Main Street between the Maple Leaf Restaurant and Judy's Sewing Shop. He opened a laundromat in front and had the ice machine in a room at the back. "Same business," he said. "Just add water." To get to his office (which was in the back, with the ice) you had to walk down a narrow laneway between the restaurant and the laundromat, past the vent for the dryers. Which meant you had to walk through clouds of steam to get to the ice—a fact that pleased Art.

Through the steam to an office that looked like the ticket bureau at the old railroad station—Art's yellowed varnished desk, Art's rubber stamps, a spike for invoices.

Art and his dog. Flannel shirt. Suspenders.

Art, who lived for ice, went to Florida once a year with Betty, his wife. The first time they went was on a bus tour of the southern United States. First stop, Memphis. When Dave asked him about Memphis, all Art said was "The ice was cloudy. They don't know how to make decent ice down there." He didn't like Orlando either: "Shopping malls everywhere." But he liked Cape Canaveral. And he liked the beach. "First thing I did," he said, "was make a snow angel in the sand."

Art.

Art, who made ice. Art, who gave Dave his first summer job. Art, who coached ball.

Art, who had been around long enough to remember the year his family got the first radio in Big Narrows. Nineteen twenty-eight. You had to use earphones to listen. And Art loved to tell the story about how, on account of the earphones, he was the only person in the house, in fact the only person in Big Narrows, to hear the report about the abnormally high tides in the Thames River in London, England. Tides so high they were threatening to overflow and burst the riverbanks. He was eleven years old. They had only owned the radio three days, and he was unaccustomed to the conventions of the medium. He got the Thames River in London, England, muddled with the Thamesville Creek, which ran through the Narrows. He was convinced the entire town was going to be swept away. He insisted on sleeping in the attic for three nights. His mother let him because he was so intense about it, though he wouldn't tell her why. He didn't see the point in getting everyone worked up.

Two years before the Great Flood, as he came to call it, two years before that, when Art was nine years old, Princess Elizabeth was born, also in London. And somehow Art got her muddled up with Elizabeth MacDonnell, the grocer's daughter, who was born the same week. Art was thirteen before he worked out that Elizabeth MacDonnell, the grocer's daughter from Big Narrows, with her brown eyes, her shoulder-length chestnut hair, and her winsome smile, wasn't going to be Queen one day.

Art.

Art Gillespie—dead now, a year and a half. No, two years. Two years since he had died.

Whenever Dave thought about that baseball game in 1966 when Kevin Campbell was called out sliding into third base, he would start thinking about Art, about the Great Flood and Elizabeth MacDonnell and about how the kids from the Narrows used to meet the kids from Linquist on Saturday nights and dance on the bridge. Art met Betty at one of those bridge dances. "Walking My Baby Back Home" was playing on a wind-up gramophone.

Art Gillespie gone. Who could believe it?

Dave couldn't. In the days after Art's death Dave would think about these things and be swallowed by a rush of panic. He would never see Art again. It felt like claustrophobia.

He worried because he couldn't remember what colour Art's eyes were. Now wasn't that a stupid thing to get upset about? But there was nothing he could do to stop himself. It upset him.

Art. Goddamn it. Art.

As the months passed Dave's anxiety slowly faded—slowly Art joined that woolly corner of Dave's brain where sorrow and regret hung out. It was a corner Dave tried to avoid, a place he was pushed into from time to time, sometimes by something someone did or said, but just as often by a smell, the wind, the colour of the sky.

The sky was blue and brilliant the autumn afternoon the letter arrived to nudge him back to Art. The letter was from Art's wife, Art's widow, Betty. Oddly Dave had been thinking about Art not an hour before he found the letter in the mailbox and sat on his front steps to read it. On his way home he had walked past a park where a group of children were playing soccer baseball—a game he hadn't thought about for years. His memories of soccer baseball got him thinking of the hours he had spent as a boy bouncing a tennis ball against the brick wall of the Big Narrows' schoolhouse. And once he got to baseball and school there was Art—guaranteed—waiting for him.

So Art was in his mind, or had been anyway, when he arrived home and found the letter and sat on the front steps to read it.

Dear David,

I am writing to thank you for your kind letter
which you sent when Art passed on. I feel awful
that I haven't replied until now, but at first I didn't
feel up to writing and then I kept putting it off.
I never seemed to have the time. Or the right
time, I guess. But I have as much time as anyone
else, so that is no excuse. Please accept my apologies.
I hope you understand.

Art always had a fond spot for you, David.
I wonder if you know Milly wasn't our only child.
Did you know we also had a son? Jack. Jack died in
1955. He had polio. He was nine years old.

You must have been four or five years younger
than Jack but I think when Art looked at you he
thought of our son. You had the same colouring.
I think watching you grow gave him a special
pleasure. He always spoke warmly of you.

The day Art learned he had cancer, they told him
he would only live three months. He came back from
Halifax after the first treatments, and he told me
they were wrong. He told me he had three years in
him. And he was right. He lived three years and two
weeks after we learned he was sick. And I think we
did all right. We did the best we could, anyhow.

Remember how we used to go to Florida? We
used to have such a grand time. Art was too sick that

last April to go. He wasn't getting around much
any more. He couldn't even play his guitar. Time
was coming when we normally went and he was
depressed and one night he said, "I can't go." And
I said, "Yes you can." And we did. I paid for four seats
so he could lie down across three of them. The first
night we stayed in a hotel in Orlando. I drove us to
Clearwater the next morning. That was the first time
I had ever driven in Florida. Your mother thought I
was crazy. She asked me what I was going to do if he
died in Florida. I told her I would buy a backpack
and have him cremated and bring him home on my
back. What was I supposed to do? I wasn't going to
sit around the Narrows and wait.

We had a wonderful time. We rented a room on
the beach and I put one of those lounge chairs out
on our deck so he could see the water and hear the
wind in the palms. He was too sick to do anything
else, but at least he was warm. At least he was in
Florida. And I didn't have to buy the backpack,
thank God.

I guess it was while we were in Florida that I really
understood he was going to die. I guess that's when
I figured there were no emergencies any more. We
had moved beyond emergencies. So we might as
well keep moving.

We had always talked about when we retired how
we would spend some money and go to one of those

fancy resorts. The Celtic Lodge or Digby Pines.
Some place like that. Two weeks before Art died,
he said, "I guess we're never going to do that." And
I said, "Yes we are. We are going to spend that
money right now. We are going to go somewhere
where we can hear loons at night." He said, "I can't
even get downstairs. How are we going to do that?"
His liver was so swollen he was having trouble
sitting up.

I told him in all the years I had been a nurse I had
never heard of anyone living longer by sitting in
one place and holding their breath. So I bought a
blow-up mattress and a line of yellow plastic rope
and away we went. We had our forty-eighth anniversary on the lake. They gave us a cottage right next
to the dining room. I pulled him to all the meals on
that air mattress. I guess we had arrived at a place
where we both realized we had to choose between
our dignity and doing something we were going to
enjoy. So we gave up our dignity. It wasn't hard.

I dragged him down to the water in the morning
and we would visit with a nice couple from
Saskatchewan and watch their kids swim. I'd pull
him back down in the afternoon and we would
watch the fishermen come in and see what everyone
had caught. Mostly I read to him on the balcony.
I would lie beside him and keep him company.
When he went to sleep I would work on the

mattress. By the end of the week it was pretty much all covered in duct tape. As I said, he died two weeks later. And I am glad we went.

I am sorry you couldn't have been here for the service. The church was full. But the house was some empty that night when I came home. I don't think I will ever get used to that. It doesn't worry me any more, though I still do funny things sometimes. A couple of months after he died I got up one morning and set his place for breakfast. Imagine that! Sometimes I'll be on my way home and I'll see something and I'll think to myself that I have to tell Arthur about that. And then I'll remember, don't be silly.

We used to read to each other at night before we went to sleep. When he died, we were about a third of our way through a book of Alistair MacLeod's stories. The night we buried him I couldn't settle because the book wasn't finished. So I went up to Art's grave with a lawn chair and a flashlight and I took the book and I read to him. After I was there awhile I heard a rustling, so I turned off the flashlight. It was deer—three deer moving from grave to grave eating the flowers. They would stop by a stone and eat all the cedar and the greenery and then move on to the next one. It was the most calming thing I ever saw. Watching nature come out and seeing how life goes on. Those three deer picnicking on all those flowers. I went up there with my chair and my flashlight and our book every night for a week and a half.

About the third night I found a baggie on his grave with a letter in it and a picture. It was from Dunn Lantier. The captain. I picked it up, but I didn't read it. I guessed Dunn had something he wanted to say to Art and I figured it was none of my business. Art was a good friend to so many people. They would call him and talk things over with him. I guess other people saw that letter during the day because before the week was over the letters started to multiply. Eventually the groundskeeper put out a box for them. There were well over fifty. I never read one of them. Though I did put your letter there. You had so many nice things to say.

I hope you don't mind.

It is funny the things that you miss. Art and I used to have a little ritual if one of us was frosted about something and we couldn't sleep. I can't even remember how it began. I think it was something left over from his childhood. When someone was peeved up, or things were rough, the other one would fix a snack. It was always the same snack: a Cadbury Fruit & Nut bar and two glasses of milk. And we always ate it in bed. We usually kept a chocolate bar handy in case of an emergency. Once or twice when we didn't have one on hand, Art went out and got one at MacDonnell's and brought it home and we would have our little picnic.

About three months after he died, I was cleaning behind the bed and I found a chocolate bar hidden on his side of the headboard. We have a bed with a dresser and mirrors built in on either side. There are cubbyholes over the dresser, and I found the chocolate bar tucked at the back of one of the cubbyholes. It really tied my buns in a knot. I wanted to have a picnic right then and there but I didn't have my picnic partner. I must have cried over that stupid chocolate bar for three months.

One night I finally decided I either had to eat it before the worms got to it or I had to throw it out. So I decided to have a picnic on my own. I went downstairs and got the tray out and a glass of milk and fixed everything just right and came upstairs. I got into bed and opened up the chocolate bar but there was no chocolate in it. Art had eaten the chocolate and folded up Kleenex and wrapped it all up again with a note. "Sorry. But I was hungry. It was truly delicious. Love you, Art." I had bawled over that chocolate bar for weeks—and I was bawling again and all I had was a handful of Kleenex to wipe my nose with.

I knew I had to do something with it. I got up and wrapped it just the way Art had, and I put on my jacket over my nightie and I went out to the garage and got a garden stake, and I nailed the wrapper to the stake, and then I drove up to the cemetery and I hammered the sucker in right beside his tombstone. I laughed and laughed while I did it.

On the way home I stopped at MacDonnell's and I bought myself a Cadbury Hazelnut bar. I never really liked the Fruit & Nut bar all that much. I didn't favour the raisins, but Art did and I never said anything. So I bought the hazelnut bar and had a hazelnut picnic. I sat in bed eating that bar and laughing so hard there were tears coming down my face.

I put up a tree this Christmas. I couldn't do that last year. When I pulled out the decorations I found a Christmas stocking he had packed for me. He must have packed it the spring before he died. I guess he knew he wasn't going to make it to Christmas. There was a bag of marshmallows that were as hard as rocks, and a necklace, and a Cadbury Fruit & Nut bar, and fifty American dollars. He always gave me American money at Christmas. I used to use it in Florida to take him out to dinner. I still have that fifty-dollar bill.

You have been more than patient to read this old woman's ramblings. I just wanted to thank you for writing. I would love to see you the next time you come home.

His eyes were blue.

Yours sincerely,
Betty Gillespie

Dave sat on the steps for a good half an hour after he had finished reading the letter. He didn't exactly cry but he must have looked messed up. Three different neighbours walked by during the half-hour he was sitting there—they all waved but none of them came up the walk to talk. Not even Jim Scoffield, who hesitated and then kept walking. "I'll see you later," he said.

Dave didn't show the letter to Morley right away. He handed it to her that night when they were in bed, reading. Morley said, "What's this?"

When she finished it and handed it back to him, she had tears in her eyes. Dave was ready for that. He smiled, and took the letter and put it in the drawer of his bedside table. Then he pulled something out of the drawer.

"Here," he said. "I thought you might be hungry."

He was holding a chocolate bar. Cadbury Fruit & Nut.